BYRON AND SHELLEY

STORIES

Glenn Haybittle

CHEYNE
WALK

Published by Cheyne Walk 2023

Published by Cheyne Walk
www.cheynewalk.co

ISBN- 978-1-9999682-4-3

Contents

Archaeology

He has dug a trench in the back garden. The trench measures exactly two metres by one and is now half a metre deep. *I'll dig down to a depth of one metre.* It is bordered by lengths of string attached to pegs which, he reasons, makes it look more like it has a rationalised purpose. *Let Mrs Dixon next door think what she likes.* The soil he digs up he removes in a wheelbarrow to the back of the garden where a mound has now formed by the garden shed. *If nothing else Eloise and Ebba are enjoying themselves.* It is the summer holiday and his two young daughters join him every day in the garden. *I'm keeping their minds occupied and at the same time showing them something of the wonders of archaeology.* His mission every day is to make his two daughters feel he is showing them a secret map. He enjoys the disciplined repetition of the labour, the physical exertion of bringing his foot down on the metal blade of the shovel and making another incision. *It reminds me of being a boy with my father in the garden. My father was always less guarded in the garden, more forthcoming.* He enjoys the sheen of sweat underneath his clothes. *Bianca always marvelled how little I sweated. She said I wasn't natural.* For a while he had to fight down a superstitious misgiving that he might unearth something with a curse attached. Treasure is often buried but so too are curses. Mostly though he disturbs nothing but worms among the clods of clay, the stones and the packed earth. The rectangular gash in the ground now resembles a grave. *You're sure this isn't an act of madness, some unprocessed rudimentary manifestation of your grief?*

'Of course, even though time is shifted about in the layers of soil, most of what we are uncovering is relatively recent history,' he tells his two daughters. They are all crouched down in the pungent hole.

'I can't see any history. Just dirt,' says Eloise.

'Just you wait. Soon we'll find something with an interesting legacy, a fascinating story. We're most happy in life when we feel we are in the midst of an unfolding story. Most unhappy when the story we're a part of seems to come to an end.' *I shouldn't have said that. Now they're both thinking of their mother.* 'Sometimes something belonging to a more distant period will work itself up among the things belonging to more recent periods. As happens in our memory. In life you can't make new things happen until you accept responsibility for old buried things.'

Though Ebba and especially Eloise seem to enjoy climbing down into the hole in the ground he catches them sometimes exchanging worried looks. His eldest daughter Ebba he knows has misgivings she doesn't voice. He suspects the disapproving attention of his neighbour, often stationed at her upstairs window, makes his daughter question the sanity of what he is doing. He has always marvelled at the freedom with which his two girls dramatize themselves in the moment without it ever occurring to them they are being watched. *Now here is our neighbour acquainting them with the unblinking judgemental eye of the world.*

'You mustn't worry about what other people think. Especially her next door. She's the kind of person who sticks her flag where it ill belongs. Like our country has done in the past.'

He has also pitched a tent in the garden. To give their field work an added flavour of authenticity. But mostly a further effort on his part to provide some distracting excitement for his daughters. They have slept inside as a family for the past three nights. He has an incomplete knowledge of the stars, so he made up names for them when they stretched out in a line on the moistening grass looking up at the night sky. He has singled out the star from which he tells them their mother now looks down at them. Eloise accepts him at his word. Ebba is less inclined to give his explanations of the world a seal of authority.

He now rubs his hand over his unshaved chin. He has always been a little vain about how infrequently he has to shave. He doesn't really know why. *Hardly counts as a worldly achievement, does it?* It occurs to him he ought to wash his daughters' clothes. *How many days running now have they been wearing the same clothes?* He often finds himself marvelling at how fiercely they attach themselves to the things they own, especially the old timeworn things. He notices Eloise's fingernails are longer than he has ever seen them. Ebba forbids him to interfere with the bathroom rituals of her and her sister. He has to deliver injunctions and reminders from outside the locked door. She has acquired a fierce body shyness. *Is it only since Bianca died that she has become aware of the barriers of sex?* Sometimes he feels overwhelmed by all the responsibilities he now has to shoulder alone.

'Why don't you try that corner with your trowel?' he says to Eloise. The inspiration had come to him last night when he remembered reading about Schliemann's quest to find the site of Troy. The aspiring archaeologist had planted a necklace of his wife's in the earth and then shown it to the press as proof that he had found Troy. So he crept out of the tent, found a necklace of his wife's in the house and returned to the garden with a candle and buried Bianca's necklace in the soil of the trench.

Eloise is reluctant to let go of her balding blue bear. It is one of the oldest of her cuddly toys, but she is devoted to it. He has noticed she holds it closer, talks to it more lately. Always in her most comforting tone of voice. He watches her now clumsily cut into the packed earth with the rusted trowel. Her little hands are still learning to handle the tools of the world and it is a moving spectacle she provides. There are always many moments in a day when he finds it hard to take his eyes off her. Her excitement when she finds the necklace almost brings tears to his eyes. Ebba however looks at him with suspicion. *You're growing up too fast.* Sometimes now he can already detect a future adversary in Ebba. A growing determination in her not to settle for any of his nonsense.

'That belongs to you now,' he says to Eloise. 'Finders keepers.'

He had argued with his wife on the day of her death. Two hours before she crashed her car. He had raised his voice to her at the breakfast table. His ugly sharpened voice had frozen with fear the faces of his two girls. Bianca had seemed distracted for a month or so before she died, as if constrained to spend much of her time in an alternate world only she could see. *She said it was that piece she was working on about fracking and the filtering of methane from oil and gas facilities into the atmosphere.* She was an investigative journalist and had formed a close bond with a woman from an environmental watchdog group. To his mind she had become melodramatically obsessed with climate change. It had irritated him. He began putting recyclable materials in the regular trash. It became a way of reasserting his masculine autonomy. He pleaded innocence but did it on purpose to annoy her. Their final argument was about this. It eats away at him now that he could be so shamefully petty. He had every intention of apologising to her when he saw her that evening. But he was never to see her again.

Perhaps I was a bit jealous of her passionate engagement; wanted to belittle it because it gave her an independence from me? He remembers her speaking of the optical gas imagery camera the woman used and how, though it made the invisible visible, it made the woman highly conspicuous and the target of threats. Bianca admired her courage. She wanted to be more active herself in the fight to save the planet. He thought she had become prey to a kind of self-righteous megalomania. He remembers a night when the subject of pollution led them to discuss the toxic emissions of every marriage, the cloud of accumulated harmful gases emitted by every household. He had argued their own marriage was, on the whole, blessed with a small emotional greenhouse gas footprint. Bianca was less convinced.

'What about your jealousy? Your jealousy is toxic.'

'You think I'm jealous?'

'I think you're a hypocrite. You yourself have a roving eye. Every wife and sister. Every mother and daughter.' Bianca had amused forgiving eyes.

'I appreciate female beauty. It's only the eye that is engaged. And a little bit of imagination. But you know I'd never betray you.'

It's probably true the thwarting of my ambition has made me insecure. At twenty-nine he had signed a three-book deal with an advance of one hundred thousand pounds. *Was I even able for a moment to convince myself I was worth that sum?* His daughters, the things they did, the things they said, often made him feel similarly unworthy of his bounty. His name and photograph appeared in newspapers. He believed someone up there liked him. But his novel hadn't sold very well. His second novel was bad and didn't sell at all. His third novel was better but sold even less. He was dumped first by his publisher and then by his agent. *Those years of teaching English as a foreign language were humiliating to my self-esteem.* He found he was engaged in a competitive struggle with almost every male he met. He felt he had shrunk six inches. *My one professional triumph was receding into insignificance, like I had been a child star: disconcerting how conclusively any moment of triumph can be comprehensively erased by subsequent failure.*

He and Bianca met at the university in Florence. When he thinks back to those days the two of them are often astride their bikes.

'Mine was green, hers was black with a basket,' he tells his daughters in the tent by the light of a paraffin lamp. 'Every day we cycled together to the university canteen in via San Gallo. You had to join the queue on the stairs. Everything I remember eating there was delicious. Even simple *pasta al pomodoro.*' He kisses his fingers in a mock theatrical gesture. Often he wants nothing more than to bring an expression of rapt attention into the eyes of his two girls, make them wriggle with smiles and laughter. They have become even more beautiful since Bianca died; a luminous depth of vulnerability has been added to their beauty. *They look as defenceless as we are in our dreams.* 'And I was in the midst of learning a new language. You both must learn new languages when you're older. It's such an exciting and liberating experience. It's like going out into the world in fancy dress clothes. Because you're a little strange to yourself everything else looks a little strange too, like something has been added to it.'

In the evenings they often cycled to *Spazio Uno*, an independent cinema, where they saw all the films of Fellini, Antonioni, Visconti, Passolini, De Sica. What he doesn't tell his daughters is that he wasn't in love with Bianca; he was in love with Giuliana, a dancer. For two years the dancer was the only thing he wanted to talk about. Every time he heard someone say her name his heartbeat increased its demand of blood. Bianca aided him in his pursuit of her. Bianca was the girl who gives and gives but keeps her own desire hidden in a secret place. The dancer, though clearly fascinated by his obsessive interest in her, showed no desire for amorous relationships. If anything, she was frightened of him, of his pursuit of her, his refusal to take no for an answer. The odd thing was Bianca began to look more and more like the dancer. She grew her hair long, dyed it black, she lost weight, she began wearing darker clothes, longer skirts, like the dancer. It was like she was making fun of him, of his refusal to look beyond appearances. Because there was no question he and Bianca shared a special bond. They were inseparable. Never bored when together. He could talk to her from his most private recesses. They allowed each other to read their diaries. When the time came for him to leave Florence she broke down in tears on the platform of the station of Santa Maria Novella. *Stations are like stages. Dramatic feeling is more readily available.* He had never seen her cry before. He was deeply moved by the depth of her feeling, overawed by this evidence of how crucial he was to her wellbeing. The force of her emotion worked a kind of alchemy on his feelings for her. She moved him to his inmost heart. His feeling for the dancer came to seem like a trick of his imagination. Nevertheless, there was always an unspoken agreement in their marriage that she loved him more than he loved her. This assumption now seems errant and he would like nothing more than to contradict it for Bianca's benefit. His most urgent wish is that he could spend another half hour with her. Tell her in plain language how deep his appreciation of her runs in him. It is maddening to him now how much time he wasted when in her company, what banal things he said when he might have spoken from the heart.

Bereavement is sometimes like wading across a succession of snowfields with no landmark in sight. You are a lone small figure in a vast barren landscape. Other times it's like a Ferris wheel ride. Like being strapped into a swinging spinning bucket. The dizzying dislocation from familiar grounded reality. The brain regrouping, recoding, re-evaluating, adjusting itself to a bewildering change in the engrained mental landscape. He is still learning to negotiate this new reality. The readjustment began on a practical level when he had to learn all the cherished daily rituals of his daughters. To begin with they didn't tell him what they expected on waking up every day, they expected him to know, and reprimanded him when he got anything wrong which he frequently did. Their entrenched hostility to change, even the smallest modification in the day's rituals, surprised him. Sometimes they made him feel he was in some way to blame for the death of their mother. Or rather that he might have done more to prevent it. When he was a teenager a baby sparrow had one afternoon flown into the conservatory. He watched its panicked attempts to find its way back into the natural world, a lurch of sympathetic horror in his body every time it thudded against glass. When, exhausted, it perched on the arm of a cane chair he walked towards it with the intention of picking it up and carrying it back outside but when he got close and saw the wild throbbing panic in its throat he recoiled. He couldn't bear to touch something so vulnerable. And it unnerved him to be the object of so much fear. Sometimes his two girls give him a similar feeling.

He suspects the death of their mother is still only half real to them. As it is to him. They are all entangled in a moment from which the consuming mystery will not allow them to leave. Everything of hers he sees in the house he expects her to pick up and use again. He doubts this will ever change. The unreality of it all was evident when they scattered her ashes in the sea. Eloise brought to the act the playacted solemnity of one of the games she plays with her dolls. The experience was real to her, but it was also pantomime. He could not begin to imagine what they were thinking when they looked down at the lifeless body of Bianca in the coffin. The face they knew

8

so well frozen in an expression that could not be coerced into a less forbidding configuration. How much damage did the vision cut into their hearts?

He hasn't yet found the will to sort through Bianca's belongings. One day he picked up a fur-lined boot of hers and was rocked back by the charge of heartbreak it sent through him. In the photograph of her he most often looks at he is carrying her in his arms. She is wearing a black cocktail dress. It's like he has made of her slender body a beautiful shape in his arms. He tries to recall on his hands the sensation of the sleek thin material infused with her body heat. His fingertips momentarily as sensitive as the antennae of an insect. Then a black cloud enters his mind. He recalls how close to him she always moved in the bed. He could feel her breathing down his neck. What once irritated him he now longs for with his entire being. *Marriage consists of so much parrying back and forth of petty irritations that sidetrack us from the deeper reality. Marriage might be the most consuming and documented experience of one's life but entire stretches of it unfold in a kind of blinkering displacing mist.* His marriage sometimes now seems to him one instance after another of him missing his cue. It was fitting that their last ever argument had been about waste.

One evening, when the digging of the trench has been abandoned and they have stopped sleeping in the tent, he enters Eloise's room to find she has spread the contents of her mother's purse on the floor. The arrangement of the bank cards, business cards, library card, banknotes, coins and receipts is like a map she is trying to puzzle out. He picks up a receipt and for a moment doesn't see what he looks at. Then he notices it is a receipt from a restaurant in Lewes. He looks at the date. *Two weeks before she died.* He has no recollection of her telling him about any meal in Lewes. He tries to remember what he did that day. *Wasn't that the day I went to London and met up with Freddie and didn't return until late?* He is still piecing back together this evening when he is in bed staring at the shadow patterns on the wall. By the time the first glimmer of dawn is showing through the window he has argued himself into the belief Bianca was having an affair. This would better explain her distracted air in the weeks before she died than the article she was working on. No article had ever distanced her from him before. And he believes he knows who with. Alex bloody Cresswell-Jones. He gets out of bed and barefooted in his pyjamas goes downstairs and hunts out the photograph he believes might contain evidence of his suspicions. It's a picture of her and Alex, the husband of her best friend. She is smiling up into his eyes, her face aglow. *When was the last time she looked at me with so much warm-blooded whole-hearted feeling?* He recalls a dinner party about six months ago when, late in the evening, Alex had demanded to know what everyone at the table's most sexually deviant experience had been. The subsequent conversation had embarrassed him. His sexual exploits played no part in his self-esteem. Bianca though had shown a surprising animation of interest. When it had been her turn to answer she told the table with a self-effacing smile that she was boring. He felt she was criticising him and that everyone at the table was judging him unfavourably. It was true he brought none of his creativity to the bedroom. Sex for him had become as routine as brushing his teeth. It had been years since he and Bianca shared a tender kiss.

Alex is probably the person he least likes in the world. He directs music videos and TV commercials and earns more money in a week than he himself does in a year. Alex is untiringly competitive and vain of his charm. He invariably induced Bianca to flirt with him and took pleasure that it was observed. He and Bianca had arguments about him in the car after dinner parties. Arguments that made him feel petty and half-grown. *Often it takes an argument to highlight harboured meanness of feeling.*

'His smile is like the smile on the face of one of Eloise's plastic dolls. And he always looks like he had his hair cut and styled ten minutes ago.'

'He's just vain but essentially harmless.'

The imprint of the photograph appears now on everything he looks at. He can't stop himself from remembering Bianca's readiness to flatter Alex. His memory begins presenting him with an entirely different film of her. She is elusive, volatile, mysterious, impossible to pin down. He realises she was always more animated, quicker to laugh and smile when they were in company than when they were alone. She becomes someone he barely knows. He admits to himself that in recent years there were more moments in an average day when she irritated him than she pleased him. He begins to feel like a tree that has lost all its leaves.

He goes to the room Bianca used as an office. It's like there is a cinder in his inner eye, blurring and blackening everything he sees. Her laptop gives off dangerous voltage. Like a witness about to speak in a trial. He paces back and forth for a while. *I think you're enjoying this in some perverse self-harmful way.* He sits down at her desk. Bianca's laptop asks for the password. He doesn't know the password. But Bianca was always concerned about her memory failing her. *I bet she's written it down somewhere.* He finds a black book in one of the drawers. All her passwords written down in her familiar sober concise handwriting which slants slightly to the left.

He is taken aback when he sees the wallpaper on her laptop is a photo of him and her together on their bikes in front of the Ospedale degli Innocenti in Piazza Annunciata. Bewilderingly he knows a moment of annoyance. His suspicions are momentarily dispelled. As if she is deviously leading him away from the scent of her guilt. He finds he wants his suspicions back. He had been set on a course with a sense of purpose. *I told you that you were enjoying this.* He spends over an hour at the computer. Trawling through her files, her photos, her social media sites. He finds nothing incriminating at all.

'What are you doing, Dad?'

The sight of Eloise, standing at the door in her pyjamas, clutching her blue bear, whips him with a smarting jolt of shame. He can sense the warmth of her body even across the room. It's a presence, this warmth of her young body that always has the power to return him to a world of love. But not today. His tone when he replies to his daughter is abrupt and causes her hurt. He tries to apologise but damage has been done. He knows he has to settle this mystery, put an end to his mental torment, separate the true from the false, legitimise or kill his suspicions. He calls Alex's wife and tells her he urgently needs to speak with her.

It is pouring with rain and his clothes are wet when he gets into the car. As he pulls out of the drive and passes through the village he thinks of all the times he and Bianca had been wet together. Being caught in rain sometimes had the effect of bringing them closer together, circumscribing them in an enlivening intimacy. He tries to remember if he has ever been caught in a downpour with any other girl in his life. He can't recall any such event. Only with Bianca had he ever been drenched, soaked through to the skin. The knife sinks a little deeper into his heart.

The drive to Lewes, the monotonous motorway, the repetitive scrape back and forth of the windscreen wipers is a smear of mundane familiarity. Or would be except for the empty seat beside him. Everything now speaks of her absence, of the sundering change in the world, even the response of the steering wheel to his hands which feel more vulnerable, even the smell of petrol fumes which seem more toxic.

He pulls up in the driveway of Alex and Mia's house. The

car tyres crunch over the gravel. It's a favourite sensation of his, the transition from smooth interminable tarmac to the jittery crunch of a gravel drive. It's like the world suddenly becomes an intimate place again. For a moment he remembers other gravel drives. But his memory is no longer his friend. His memory has become like a war-torn place. He notices Alex and Mia have let their front garden grow wild. There is a tall weed with blue flowers that catches his eye. He is spotted with raindrops. A cold presence on his face. He braces himself on the doorstep. He has never been quite sure that Mia likes him.

'I hear you're digging a large hole in your garden.'

'Who told you that?'

'Ebba. You were in the bath.'

'She didn't tell me you called.'

'Don't worry, there isn't any kind of conspiracy. You're struggling. I remember when my father died. Death floats regrets up to the surface and they won't go away. Regrets are like slicks of spilled oil. That's how I thought of it. And our old freedoms are like seabirds that doused in this oil can no longer fly. We want to believe we have no regrets but it's not true. How can it be? For anyone. The purpose of feeling I've found is to lead us to new knowledge. So even if you're feeling regret or guilt ride with it for a while and the outcome will not be a negative.'

He is not really listening to her. He is steeling himself for what he has to say.

'I don't quite know how to put this.' He runs his palms over his tightly crossed legs. 'Alex and Bianca. I found a restaurant receipt in her purse. A restaurant in Lewes.'

It takes her a moment to understand what he is implying. Then she looks across at him with something close to contempt.

'Alex was having an affair, but not with Bianca. He was

having an affair with a twenty year old stylist. I told Bianca about it during a lunch in Lewes. There's your receipt. Your mind has become very twisted to arrive at the idea that she would have an affair with Alex. You must not have known Bianca very well if you think she would have betrayed me like that. Do you know that even when Alex was having an affair we made love more often in a month than you and Bianca did in a year? You're lucky she didn't have an affair. Look, I don't mean to make you cry. Though perhaps that's what you need. You're looking for a hole in the fence. That's understandable. Grief pens you in. I think you're trying to love her less so as to miss her less. And I don't think that's the way forward.'

Synchronicity

'With a traffic warden. Do you have any idea how humiliating that is? I had to tell my mother my wife has betrayed me for an Italian traffic warden.'

Jamie does his best to convey some sympathy to his teacher. Even though he has the suspicion that he enjoys his anger. The energy it gives him. Maestro is a prolific generator of energy, both of a positive and negative charge.

Fields of sunflowers sway in delicate continuous motion on either side of the road. Jamie is impatient to get out of the car, to breathe some fresher air.

'What's going on? Am I mad? Am I going mad? Is it my wife's betrayal that has led to this onslaught of synchronicities in my life? Have I told you this? When I moved into my apartment in Florence I inherited the complete works of Carl Jung. You've seen them. All those green spines on my bookshelves. One August I caught pneumonia. I couldn't go out landscape painting. I had to stay in bed. So I read Jung. Of course I skimmed a lot. Jung is heavy going. But he might be the greatest mind of the 20th century. And his theory of synchronicity is perhaps the most exciting of all his ideas. This synchronistic odyssey of mine began with the appearance of the dwarf drummer. He flagged me down. I was on my bike. I was looking up at the moon and he flagged me down. In Piazza della Signoria. The site of the bonfire of vanities. That's what's happened to me. There's been a bonfire of my vanities. The dwarf drummer was the messenger. Look at what's happened in sequence. I discover my wife is betraying me. With a traffic warden who writes poetry. Awful poetry. You saw it. I showed you his poems. Have you ever read such hackneyed tripe in your life? How could my wife be taken in by such drivel? I feel ashamed on her behalf. She's a bright woman. You know that. Is he some kind of necromancer? Has he cast a spell? His name is Angelo. And he always dresses in black, except when he's in his uniform. You know who the black angel is? Has my wife succumbed to Lucifer? But, tell me, who is my wife in my big picture?'

'The Madonna.'

'Exactly. And what happens within a week of my wife betraying me?'

'A church commissions us to paint five altar paintings.'

'Five large canvases celebrating the Holy Virgin to fill the apse of the Church of the Immaculate Conception in Alabama. I have to paint the Madonna again. I have to return to the image of my wife except she's no longer innocent. And then arrives the offer of the farmhouse in France for the Easter break. We're three miles from where my wife and I took refuge after I stole her from her husband in Paris. We were at our happiest here. I've been returned to holy land. Of course I stole my wife from another man. That was my sin. Ben is probably right about one thing. Most of his Eastern ideas are poppycock but karma is a powerful idea. What do you think of Ben and his Eastern ideas?'

Jamie shrugs. Maestro wants him to betray the affection and respect he has for Ben. Ben gives Jamie the feeling some people know in church. A peaceful feeling of faith that the future will be fruitful and meaningful. Ben is someone who creates harmony. But he can't display too much admiration. Maestro is easily roused to jealousy. He doesn't have to answer because Maestro, never silent for long, soon resumes his dialogue.

'Ben wants me to be a mentor. He had his guru at the community for fifteen years and now he has me at my studio. He needs a mentor in his life. Someone to beat a pathway for him. But he sees me as a mentor, not as an artist. I like being looked up to. Who doesn't? It's a good feeling to be made to feel you have the answers. But it can be exhausting too. First and foremost, I want to be an artist. That's what none of you understand. You just want to steal all my secrets.' Maestro suddenly stops the car. 'I remember this street,' he says. 'The house where we lived is just around the corner. That's the bar where we had our morning coffee. Let's get out and take a stroll around.'

The village seems to Jamie to be shrouded in decades of dust. A place of leakages and slow drips. Every brick loosening itself and flaking. Weeds pushing up everywhere you look. 'It's strange to imagine you living here,' he says.

'Why do you say that?'

'I don't know. It's a kind of nowhere place.'

'And life has brought me back to this nowhere place. But there's no such thing as a nowhere place. You should know better. You grew up in London. You're too attracted to surface glamour.'

On the other side of the road there's a woman with an ugly birthmark covering half her face. She's holding a bunch of wildflowers. The image is unsettling in its blend of beauty and ugliness. Jamie catches her eye for a moment. He's not quite sure if he wants to dismiss the moment as meaningless or, in imitation of his teacher, read into it a mystical sign of personal significance. For a moment he considers alerting Maestro's attention to her. But Maestro has resumed his narrative.

'Sometimes I feel like Ben and Giulia have summoned this commission. They want to do it much more than I do. I'm far from sure we have it in us to do these paintings. I feel exhausted. The traffic warden has worn me out. Really, I should do all five paintings myself. You're all still students after all. You don't understand how difficult it is to finish a painting. The paintings you do at my studio aren't finished paintings. They are exercises. You might stop working on them, but they could all be brought to a higher level of accomplishment with patience and discipline. But I'll only have time to do the Crucifixion and the Immaculate Conception. I'll have to entrust the Angel of the Lord Appearing to the Shepherds to Ben and Giulia. You and Nadia will have to do the Nativity. We'll decide what happens with the Archangel Michael Vanquishing Satan when we've finished the other four pictures. Perhaps I should let Doug do it. But he's eccentric. That said he's only the Catholic among us. You don't care much for Doug, do you? Too macho for your fey English sensibility? You know he killed his best friend? Of course he didn't mean to. At least that's the official version.'

The task while they spend three weeks in the house in the south of France is to complete five small painted sketches of the paintings they have designed to show the bishop in America. The farmhouse is a history unto itself. A timeless atmosphere seeps through its topsy-turvy maze of echoing rooms. There isn't a single clock inside its rough-hewn stone walls, beneath its heavy oak roof beams. It becomes a spooky forsaken place at night. Despite the thickness of the white-washed walls, Jamie hears constant purposeful movements elsewhere in the dark. As if ghosts are on the prowl.

Maestro surprises everyone by finishing his painted sketch of The Immaculate Conception in three days. The small painting of the exalted woman is so beautiful it appears closer to the eye than most things looked at. Jamie can't stop looking at it. The otherworldly glimmer of it. The praise Maestro receives seems to embarrass him. He fends it off. Perhaps because it isn't life-size, and he has been trained to draw and paint everything life-size. As if anything on a smaller scale is unworthy of praise. He complains that he has been turned into a miniaturist.

At the wobbling wooden table in the garden where the girls have served lunch Maestro draws everyone's attention to the peacock fanning out its rainbow feathers on the lawn. 'Is Jamie our peacock? Are you a little too obsessively a ladies' man, Jamie? I'm putting you on the spot.'

There is a smile on every face at the table. A smile at his expense. He catches the eye of Kira, who Maestro has invited along on the trip to be the model for the Virgin Mary. It's always distressing to be singled out for criticism by his teacher, to be made to feel you are lacking in seriousness. It is true Jamie has an eye for the ladies. He keeps count of his sexual conquests. As if each one is an exam he has passed for which he now owns a certificate confirming his worth. At the final reckoning he can't help believing it is a calculation that will define his measure of success in life. Though he argues with himself that quantity is not more important to him than quality. There have been forty-three so far. Forty-three girls willing to take off their clothes for him. He feels there should have been more. Often he finds himself dwelling on the missed opportunities. It's the women who have eluded him he realises that have the most power to determine how he thinks about himself. As if every desired woman that eluded him has diminished him in some way. Maestro at fifty has only ever enjoyed the sexuality of two women. He seems to take a puzzling pride in this scarcity of carnal knowledge. He who is so ardent and resourceful about acquiring other forms of knowledge. He has been hampered by a strict religious upbringing. For Jamie the run-up, the imminent anticipation of undressing a female for the first time is the most excit-ing gift life has to offer. He doesn't understand all the moral scruples Maestro creates to make this a remote possibility for himself. Jamie likes to believe it is his admiration for women which makes him want to sleep with them. He was taken aback when a girl once told him that his desire to sleep with as many women as possible was more an indication of his competitive insecurity with other males than an expression of admiration for the female sex.

'I blame my mother,' he says, thankful he has come up with a witty response. It's what his teacher most favours, the quick witty response.

There is a scorpion on the whitewashed wall by his bed when Jamie enters his room, like a black inked hieroglyphic. Even when he stands close to it and expects it to scuttle off to some place of shadow it makes no sign of acknowledging his presence. He can feel its darkness settle upon his skin. For some reason he recalls the woman with the livid birthmark on her face. She and the scorpion are as if part of the same narrative. His first thought is to turn it into a synchronicity for Maestro. Maestro's obsession with finding buried meaning in the passing moment is contagious. Everyone wants a part to play in the mythology of mysterious sequenced and connected events he is composing.

Jamie's intention was to take a nap, but the scorpion is a sinister presence that he knows will not allow him to close his eyes. For a moment he contemplates killing it. He pictures himself perform the act. But there is a superstitious reluctance in him. He thinks of the disapproval the act would incite in Ben with his Buddhist beliefs. And he realises he might believe in karma without knowing it. He decides to read in one of the cane armchairs in the upstairs conservatory. At the top of a stairway he sees Kira open the bathroom door. Her hair is wrapped in a white towel and she has another white towel tied around her waist. Her breasts are bared. It is a vivid charged moment as if lit by a sheet of lightning, soundtracked by a peal of thunder. The vision puts him in a trance of longing. When she sees him at the foot of the dark stairs he lowers his eyes. But he is aware of a shared thought moving between them. There is an acknowledgement he has momentarily entered her secret life. He is embarrassed, whether on her behalf or his own he cannot say.

The afternoon painting session is conducted in an atmosphere of harmony and intimacy and high tide concentration. They work together in close stirring friendship. They perform the alchemical act of creating three dimensions on a two-dimensional surface. To the accompaniment of Thomas Tallis' *Spem in Allium* which Maestro plays over and over again on the CD player. The fumes of turps and white spirits thick and heady in the north lit room. Kira, standing on her podium in her red robe, is beautiful to look at. He watches the occasional fidgeting of her hands. The lightness in her fingers when she takes hold of the cloth. The work he does goes deep into his body, like the heat of a fire. He feels he has a gift for the world. A rare and precious feeling. The fields of sunflowers he gazed out at earlier are part of the moment as is the glimpse he caught of Kira's bared breasts. Ben and Giulia encourage the flirtation between him and Kira. They are always eager to promote love in the world. He begins to feel he and Kira are talking to each other without words. This world Maestro has created for him is a beautiful world. This world that gives him something lofty he can aspire to. The troubling feeling he had yesterday while food shopping in the local town is gone. The feeling of possessing no useful purpose in life while he watched people in the market apparently leading more constructive lives than him.

When, later, he is leaving the bathroom and Kira is still modelling, he is drawn to stealthily enter her room. There is a rucksack on the stone floor by her bed. He sees a pair of black lace panties and with trembling hands delicately removes them and brings them to his face. A hot surge of guilty excitement in his blood. It feels like he is committing a crime. As he replaces them in the rucksack the pattern on the black lace reminds him of the scorpion. And then he thinks of the woman with the ugly birthmark on her face. The scorpion, the woman with the birthmark and the black lace panties. The unfolding story of his own experience of synchronicity. He is reminded the woman was holding flowers. Surely a positive sign.

The next day, Sunday, they take the morning off. They drive in two cars to a local monastery. Kira and Doug are in Maestro's car. Jamie is in Ben's car with Giulia and Nadia. They talk about Maestro, his obsession with synchronicity and the five big paintings.

'I've got a feeling we'll never do these five big paintings,' says Jamie.

'Why must you always be negative?' says Giulia, smiling up at him in the rear-view mirror.

He lets Giulia know with a frown that he doesn't like being perceived of as negative. 'Do you believe in this map of synchronicities he's creating? That it has any coherent meaning?'

'Guru used to say that knowledge is always a gift from beyond ourselves and often arrives in the form of signs,' says Ben. 'Except ego and vanity often blind us to these signs. That's why animals are better at sensing and interpreting signs than human beings. They don't have ego or vanity to distract them.'

Giulia smiles. She likes it whenever Ben quotes his former spiritual teacher.

'I've got a feeling he'll eventually use some perceived synchronicity as an excuse to abandon these paintings. He doesn't want to do them. They frighten him.'

'They do frighten him. But I think how well the sketches are turning out has given him more confidence. His eagerness to work is evident.'

'I can't help feeling all his synchronicity is just poppycock. Like trying to reduce life to a crossword puzzle. Something that can be completed. Why does every encounter have to possess a mystical meaning? It's like reading significance into that car in front's number plate.' As he says this he realises the plate contains the numbers of the day and month of his mother's birthday. He announces this to the car with a wry smile.

Inside the monastery his voice has an echo to it. As if everything he says has an added secret significance. He tries to sit next to Kira, but Maestro has commandeered her. While the monks chant Maestro frequently whispers something in Kira's ear. Maestro has trouble staying silent and still. It's like he has to plant a flag in every passing moment. It's an admirable trait in many ways. It's like he never allows himself to be bored. Jamie is too easily bored. He knows this about himself. He feels now as he did as a schoolboy in chemistry or maths class, bored and restless and eager to be outside. He sits with his legs and ankles crossed. The chanting is beautiful for a moment. But the moment goes on too long. The moment becomes minutes, long slow dragging minutes. He begins to feel it's an experience he isn't equal to. As if his sensibility needs further refinement to receive the choral messaging of the monks. Afterwards he will have to fake enthusiasm for the monks to Maestro. He often has to fake enthusiasm for Maestro. Maestro frequently demands bigger feelings than he is capable of mustering. He is not a thinker of big thoughts like his teacher. Maestro often makes him feel he is not a sufficiently serious person. He suspects this is true. The most exciting moment is when the chanting is over and he steps outside the monastery into afternoon sunshine. He feels like he is opening his mouth to a shower of spring rain.

When they return to the farmhouse there is a black snake with green markings coiled in the front courtyard. They watch it slither off into the shrubbery. But it unnerves Maestro. He drinks excessive quantities of red wine that night and is eager to lose his temper. He keeps returning to the theme of the serpent in the garden. He has to make sense of it. He goes over again all the strange signs he has encountered since the discovery of his wife's betrayal. He eyes everyone with suspicion. They sit close to the firelight in the cavernous dining room. Unfinished history seems a presence in the shadows.

'What does it mean, that snake? Does it mean we have a snake in our midst? What do you think, Doug?'

Doug shrugs his shoulders, but he has a knowing look on his face. His boots, as always, are caked in mud. There is a hiss and crackle in the fire and a flame suddenly shoots up high, giving a glow to all the faces in the semi-circle before the hearth.

'Did you see that? The fire has spoken. The fire has given a warning.'

Jamie is careful not to draw attention to himself. He tries to shrink himself into irrelevance. He does not want to offer himself as a target for Maestro's drunken building fury. Kira announces she is tired and goes to bed. She takes the pulsing warm beauty of the world with her. Or that's how it feels. As if only Maestro's irascibility and the erratically lit smoking darkness remains now. Maestro opens another flask of red wine and demands Doug tell everyone about the night his best friend was killed. 'Doug was driving the car when it crashed. Tell us about the crash, Doug. Don't go shy on us. It's therapeutic to talk about these things. Were you in your cups?'

There is a moment of high tension. Doug is its source. He emanates a threat of violence.

'But why has fate brought me back to this place where I was happy with my wife? Who can explain that to me?'

'I think it's a sign you need to talk to your wife,' says Giulia, providing Maestro with the prompt to finally let loose the full force of his anger.

'I'll never talk to her again.' Maestro stabs the air with his forefinger. 'Why can't you women realise actions have consequences?' The rant, directed at Giulia, continues for several minutes. Bright red in the face, Giulia leaves the room, followed by Ben. Jamie too gets to his feet.

'You English!' says Maestro with withering scorn. 'Always banding together.'

The look of contempt he receives from his teacher produces a confusion of hurt and anger in Jamie. He feels a need to proclaim his innocence. He is as if magnetised to Kira's door. His heart becomes the loudest noise in the house. Every creak beneath his feet makes the hairs on his neck stand up. There is a thin wand of light beneath her door. He debates whether he should knock or simply open the door and invite himself into her bedroom. Maestro, downstairs, might hear the knock on wood. He knows he is encroaching upon forbidden ground where Maestro is concerned. He opens the door without knocking. Kira's startled face, lit by the candle by her bed, makes him feel there are dangerous forces within his body. He places a finger to his lips in what he hopes is a comic endearing manner. Then he gently closes the door behind him.

'All hell has broken loose downstairs,' he says, sitting down self-consciously on the edge of her bed. His intent is to make himself appear harmless, to grant his entry into her candlelit bedroom the benignity of an ordinary occurrence. 'Maestro has had a nuclear meltdown. Synchronicity again.'

'Synchronicity – it's just a fancy word for coincidence, isn't it? We all look for coincidence at times. The occurrence of coincidence suggests we're on a trail. And we all want to feel we're following a trail. At the end of every trail there's some kind of reward, some form of treasure.'

He looks at her with new admiration. 'This is the first time you've spoken your mind,' he says.

'What you mean is, you didn't know I had a mind. I'm constrained here to play the role of Woman through the ages. Stay still, stay silent. But back to synchronicity, it's the business of the brain to make connections. Even if most of what goes on in our heads is completely beyond our comprehension. The known part of ourselves is a pathetic little creature compared with all that's unknown within us. Synchronicity is Maestro's way of trying to plug into the unknown realms. It's all true when it's inside him; it becomes false when he tries to explain it. That said I like the way he makes theatre of his mind's quest for meaning. It's entertaining and he's an accomplished performer. But the moment we try to put feelings into words we begin deceiving ourselves. Isn't that why you paint? So you don't have to use words?'

She smiles, a private smile, meant for her alone. Then she sits up in the bed, pushes down the sheet and reaches out for her tobacco on the bedside table. She is showing him her naked thighs but with no more self-consciousness than she might show him her knuckles. This revealing of intimate flesh contains no kind of invitation on her part. It's as if she is distant from her body. She begins rolling a cigarette in her lap. He watches her lick the paper and the glimpse he catches of her tongue deepens his desire to know the taste of her. The smoke she exhales when she lights her cigarette up drifts over his face.

'One thing I've noticed about you is that you walk almost on tip-toe as if you want to make as little noise in the world as possible,' he says.

'You know nothing about me. Just as I know nothing about you.'

His eye is drawn to a small bruise on her thigh. He can't help reaching out and touching it. She doesn't seem to mind him touching her. She is lazily pliable like a cat allowing itself a caress. But there is no sign of her wanting any kind of embrace. He moves his fingers up and lightly traces the border of her cotton panties. She opens her thighs a fraction. He continues moving his fingers in the vicinity of her knickers without ever encroaching inside. He marvels at the mysteries of the human hand, its fluency when it knows what it touches, its hesitations when it doesn't.

He has been caressing the inside of her thighs and her navel for a while when there's a creak on the landing outside the door.

'I want to go to sleep now,' she says.

The next morning he wakes to the sight of Doug in his muddied boots standing over his bed.

'Maestro says you do not have sexual relations with the Virgin Mary.'

'What?'

'Sexual relations with the Madonna are not allowed. He wants you to pack your bags and leave. You're to leave the studio as well. Ben and Giulia are going to drive you to the station.'

'I didn't have sex with Kira. I didn't even kiss her.'

'In my experience not much in life is changed by anything we say. Anyway, this isn't a criminal investigation. Maestro has made his decision. You no longer have a role to play in this project or at the studio. You have to respect his decision.'

His heart is thumping at the prospect of confronting Maestro. But there is no sign of him when he goes down to the kitchen. No sign of Kira either.

'They've both gone into town,' Ben tells him.

The big stove is burning but there is a chill in the cavernous room. He sits down at the huge wooden table with Ben, Giulia and Nadia.

'I'm afraid you've become the snake in the garden.'

'I was the peacock yesterday,' he says with irritable mockery. He gets to his feet and paces over the flagstones. The muscles in his legs feel like he is climbing a steep hill. 'But what's the story? I didn't do anything. We talked. That's all.'

'I think Doug heard you in her room. Then Kira told him what happened.'

'So he knows nothing happened.'

'You made a move on his muse. Forbidden fruit. That you didn't succeed is beside the point for him. The intention was there.'

Ben and Giulia drive him to the station. He looks out at landmarks that have become familiar to him. The scraggy mongrel chained up outside an isolated weatherworn house, the handwritten sign offering eggs outside a barn, the roadside altar to the Virgin Mary always bedecked with fresh flowers. It occurs to him that the life he has been living for three years is over. He has lost his home. His mind swarms with all the rituals he is on the verge of losing. He has taken too much for granted. Never has he been so keenly aware of how much affection he holds for Ben and Giulia whose everyday presence in his life is about to end. He's at the beginning of a new story all of a sudden.

It is market day in the town. The inhabitants in their faded clothes. This going to market is one of the routines that give their lives shape and substance. He feels cut adrift from the mood of collusion in the day. The progress of the car is slowed down by heavy traffic. He looks at his watch. Ten minutes until the train to Paris arrives. Three minutes when they pull up outside the station. As he removes his luggage from the boot of the car he sees the woman with the ugly birthmark on her face. Today, she is not holding a bouquet of flowers. Her presence angers him. *It's all very well you appearing again and looking across at me but what does it mean?*

The Day David Bowie Died

Marg is thinking again how little she likes the name her mother and father chose to give her. A name felt to be inappropriate is like a shallow root. She sometimes blames her name for why she feels so unsteady on her feet in the world. Closer to the truth would be she is unsteady on her feet because she favours shoes with tall thin heels that make her look thinner. Her mother told her recently that she walks like someone who has had too much to drink. 'Where is your poise, where is your self-regard?'

Tonight, she *has* had too much to drink. Three quarters of a bottle of sparkling white wine consumed in the solitude of her bedsit. She has nothing to eat in her kitchenette except a withering avocado. She is sitting on the floor, on the carpet that is worn down to its weave in places. She likes sitting on floors. It's a facet of her anarchy, her determination not to conform to the world of her mother. Her laptop is open on a dating site. She has been looking at girls more than boys. The small television is on but muted. An image of David Bowie appears on the screen with text beneath announcing he has died at the age of sixty-nine. She turns up the sound. A man being interviewed says, 'Bowie changed the world.' Marg has always nursed a dislike of David Bowie. Because her father idolised him. And her father abandoned her. When she was ten he vanished into oblivion. He evidently didn't care if he ever saw her again. She has never been able to understand why he identified with Bowie. It's her contention that Bowie owed much of his success to his haircuts. He had great haircuts. And he was glamorously thin. She's willing to grant him that. Her father did not have a great haircut and he wasn't thin. He was stocky and had an everyman haircut. In every image she has of him he appears keen to present himself as a model of convention in his high street attire. He didn't even smoke. She once discussed the mystery of his empathy with Bowie with her mother, but her mother was unable to provide any insights.

'Do you think he might have been secretly gay?'

This question embarrassed her mother. Marg realised the implication was humiliating.

'Or perhaps it was Bowie's so-called talent for reinventing himself which he longed to emulate?'

Her most vivid memories of him are at the wheel of his car singing along to David Bowie songs. 'Rebel Rebel', 'Boys Keep Swinging', 'Changes'. She associates the songs with oppressive intimacy, the feeling of carsickness. In her memory they are driving to the bungalow in Dymchurch where they holidayed every year. She can recall the brand logos of the cans and boxes and packets in the kitchen cupboard. The groceries we were raised on can be no less affecting in memory than the toys we played with, the friends we made, the places we made camp. There was no TV in the bungalow so, of an evening, they played card games. She remembers Old Maid in particular and the magical properties the cards held for her. But she also recalls the humiliation of losing, of being left the old maid, of being the subject of her father's teasing mockery. Childhood contains prophecies of what awaits us as an adult. No doubt about that. Powerful totems are bound up in trifles. Marg expects men to abandon her, expects to be made to feel like the old maid. Perhaps deep down she even covets and encourages this outcome as if secretly she wants to prove her father right for abandoning her, for making her feel like the sour wrinkled unlovable old crone on the card.

There is footage now of Bowie as Ziggy Stardust on the television and then of a small crowd gathered in front of the mural of Bowie which is not far from her bedsit in Brixton. She decides to take a selfie in front of it and post it on her social media sites. It takes forty minutes of preparation in front of the mirror before she has a face she wants her camera to commemorate.

Most of the people congregated in front of the spotlit mural are as young as she is. They have come here, like she has, to become part of a crowd, to take part in and person-alise a moment of history. It is rare one is able to identify a moment of history. She looks around for someone she knows and then for broadcasters, television crews. She is struck by how many beautiful girls there are, many wearing Aladdin Sane face paint. People continually arrive with flowers and candles. She has the feeling of being part of a congregation in front of an altar. Only a hymn is missing. She thinks it would be more emotional if everyone began singing one of his songs. Why does no one think of that?

'Sad day, isn't it?'

She hadn't noticed the man until he talks to her. He has the appearance of a man who goes unnoticed.

'Most people look like they're having fun,' she says.

'Well, nothing wrong with celebrating him, rather than mourning him.'

'I doubt if most people here have given him more than two minutes thought in their lives. They just want to be where the cameras are.'

'Is that your reason for being here?'

'I've given him quite a lot of thought in my life,' she says, lighting a cigarette.

'What's your favourite of his songs? No, don't tell me. Let me guess. Rebel Rebel,' he says. 'Now tell me I'm wrong.'

'You're wrong.'

'Shall I tell you my favourite Bowie moment? It was the first time I ever saw him. He was performing 'Starman' on *Top of the Pops*. And what I loved was the seething discomfort he caused my father. My father was fascist, racist, homophobic, jingoistic. Everything socially reprehensible he flew the flag for. He was only though a loudmouth in his armchair. Out in the world he was as submissive as a computer program. I could tell he thought about smashing the television while Bowie pranced about in his glittering hot pants. He was itching with impotent violence. I felt the world was changing before my eyes. Bowie was ripping the world my father cherished to shreds.'

'My father idolised him.'

'Lucky you. It must be great to have a cool father. In my experience nothing can undo our attempts to appear cool as catastrophically as the proximity of our parents.'

Many of the people around them are taking selfies. She has a dizzy moment. Her body telling her how much wine she has drunk, how little food she has eaten.

'You don't look like you'd be a fan of Bowie.'

He looks hurt for a moment, aggrieved. She registers his receding hairline, all the wrinkles on his face. He is one of the oldest people in the crowd. Only now does she become aware of this fact. He is old enough to be her father. And like her father you would never know by looking at him that he felt any connection to David Bowie. Can she even say for a dead certainty he is not her father?

'Is there a wife and daughter in your life you abandoned?'

'I suppose that might make me more interesting. Truth is, I'm incapable of starting anything new. I guess that's one of the things I admired about Bowie. He was always starting afresh.'

'Didn't he just change his haircut and hair colour every few years?'

It's not entirely clear to her how it comes about that she enters her bedsit with the man. She has these memory lapses when she drinks, when she doesn't eat. There's a lingering feeling that fate has sent him as an emissary of her father. That he might unlock some mystery about her absent father. When she takes off her coat she realises she has too much naked flesh on display. Her short thin dress skimming over her body when she moves. She sees him register the discarded dirty panties on her unmade bed, the deposits of candle wax everywhere, the almost empty bottle of wine and, when she opens her laptop, the dating site on the screen.

'I suppose we ought to listen to him,' she says, trying to keep her voice offhand and relaxed. 'Choose a song.'

'How about 'Time',' he says. 'Time, he's waiting in the wings, he speaks of senseless things; his script is you and me.' He recites rather than sings the words. Only now does she get a good look at him. He is bigger than she thought, his body more powerful. His thinning hair is combed to one side. His shoes are scuffed, his trouser hems frayed, the scarf knotted at his neck discoloured with age. His lips are in constant movement, as if he is swirling about saliva inside his mouth. He is not a man who expects improved circumstances. And in his eyes or perhaps it's in the fidgety line of his mouth there's a hint of something unstable about him. His face reflects an excessive mental concentration. His attention has the effect of magnifying her to herself, in a way she doesn't like.

'You don't even know my name,' he says. He smiles. He is missing a tooth. He takes off his scarf and then his lumber jacket. Tosses them onto the room's single armchair. She knows he is picking up her discomfort, her desire to reverse the decision of inviting him into her life. 'What's your father's name?'

'James.'

'And if I told you my name is also James?'

Her unease grows, prickling all the nerves of her body. His

presence among her things has become like a snake slithering around in the shadows. She sits down on the edge of the bed and watches him walk over to the kitchenette where dirty dishes and mugs fill the sink.

'Bottle opener's here,' she says. 'Why don't you open the wine and take the bottle with you. The thing is, I'm not feeling so good. And I have to get up early tomorrow. So I might have to ask you to leave.' Her voice sounds childish in its wheedling plea. It frightens her how small and meek he has made her.

He is opening the bottle of wine. All his attention focused on performing the task with a professional flourish as if his manhood is under scrutiny. He has taken no notice of what she said. He rinses two mugs under the tap and fills them almost to the brim. He walks up close to her and hands her a mug branded with the emblem of a heart. She frowns but she has never been able to openly express anger with men. It always remains knotted up inside. Only with her mother is she capable of losing her temper and striking out.

'Your father loved David Bowie and he abandoned you when you were young. And you think I might be able to help you understand why.' He is tapping his foot to the music, not quite in time. She is aware of a difficulty he has inhabiting his body. As if his body is not quite under the jurisdiction of his mind.

'I don't think that's true.'

He has a way of creating uncomfortable pauses. In every silence she has a sense of shadows gathering and moving.

'So how long have you lived here?'

'Only a few months. I move around a lot.'

'I've lived in the same place for years. Decades. Unemployed at the moment. I haven't downloaded the app. I've missed out on the updates. Can you tell by looking at me?'

She has a talent for producing laughter when men think

they are being witty. It's her go-to ploy to flatter men. But she has the discomforting sense this man has no vanity to flatter. She risks an ostentatious yawn. She feels it is imperative she does nothing to anger him. She is holding tightly on to her house keys. She has begun to think of what she might have in the flat to defend herself with. There's a pair of scissors somewhere. And a kitchen knife. It's hard for her to work out how legitimate her rising panic is. If this is a critical moment in her life or merely a comic anecdote she might offer up as light entertainment in the university canteen tomorrow.

'We could try dancing, if you want?' He holds out his hand. She looks at the dirt beneath the long yellowing nails. The panic now arrives, like a gust of cold wind in an underground tunnel. She gets to her feet, pushes past him and leaves her home.

It is January, but the bitter cold only becomes a new consideration when she has reached the end of her road. Not far away, she hears raucous jeering male voices. A dangerous overload of testosterone. She avoids looking at the people in the cars that drive by. She tries not to be noticed. Aware people are looking at her. Wondering why she is so under-dressed. London does not seem like an affluent city tonight. It seems aggressive and menacing, like a dirty syringe poised to enter a vein. She feels everything is rushing towards her. She watches two young girls hail a taxi. Sees herself in the act, on other nights when her blood was warm with sensual expectancy. She knows some relief when she reaches the house of a friend. He is a boy who likes her. A boy whose sexual advances she has always playfully fended off. But he doesn't come to the door. She rings the bell again. She can't believe he doesn't come to the door the one time she needs him. Her teeth are chattering. Her hands are chalk white. She thinks of the hot water bottle her mother had occasionally brought her when she was ill. That sudden surprising catechism of intimacy with one's own body.

She enters the shop owned by the Pakistani couple at the end of her street. The husband likes her, the wife doesn't. Luckily, it's the husband behind the counter tonight. She tells him she has locked herself out of her flat and asks if she can stay a while to warm herself up. The man is not as kind as she expects. He makes her feel she has overstepped a mark. She looks up at the silent television. There are images of a desert city ravaged by war. Children in torn clothes, covered in dust, squatting in ruins. Bowie didn't change the world, she wants to tell the man interviewed on the news. The world hasn't changed. The world never changes.

She wants to believe the man will have left her home by now. Surely, he will assume she left with a purpose. He might think she will return with a friend or even the police. She tries to picture him perform the act of leaving her home, returning to wherever he came from. She sees him rifle through her bag, take the contents of her wallet. She feels she doesn't care if he steals her money and bank cards. Just let him be gone. She can't rid herself of the disbelief of how this evening has panned out. She should be at home, tucked up in bed with her Don DeLillo novel. It's like she has stepped through a door that is no longer there when she turns to go back to it, compelled to wander into a counterlife. And this counterlife feels more intimately raw, closer to the truth of who she is behind all her everyday interactions and social media role playing. She is shaking from the cold and her teeth are aching again when she sees the light is still on in her room. She looks up from the kerb for a sign of him at her window. She has difficulty opening the front door of the house because her hands are trembling so violently. She creeps as quietly as possible up the stairs. An intruder in her own home. Outside her bedsit she presses her ear to the door. It takes a while for her to hear anything beyond the pounding of her heart in her ears. She thinks she detects some faint movement inside, more a displacement of air than a clear sound. To be standing outside her home, unable to enter, brings a shadow of madness into her mind.

She musters all her indignation and anger. She inserts the key in the lock. Her heart is pounding with an intensity that shifts the shapes of everything she sees. For a moment she thinks she sees a ghost image of him. He is smiling at her with his dandruffed hair combed to one side. But he is not here. She waits for her home to return to its familiar welcoming appearance. But it refuses to comply. Everything looks and feels different. Dirtied. Repossessed. He has stolen her home from her. She kneels down on the floor by the small bar heater and as the elements begin to emit their orange glow she knows she will have to find somewhere else to live.

Mother Love

The iron wheels hammered, the floor swayed, the occasional light flickered past in the rural night outside. Life had backed me into the urine stink of the WC of the night train from Florence to Paris. My mother had suffered a breakdown, some kind of estrangement from self. She had threatened to commit suicide.

'She told me she was going to throw herself down the stairs of the nursing home.' The anarchic threat on my mother's part was a source of amusement to my sister, in part because the stairs at the home were plushly carpeted and widely spaced apart but also because our mother was a woman who never let herself go. Never in my entire life had I ever seen her run or dance. Neither was she a person we thought of as thinking big thoughts. She acted and thought along conventional lines. Decorum had always been her mantra. I participated in my sister's amusement but afterwards I felt bad for laughing. I knew, perhaps as my sister didn't, that when you're suicidal you go through all the options, trying to find the least painful, messy or terrifying. I understood that, though throwing herself down the stairs wouldn't achieve the desired result, my mother was unhappy enough to seriously think of ending her life. So I was on my way back to England.

She threw her arms around me with a beatific smile when I entered her room at the nursing home. For the first time in my life I was her saviour. At the same time I struggled to recognise her in this new emaciated impassioned woman holding herself close to me. We hadn't seen each other for two years. Not since we sat together by the Grand Canal in Venice and tears came to her eyes. My father had recently died and I had never seen her cry before. We were about to part company. I was to return to Florence and she had a flight to catch back to England. It bothered me afterwards that I had offered her so little comfort, that there had evidently been an occasion I had failed to rise to. She often made me feel I was cold hearted. I suspect I probably made her feel that she was cold hearted too. We weren't good at enlivening or consoling each other. I stiffened now as she embraced me. This rapturous display of affection embarrassed me. It had no precedent. My mother wasn't given to expressing open emotion. There was always some vital part of her that stood aside. Probably I had inherited this trait from her. I couldn't receive this great gust of released energy without a physical resistance over which I had no control. It was the first sign my mother had undergone some revolutionary revision in her identity. There were very few of her possessions in the room. She was without her props. Our belongings perhaps form a bigger part of our identity than we realise. They are what survives of a life after all. She began whispering to me conspiratorially. She told me her room was bugged and led me out into the garden with its serpentine gravel paths, rhododendron bushes and wooden benches. There she told me the staff at the nursing home subjected her to humiliating tortures every night. They all wore surgical masks while inflicting pain on her. It was hard to follow what these tortures consisted of. She spoke of masking tape, leather straps, manacles and needles. There was a sinister plot, she told me, masterminded by a man with a burnt face, to rob her of everything she owned. Agitation had brought a new quickness to her eyes as if the world had brightened and become a more intimate presence for her. Clearly she had entered a new dimension of belief, but this was no religious conversion. It wasn't so much the things she was telling me that came as a shock as the realisation of how easily she could slip free from all the ideas I harboured about her. I had to admit I had never made much effort to know her, to understand her. Not that I ever felt she had any pressing desire to be understood by me. Now I was forced to acknowledge how erroneously the picture we have of the people we think we know well reflects the reality as they themselves see it.

There was a breath of salted sea air and she looked like Miss Havisham among the flowering rhododendrons. I have to admit I liked her new look. She had ceased to look like a woman holding a pose in a mail order catalogue. She now looked like a woman who went out in the rain at night.

My relationship with my mother had generally been one of conflict. The first time I recall her embarrassing me was at a dinner party at our home. I was about twelve and caught only a glimpse of the proceedings. I didn't recognise my mother in the woman presiding over the table. It was like she was making an exhibition of herself. She spoke louder and with more animation and amusement than usual. What made me ashamed of her was her innocence. She had no idea how fake her performance appeared. I felt sure all the guests would laugh at her when they drove home in their cars. However in recent years, since my father died, I had mostly ceased to dwell on the critical perspective of her. I preferred to think of the moments when she had surprised me by revealing herself to be a presence for which I was grateful.

To be in sole possession of my parents' house reminded me of the excitement this state of affairs brought with it when I was a teenager. The anticipation of the forbidden becoming permissible for a heightened stretch of time. I knew a familiar crazed feeling of wanting to smash everything. It was too easy for me to regress back to the teenager in me. I hadn't grown up much. This always became clear to me when

I found myself surrounded by the familiar possessions of my parents. Family history was an oppressive force in my life. I rarely gave it much thought. People sometimes said of me that they couldn't imagine me with parents. I embraced the observation as a compliment.

I had never married or even come close. My longest relationship lasted little more than a year. There was little inspiration to be taken from the marriage of my mother and father. Open displays of affection were as if strictly outlawed. Neither were there any long heartfelt conversations. My mother and father didn't seem very interested in each other. It was incomprehensible to me that my mother and father who had nothing to say to each other could share a bed. But every marriage is a mystery. No one knows what goes on in private, perhaps not even the participants. My father sometimes pulled a face when my mother wasn't looking. I can't say I liked it when he did this even though his aim was often to earn a complicit smile from me or my sister. These surreptitious gestures of protest made him seem only half grown as if he had little more authority than a child in a classroom. It was my mother who enforced all the censorship. My father had little to say for himself except when he watched the news. Then he revealed depths of anger and resentment which were a source of embarrassment to everyone else. Later, he decided to learn to play the drums and bought himself a large kit and soundproofed the spare room upstairs. He worked off some of his hoarded rage on his drum kit and became more companionable. Me and my sister sometimes sat with our mother in front of the television. It always came as a discomforting shock whenever something on television made my mother laugh from deep within. She so rarely gave any hint of being unable to control herself. So rarely dropped her guard of self-possession. It was like she was being tickled against her will.

In middle age my mother, never a cook and clean woman,

started up her own business. An employment agency which quickly flourished. It became obvious she was in her element orchestrating a world in which she had the last word. She also offered a computer training course at a time when most people still didn't own a computer. But she sold the business too early. Two years after the sale, when it became clear the computer was to become a universal fulcrum of daily life, the business was worth an additional million pounds. The business acumen she prided herself on had let her down.

Ballet was the love of her life. My father was compelled to accompany her to Sadler's Wells or the Royal Opera House at least twice a month. If she nurtured a secret thwarted ideal of herself it was probably as a ballerina. The closest she got was to run a keep-fit class. There she pumped her body in an exemplary fashion for an ever-increasing miscellany of women in leotards and pastel-coloured leg-warmers. It was so successful she was interviewed on television for a local news program. To my mind though she had the wrong opinion about everything. She wasn't sympathetic to migrants, refugees, political prisoners, the poor, the weak, the persecuted or the homeless. She sided with border guards, riot police, with the hard of heart and the unscrupulously ambitious. She had no affinity with animals. Both our dogs bit her – a response to her lack of supportive feeling I fully understood and applauded - and were put down as a result. Something for which I found it hard to forgive her. She had never made any pleas for understanding. Take me or leave me was her attitude.

Within a month I had seen to it that my mother was put on different medication and then brought her back to her home. It quickly became clear I would not be returning to Florence any time soon. My sister had a marriage, a job and two daughters to occupy her. I had no such excuse. I could continue my translation work and endeavours to write a decent novel just as easily in England as Italy. As a child my mother had left me to my own devices. This was still true of my life. At fifty I was responsible for no one's wellbeing except my own. My mother had never found within herself any impetus to form a friendship with me as a child. I had failed to create any kind of charmed conspiracy with her. I had remained a household duty for her, as was the case with my sister too, a duty she didn't evidently much enjoy. The phrase she most often said to me as a child was 'Later, dear.' This 'later' never arrived. Perhaps it had finally arrived now. As if the love I always felt I warranted but that she had withheld might now be forthcoming.

At least once a day she asked me if I believed her about the tortures she had undergone. She always looked anxious when she broached the subject. I think she needed to believe the tortures had been factual. The only alternative was to accept that she was losing her mind.

With the new medication the raging storms in her head began to abate. She started to do again the things she had always done. She read novels about Tudor England, Renaissance Italy; she watched her DVD collection of ballets and Shakespeare plays. She began driving her car again. But her memory more and more often failed her. I always had to be by her side. Remind her where to take a turning, what was missing in the supermarket trolley. It was a new experience for me to be needed by her. It was distressing to watch her make mistakes out in the world. She had always prided herself on her social poise. That said my mother had spent her life putting things out of her mind. You might say she had been courting dementia for years.

One day she mistakenly used her credit card instead of her debit card at a supermarket checkout and the pin number failed three times, each time causing her more distress and humiliation. In life it's hard to find the right words no matter how alert the mind. Words are rarely reliable. But we expect numbers to behave. We expect numbers to provide a solid foothold. My mother especially was prone to calculate her net value in terms of numbers. It must have been mortifying when she could no longer trust numbers.

Then came the afternoon she told me she had decided to have the swimming pool in the garden filled in. The prospect of the ruckus workmen in the garden would create made me lose my temper. I used the garden shed as my study where I was working on the revisions of my novel suggested by my editor. Nevertheless my anger was disproportionate and aggressive. I suspect in part it contained some resentment that she was stopping me from going back to Italy. I told her if she insisted on having the swimming pool filled in I would return to Italy. Half an hour later she opened the door of the shed where I was working. Her body language was sheepish. She told me I was right, apologised and we shared a hug. I had never known her so humble, so defenceless. It should have been me apologising. I had shouted at her in a blaze of unwarranted fury. It was the first time I had ever won an argument of consequence with her. I think I broke her will that day. It was the end of the iron lady. She became nicer as a result but much more vulnerable.

'Don't you think you can work just as well here as you would in Italy? Or perhaps we could both live in Italy together?' She was shy when she offered this hypothesis. It was the first inkling I had that she felt some guilt for separating me from my former life. I should have agreed with her to make her feel better. Instead I opted for a bemused expression. I regret that now. Now that I sometimes find myself wishing there might exist a time or place where all is forgiven.

It was at the beginning of winter that a tiny growth on her nose was discovered to be cancerous. Surgery was recommended. Instinctively I was against it. At a time when she was undergoing an ever more alarming estrangement from self the last thing I thought she needed was any kind of alteration to her face. Surely, even for a well-balanced mind, there can be few more unnerving experiences than to stare at an unfamiliar face in a mirror. But the operation went ahead. In the consulting room, after the doctor had explained the procedure, she took my hand. Her hand in mine felt heartbreakingly vulnerable. I felt the quickened pulse of her fear in the contact. It was another of those moments when I felt I didn't impart the necessary comfort. What we achieve when there's love in our heart never feels enough. I left her there alone. I walked out into the car park with its puddles on the pitiless concrete and border of anonymous shrubs and nettles. One of the world's many desolate places.

The operation ran into difficulties. They had to graft a substantial portion of skin from her forehead onto her nose and she returned from the hospital looking like an entity from a low budget horror film. Her face was almost entirely covered with bandages and blood seeped out into the cloth from her forehead. The sympathy I felt for her was at high tide, swilling over my bulwarks. Every mirror now had only unkindness to give her. For three months she didn't leave the house. I took over duties in the kitchen. Only the meals I cooked differentiated one day from another.

I don't recall there being a specific morning to which she woke when she no longer knew who I was, when she no longer had any knowledge of what she had once loved and hated. She stopped brushing her hair, changing her clothes. She began violating all the sacred codes she had lived by. It became apparent, even if she herself didn't realise it, she was now in the midst of the fight that eventually faces all of us, the fight we cannot win.

One day I looked inside a notebook of hers. She had been teaching herself French. *Il y a en deux*. She had been studying

Shakespeare plays. *What qualities does Lady Macbeth possess? Ambition, confidence, strength of purpose.* These were qualities I knew she esteemed. It made me smile to realise she had probably identified with Lady Macbeth for a while. But there was something heartbreaking about these efforts of hers to engage her intellect. I suspected the great regret of her life was that she had never discovered what her intellect was capable of. She once told me that given her life again she would not have children. I didn't at the time ask her what kind of life she imagined for herself instead. I wished now I had, I wished I had been a better friend to her. I decided to leave the notebook by her bed. 'If your memory comes back write down anything you want to say,' I said. She didn't know what I was talking about. I might as well have been talking Italian, which I sometimes now did to amuse myself and amuse her.

Two years passed in which there was no further significant deterioration in my mother's mental health. There was a scar on her forehead and her nose was crooked after the operation. To me it felt like we were both imprisoned in a tower. Awaiting sentence. More and more my task became to keep her entertained. I became a kind of court jester. It worried me how much I enjoyed deploying a madcap persona. There sometimes seemed more truth in it than how I had always felt constrained to behave in the outside world. She could still take momentary pleasure from the moment. The only emotions she appeared now to have access to were rudimentary and short-lived. She no longer had any sense of time. Even her sense of place was subject to constant revisions.

One summer afternoon I removed my mother's shoes. Holding her dry swollen feet with their weak charge of warmth and clipping her yellow toenails for the first time required a deep breath and some fortitude on my part. Then I grew accustomed to the chore. Just as I grew accustomed to the sight of her naked body. But today I wasn't cutting her nails.

I had brought my mother out into the garden. We were both barefooted now. I pressed the play button on the machine and there was music. I began dancing and soon my mother emulated me. She concentrated hard on copying every move I made. We danced among the buttercups on the unmown grass. It was like her dementia provided us with an alternate life where we could do stuff we could never have done in the other life. I couldn't remember ever seeing my mother look so enamoured of life. Neither could I remember ever seeing her dance before. It was sad that this kind of exalted abandon was only available to her now that she had so little memory of who she was.

'You're a nice man.'

I was sitting opposite her at the kitchen table. Even in former times when alone together we usually had to think about what to say next. Conversation between us didn't come easily. Often now I wasn't entirely sure she saw the person she was talking to. She could make me feel no more substantial than a wraith in sea mist. I could sense how much effort it cost her to think herself into my presence. Now that she was no longer able to impart design her spoken words seemed to float above her on the air, mysterious weightless home-less things. I had just given her her medication. The most straightforward recognitions eluded her, but she always iden-tified this as a daily ritual and seemed to take pleasure in the accomplishment of swallowing her three pills. She counted them off on her fingers. The smile she now often wore was disarmingly good natured. As if there was no sacrifice she wouldn't make for her son. Except she no longer recognised me as her son. I'm not sure, when she was in full possession of her faculties, she ever thought of me as a nice man. I certainly hadn't been a nice man the previous night. I hadn't been able to concentrate on the novel I was reading in bed because she was conducting a surreal running monologue with invisible friends, the ladies as she called them. Finally I could no longer master my irritation. I went into her bedroom and shouted at her to be quiet. She was both mystified and frightened by the sudden fact of me and my unkind rules. Though nothing I did had any emotional consequence for her, this wasn't the case for me. I felt deeply ashamed of myself afterwards. I was reminded of how surly, judgemental, argumentative I had always been around her. Our relationship often felt like a long drawn out border war, with the occasional ceasefire. In this war she was the greater power, possessed of better weaponry, more resources. I was like a barefoot kid throwing stones at an enemy with expensive hardware. Neither of us ever accepted or even shared the blame for our hostilities. I read somewhere that you should treat every living creature as if it had once been your mother in another life. I though had always treated most living creatures much better than I treated my mother.

Now I had from her what I always believed I wanted – unconditional surrender. Needless to say, there was no satisfaction in the achievement. Instead I realised I should have accepted her as she was instead of trying to bludgeon her into submitting on my terms. I wanted now to make amends. Except she was no longer capable of appreciating any change of heart in me. It was bewildering to realise nothing I did would have any emotional consequence for her. For her continuity was restricted to a short scatter of blurred frames. There was no big picture. No feature film. The narrative began anew every morning. There was still an animating presence inside her mind, but she no longer met herself there. She lived in a world almost bereft of recognition. What had once been reality was now as if nothing but a forgotten fiction. Only the moment mattered to her. Let the moment therefore suffice, I thought. That got me thinking about isolated moments of beauty in my own life that have had no apparent consequence.

Especially a girl I shared an enlivening kinship with. There I had been longing to hold her, but she didn't want to be held by me. So much of our life is the circling of a dream. The dream, a changeable elusive presence, is at the heart of our identity, it is the fabric to which all our qualities are stitched. Did it matter that the dream never found fruition in the physical world? The important thing was never to relinquish it. It's the dream which keeps beauty as an animating source of strength in our lives, which reminds us we are connected to a larger reality. My mother was no longer circling her dream. She had lost all contact with it.

I began looking through old family photographs. The old garishly coloured photos reminded me of how rarely I was able to find her as a child. As if even back then she had been preparing the way for what was to follow. Then it surprised me how extensively my mother had travelled. There she was smiling outside the Taj Mahal, standing in a familiar pose in front of the Weeping Wall, squinting in the sun while leaning against a rail on a boat on the Nile. I found it hard to grasp that she had inhaled the dust, used the currency of these far-flung places. It was easier to believe she was standing in front of backdrops of a photographer's studio. She had perhaps possessed more pioneer spirit than I gave her credit for. All the photos made me sad, as if she had already died. There's something soul destroying about the hard evidence provided by a photograph that never can the clock be turned back. There was a more recent photo of her in the garden of Virginia Woolf's house at Rodmell. I had taken it and she was smiling. It was an affectionate smile. I remembered well that day. We had made a memory of quiet enchantment together. I had succeeded in infecting her with some of my love for Virginia Woolf and it had brought us into harmony for a couple of hours. I remembered telling her how often I thought of Virginia Woolf's suicide. Trying to imagine that final walk of hers across the Sussex downs to the River Ouse. The bottomless loneliness of it.

She now spent most of her time in bed, talking to the ladies, her invisible friends, when she wasn't sleeping. I began pretending I too interacted with the ladies and that the house was a hotel. I invented a staff. Francesco, the dessert chef, was her favourite. He liked his drink and was generally untrustworthy. One of his nightly concoctions was always something inedible. I announced the fictitious choice of dessert menu every night with a teasing show of suspense.

'For tonight's menu Francesco has come up with the option of wild oxen testicles marinated in crushed banana and cinnamon or, if you'd prefer, tiramisu.'

I'd always get a smile out of her and the right answer when I played this game. I felt rewarded when she grinned as if I had helped her escape for a moment the dark place her mind had become. She could just about grasp the gist of my sentences. I was aware she believed everything I said.

'When I was young you had the power to create the world I lived in. Now it's the other way around. I create the world you live in. Our roles have been reversed,' I said. I couldn't help thinking that once upon a time she had tied my shoelaces, pulled sweaters over my head, washed my hair, lifted me up into her arms, scolded me, observed me closely day after day.

'When will my sister be back? Do you know? They told me she was coming back soon.'

Her sister had died a year ago, in America where she had lived all her married life. She too had been struck down by dementia. My mother had not been able to register the fact.

'What do you remember about your sister?'

'Remember, yes. Are those men still in my room?'

'What men?'

'There was a man with a burnt face. He frightened me.'

'I sent him away.'

'Did you. Oh, you are a lovely man. Do you live here as well?'

I thought it strange that she could barely remember anything that had happened to her, was no longer able to understand things she had once understood but could remember and understand words, their meaning and how to put them together to form sentences. Her sentences rarely failed her. She knew the meaning of words, how to order them but she could no longer put them at the service of an identity. Language, not experience, it appeared, was the last thing to leave the mind.

'I've moved in to look after you. I've been here three years. Can you remember my name?'

'Flora.'

'That's your name.' I smiled. My mother smiled back at me. There was personality in her smile, though not a personality I recognised as belonging to my mother. She was like a puzzling anagram of herself.

'I'm going upstairs now.'

She hesitated at the door for a moment. Then she returned to the table and, awkwardly, from behind, put her arms around me.

Needless to say, I had no social life. I couldn't leave my mother alone for more than half an hour. Like her I was moving further and further away from my former life. There was a growing sense that I would not get it back. We were both of us passing time, not living. The irony was that while my mother was losing all her memories, no longer living in time, I felt myself more deeply aware of time, shackled by it. I was taken to a deeper tier of reminiscence, constrained to inhabit my memories more intensely. They were all I had in the way of intelligent company. I suppose the mystery of my life is why I never married. How it came about that I never arrived at this crossroads. This was the convergence point all my memories seemed to lead to, this path I had never taken. My mother was always jealous of my girlfriends. She liked to belittle me in their presence. As if she couldn't understand what possessed them to see any virtuous or reliable qualities in me. Annoyingly I couldn't help agreeing with her on this point. It was like she didn't feel any need of me but at the same time didn't want to relinquish me to another woman either. As if she had known all along that this moment when I became necessary to her would arrive.

At the kitchen table again, I handed my mother a photograph of herself as a teenage girl.

'Who is this?'

She looked at the photograph. It widened and then clouded her eyes. She was clutching the cross she wore around her neck. Rubbing her thumb over it constantly. 'I don't know,' she said.

'That's you when you were in your teens. Before you were married. You once had a job as an usherette in a cinema. I bet you didn't know that. You lit up pathways with a torch. Like you were enacting an existential metaphor.'

I smiled, but she looked troubled and I stopped the photograph game. My mother was mostly immune now to passing grievances, temporary embarrassments. Except when the carer arrived twice a week to wash her. Only then did her stubborn resistance to entreaty, so familiar to me, return. My mother was no longer an object of study to herself. There must be relief in that – or would be if she still possessed the tools to appreciate the relief. She was like an animal now, bounded always by the moment. She had even acquired an animal smell, a raw musky odour which began to fill the entire house.

My mother walked into the sitting room where I was on my laptop still working on the final edits to my novel. She handed me the broken chain of the cross she could no longer wear around her neck.

'It's okay. I can fix it,' I said.

But I couldn't fix it. One of the middle links had snapped. I held it in the palm of my hand and for a moment it seemed charged with all the unfulfilled wishes of my mother's life. I searched her dressing table for another chain I could use to restore to her her cross. It upset me more than it should have that the chain was broken and I couldn't mend it. Even though my mother had already forgotten about it at dinner that evening.

One evening when I went into her bedroom to check on her there was a smiling lucidity in her eyes that questioned my own eyes. It alarmed me as if a moment of judgement had arrived.

'One day you'll write about all this,' she said.

That her mind had returned to her body turned me inside out. I was frightened for a moment as if a ghost was speaking to me.

'Have you come back?'

She smiled up sadly from her high bank of pillows.

Now was the time to say what was in my heart. To say what I might most regret not having ever said. We had spent a lifetime of saying little of significance to each other. Here was the chance to make amends. It might be the last opportunity I ever had. But I was paralysed by the lack of any precedent for honest displays of feeling between us. I smiled back at her, but it was as if I had lost the power of speech. Then the moment had gone. The blank bewilderment returned to her face.

I was frustrated with myself in bed. I thought how little effort I had made to know my mother. How rarely I asked her about her life. As if the vast silence into which she had retreated I myself had helped create. I should have shared more with her, shown more interest. I never told my mother the stories I told my friends. A secret lost its excitement and depth of meaning whenever I contemplated sharing it with my mother. I had always treated my mother's interest as white noise. I answered her questions with irritation which she pretended not to notice but which I now realised had probably hurt her. I rarely sought to entertain her. I should have behaved like an adult and not a sulky child. I could never make my mother angry. But I wasted a lot of time and energy trying.

I sat at the kitchen table listening to the shrieks and complaints of my mother in the bathroom while the carer showered her. The water was too hot, then too cold. I found I enjoyed my mother's determination to put up a fight.

My mother returned to the kitchen table with a lost and dazed expression. She looked more gaunt, more vulnerable, more pared down to the bare bones with her hair wet. She always sat at the same place at the table. It was one of the things she was careful to remember. Then, when she was in her chair, she walked her fingers over the table, counting aloud to five each time. Her wedding ring was loose on her finger. The branching of the blue veins and the black bruises on her hands ever more visible. She repeated the ritual several times, fascinated by the spidery movements of her fingers. Her only guide now was her nervous system.

'You were making a lot of noise in there. But you must be feeling better now you're all clean,' I said. The previous night she had had a kind of seizure. Her body locked in a fierce struggle to make it through to the next minute in time. I saw the ghost of death appear momentarily on her face. It surprised me that, however foolhardily, I felt equal to whatever was forthcoming. It never occurred to me to call an ambulance. As if this was a journey me and her had to undertake alone together.

The carer busied herself with the dirty clothes. My mother left stains everywhere now, like a last unconscious attempt to leave her mark on the world. While the carer removed her latex gloves she said, 'I think it's time you thought about putting your mother in a home.'

I looked at the woman and before I knew what was happening there were tears in my eyes. I couldn't help myself. I was aware my mother was watching me. Watching me with the uncomprehending curiosity of a wild creature. The carer saw my tears and gave me a hug, but it felt like a perfunctory gesture on her part and there was no consolation to be found in her arms.

The open suitcase sat on the bed. For a moment I felt as though I was staring into future time. Experiencing the moment already as a memory. As if my mother had long since vanished. The pungent smell of the fermentations of her body was thick in my nostrils. I had come to associate the smell with affection. As if the better part of my nature resided in it. I hurriedly packed items of my mother's familiar clothing, trying to recall the things she liked best, the things that brought her comfort. Every article of clothing now conveyed a secret history of sadness. There are epiphanies hidden in ordinary things. Awaiting their moment of revelation. My hands were prickling with guilt and sadness when I picked up her fur-lined boots. It was my job every morning to help her put them on. I was conscious that whatever I packed would be accompanying her on her final journey. What was left behind she would never see again. I listened out for any movement downstairs. I didn't want her to catch me in the act of packing the suitcase. The truth was, I was in the midst of tricking her, of performing a shameful act of betrayal. I had promised her I would never put her back in a nursing home. It was a different home, not the one where she believed she had been tortured every night, but nevertheless I was breaking a pact. I had sat her in front of a Rudolph Nureyev DVD down in the living room. As I packed her things I became aware of how much I had come to enjoy many of the rituals I shared with her. She enabled me to act without self-consciousness and it was a liberation to be able to do things without critically watching myself. Earlier I had danced her around the kitchen table to Chopin's Mazurka from *Les Sylphides*. The habit of looking after her, of keeping her entertained had given my life structure and purpose. For the first time in my life I had been able to sustain a liking of her without reservations.

The dreaded day arrived. I helped my mother into her coat. I put on a show of excitement, pretending we were going on holiday together. Deploying all my acting skills to trick my mother, to reassure her when a look of fear entered her eyes. I feigned excitement when it was guilt and heartbreak I felt. The effort of the deception involved was exhausting. I was conscious of the momentous nature of the moment. I was about to escort my mother from her home to which she would never now return. There was a moment as I walked with her past the garden's cherry tree when I considered sending the taxi away. It was as if I had the smell of incense in my nostrils. Wasn't it more than possible that somewhere deep inside her ravaged mind my mother might at some point register this awful betrayal on my part? Her brief return to lucidity the other night was an indication that momentarily she did at times regain memory. While the taxi driver behaved as if he was participating in a moment that was nothing out of the ordinary a shameful sadness lurked inside that I sensed I might never be able to step outside of again. I found myself wishing she would put up a protest or begin crying, pull more at my heartstrings. Then I know I would have taken her back home. But her face was a blank canvas. Not once had she cried since her mind began failing her.

Two rows of broken shrunken old people sat in armchairs against the walls. Open mouthed and staring into private voids, their skin the colour of ready salted crisps. My only consoling justification had been an idea that she might find more animating likeminded company in the care home than I was able to provide. I saw this was unlikely to be the case. We were shown to her room. She kept close beside me. I noticed the big iron radiator which reminded me of all the depressing rooms I had been forced to sit in during my lifetime. I was still tricking her, making believe the care home was a hotel and I would be staying there too. But the act of separation had already taken place. I had no role to play in this new room. I would soon cease to be her familiar friend. I took my mother outside for a walk with the intention of going down to the seafront. I wanted one last moment of intimacy with her. However, she was sulky. She pushed me away when I put my arm around her. I realised she hadn't spoken a word for at least ten minutes. That she had a forsaken private grimace on her face. It felt like I had undone all my commitment to looking after her. There was no acknowledgement on her part when I left her. I turned once to look at her sitting mute and bewildered in an armchair facing a giant TV screen on wall brackets. When I came in sight of the sea I tried to feel some excitement at being free again.

I visited her twice in the care home. Both times the smell of boiled vegetables and custard behind the herbal detergent stink was sickening. The ready smiles and upbeat activity of the staff seemed playacted like they were acting in a TV commercial. On neither occasion did my mother acknowledge my presence. Her mouth was drawn tight. There wasn't a trace of personality in her eyes. She looked like she had now forgotten how to laugh, forgotten even how to smile. Each time she was sitting in a different armchair. I felt she hadn't found a foothold in this place. I knelt down in front of her on the carpet, but she refused to look at me or say a word. I felt she disliked me. That I was an untrustworthy stranger to her. Though the thought did cross my mind that she knew me and wanted to make me pay for the wrong I had done her. Her thinning hair had been tied back with an elastic band which showed her scalp and made her look like a stranger impersonating my mother. Each time I turned to look at her before leaving and each time the sight of her, the forlorn helplessness of her expression branded itself on my heart.

Then I received a call from the nursing home. They were going into lockdown because of Covid. I would no longer be able to visit her. It occurred to me that the people ministering to her needs would now be wearing masks, as she had imagined in her hallucinations of torture in the previous care home. She had prophesised the future. A week later I received another call. My mother had died. She had fallen down the stairs. Initially they thought no damage had been done. They had taken her to hospital to be checked. But, twenty-four hours later, she had died 'in her sleep'. I'm not sure I believe it's possible to die in your sleep. How can anyone sleep through such a momentous event as their death? I found myself picturing her lost and desperate, standing at the top of the stairs in the middle of the night. I didn't notice at the time but the stairs in this home were narrow, steep and thinly carpeted. They could do damage to brittle bones. I pictured her throwing herself down those stairs on purpose.

I went into her bedroom. I looked at the photograph of her smiling in Virginia Woolf's garden. A memory that now only I possessed. I looked at all the flotsam that had survived her. Elastic bands, hand creams, lipsticks, biros, stockings, slippers, hair brushes, a box of tissues, tubes of ointments, a cuddly toy. It made a mockery of the nature of life to me that she had gone forever but all this trivia remained. Then I picked up the broken chain and the silver cross I had been unable to mend and looked at the empty bed. I felt I had failed somewhere along the line. That I didn't know how to love the people to whom I owed love until they disappeared.

Then the prophecy she had made came back to me. 'One day you'll write about this.'

Fabio and Eva

It's more likely than not that I died in 1943. That is, I died as Eva Rosenthal, a ten year old Jewish girl native of Hamburg, Germany. I can't claim to know what it means to be dead. Except I now have this hunch that we never are dead. Rather that we are in continual transit and transition from one birth chart to another. You see, I am writing this as Fabio Lombardi, a fifty-six year old man living in La Spezia, Italy. A married man of modest ambition and means. A Catholic by birth who hasn't set foot inside a church for years. I woke up as Fabio while in the midst of an altogether different life. Now I am terrified of falling asleep again. For reasons which will soon become clear. So I keep myself awake. I have been awake for four consecutive days now. Fabio had rarely given much thought to the idea of reincarnation. Fabio wasn't much inclined towards abstract thought. But when I did think about it I assumed, like most people, we would be reincarnated into the future. We are fixated with the idea of forward progress. It's our mantra. Even though life teaches us this stubborn notion is mostly fallacy and ends in disappointment. However, it never occurred to me that reincarnation might rocket us backwards in time.

Of course when I was Eva I had no knowledge of Fabio, no recollection of a different existence at all. But, as Fabio, the German faces in archive footage of the war years always fascinated me. Especially the faces of individuals caught performing the sieg heil. Here they were preserved for all posterity in one shameful defining moment. It always bewildered me how much insanity was charged into that gesture. Especially bearing in mind the outward appearance of normality of the faces. Clearly it was possible to be both normal and insane. I had often wondered as Fabio what these people were like in their daily lives. As Eva, I was to find out.

We lived in Hamburg. My father was a shoemaker. He made beautiful shoes that were famous throughout the city and even beyond. His clients included film stars, footballers, politicians, financiers, musicians. He encouraged me to pursue the gift I had for music. Sometimes the piano was my best friend, but it could also be my worst enemy. It made challenging demands on me that I met and failed to meet in equal measure. What my fingers could achieve on the keys was both a source of wonder and triumph and wretched frustration.

When Hitler came to power my father's attempts to appear strong and wise made me want to give him something from deep inside. It was the first time I felt myself reaching out with my entire being. He liked me to wear ribbons in my hair. He said then I looked like an angel from heaven.

Noticeably more and more members of the community began giving Hitler their support. His leadership skills weren't proving to be incompetent as my father had predicted. If my father had a fault it was that he was too optimistic, too good natured. The symbols of the Nazi party were everywhere you looked. Hitler's hateful eyes watched you from posters in the streets and there was even a painting of him in the classrooms. At school my companions began shunning me. Even my best friend, Steffi stopped talking to me. We had created our own world together. We shared secrets. We shared our every recognition of a new connection. We excited each other. She was the only person I talked to about the things that were important to me. Now I often caught her speaking behind her hand while looking across at me with a cruel grin on her face. Then there was the day I was walking Nana, our dog. I liked to walk as far as the bookshop where two kittens always lay curled asleep in the window among the display of books. In the square on my way home three older boys who lived nearby jeered at me. The woman who worked in the local butchers walked by. I was accustomed to seeing her in a blood-soaked apron sawing at a leg of beef. She was an intimidating woman. I thought she might intervene, reproach the boys for being abusive to an innocent young girl, but she didn't. She pretended not to notice. The shortest of the three boys asked his two friends if a dog owned by a Jew made the dog Jewish too. He gave Nana a nudge with his foot. Then I saw something more menacing enter his eyes. I knew in my stomach something horrible was about to happen. And it did. He gave Nana a hefty kick. Nana yelped then snarled at him. He gave her another kick, putting more disgust into the blow this time. His friend spat in my face. I remember I was wearing my red coat with the wooden toggles.

I didn't tell my parents what had happened. But I woke up every morning sick with apprehension. I dreaded leaving the house. At school I was subjected to one humiliation after another. Even from some of the teachers. My father's beautiful bottega window was defaced with ugly words and a whitewash image of a grotesque hook-nosed bearded man. He was no longer selling many shoes. My parents began arguing. I could hear their hushed irritable voices through my bedroom wall. My mother wanted to leave Germany. My father opposed the idea. It was the first time I sided with my mother against my father. My mother made me tell my father what I went through every day at school. When I heard myself speak of the cruelties I suffered they seemed petty as if I was making mountains of molehills. I was therefore surprised how sympathetic my father became.

I retreated back into childish things, toys and dolls I had outgrown, in an effort to take refuge in the oblivion of early childhood. The piano became a conveyor of lies and deception. The music it produced wasn't true. There was no beauty in the world. Everything was ugly and cruel. The deepest layer of my being was constantly laid bare. Sometimes at the deepest layer of my being there seemed to be terror, terror of the ugliness of people; sometimes there seemed to be love, love for my father, my mother and my dog. At school only one teacher stopped the unkindness of my classmates towards me. Only one of my old friends sheepishly nodded a greeting to me. No one wanted to be called *Judenknechte* – lackey of the Jews. It was a new word that entered the school classrooms. All the cruelty inflicted on me was passed off as a passing joke by its perpetrators as if it was of no more consequence than a gust of wind. They had no idea how much sundering unhappiness it caused me.

It was the middle of the night. The pounding on the door of our apartment woke me up. Or perhaps it was the hysterical barking of Nana. I walked out into the hallway. My parents were standing there in their nightclothes in the electric light. My mother was telling my father not to open the door. Outside angry abusive voices demanded to be let in. Sweat started out of my armpits. The aggressive banging wouldn't stop. Nana's barking became still more frenzied. I had never before seen my father's face with so much fear on it. I didn't recognise him. We all stood staring at the door. My father stepped forward as if to open it and my mother hissed at him and pulled him back. When the blade of an axe pierced the oak panelling, my mother screamed.

The faces of the four men who blustered into the apartment were contorted and flushed. They looked like devils from a medieval painting. Lips drawn back over flashing teeth, eyes narrowed and ablaze with determined malevolence. There was nothing recognisably civilised about them. They brought with them a suffocating stench of alcohol. They entered our apartment with a goading sense of entitlement. One held a crowbar, another a hammer and a can of petrol and then there was the overweight young man with the axe. They weren't wearing uniforms, but it was clear they loved their fuhrer and there was nothing Hitler approved of more than hate. Hate had become righteous. Even the churches were draped in Nazi banners. The terrifying unreality of hostile strangers suddenly invading my home made my legs tremble so much they seemed to belong to someone else. The first thing they did, while spitting out insults at my mother and father, was to rip out the telephone wire. Then one of the youths spun my father around and struck him in the face with his fist. My father tried to reason with them. They weren't interested in reason. They had only contempt for reason. They took it in turns to hit him. My mother stood with her arm around me. We were both shaking. My father was repeatedly kicked as he lay curled on the floor. One of the men gave my mother the hammer and told her to smash the glass of the mirror and all the crockery. She refused. The man slapped her and tore at her dressing gown. The piano made awful noises when they hacked at it, noises eloquent of how violently insane the world had become. Nana was hysterical. She bit one of the boys when he kicked her. He picked her up, marched over to the window, opened it and threw her out. Her bloodied body was still on the paving stones the next morning.

They left after someone had set light to the bedclothes in my parents' bedroom. It was me and my mother who put the fire out. My father was beaten so badly both his eyes were swollen shut and it was painful for him to breathe. My mother's dressing gown hung off her body in rags and tatters and you could see her underclothes. There was blood on her chemise. Every cabinet, wardrobe and cupboard in the apartment was overturned. Every piece of furniture butchered. Every window broken. Wires were ripped out and cut. Everything breakable was broken. The apartment looked like a scrapyard. The piano, radio and gramophone had been mutilated. All the phonograph records broken. My mother and father's clothes had been torn and cut. Books had been ripped up. Photographs torn in half. They even broke some of my toys, shredded my books and slit my mattress. Shards of broken grass and crockery crunched underfoot wherever in the house you walked. We all had to sleep with icy winds blowing through the shattered windows.

My father's workshop was also ransacked and destroyed. All his tools and materials destroyed or stolen. He fell to his knees when he saw the damage. Some of the older Germans looked at us with sympathy but they seemed listless and irrelevant bystanders in this new world. I could sense my father felt deeply ashamed of being so helpless to protect his family and his home. He barely spoke. Then his resolve was tested still further when he discovered his father, my favourite grandfather, had been beaten to death the previous night. Nazi thugs had entered his home too. My mother was still trying to console my father when two members of the Gestapo arrived and arrested him.

My mother soon learned he wasn't alone. Every other Jewish male she knew had been arrested as well. She discovered later he had been sent to Dachau, the fearsome concentration camp not far from Munich. My mother was told the best way to get him released was to prove the family possessed papers to emigrate. She took me with her to one office after another. In most of these buildings we were treated with unkindness. My mother couldn't keep her indignation to herself. Often now she spoke to me as if I were an understanding adult. She no longer bothered to use her soothing voice on me. For example, I learned from her that the insurance money owed to my father for the fire at his workshop was confiscated by the Nazis and the same happened to all the many Jewish families whose property was damaged that night. The Jews were even made to pay for the petrol that had been used to set fire to their shops and businesses and synagogues.

I barely recognised my father when he finally came home. His head was shaved, he was hollow-eyed and there was no colour on his grizzled face. He looked weightless, like a scarecrow. He wouldn't talk about what he had suffered. Only that he had experienced things that made him despair of humanity. His head sagged to one side. His voice became flat and mournful. In former times he had loved to laugh. It was one of his favourite things. This changed. In former times he sang songs while getting dressed and he would change the words to fit us, his family, into the song. This too changed. It was like he had forgotten lots of things about himself. Things that made him loveable. I watched him more closely. The way he crossed one leg over the other when he sat down, the way he fiddled with his shirt collar, the absent way he ate his food. He talked to us now as if from a distance. He had lost authority. Even I could tell some of the things he said were silly. He was opposed to leaving Germany. He didn't want to leave his mother alone.

'Soon things will go back to being normal,' he said. 'People will tire of Hitler and the Nazi thugs.'

'We'll be dead before things return to normal. We owe it to your daughter to leave.'

I didn't like being turned into a bargaining chip.

'I have to believe in normality,' my father said. 'What else is there to believe in?'

After that night – *Kristallnacht* as it came to be called – I had grown closer to my mother. Even months later it was like he was still kneeling down in the midst of the wreckage of his workshop. It was a moment he couldn't escape from.

The next bad thing to happen was he was ordered to report to the Gestapo. He was told they had found a buyer for his shop and our apartment. The price offered was a pittance of their true value. They demanded he sign papers. He refused. So he had to report to the Gestapo every morning and was kept there all day, forced to press himself against a wall. Sometimes they made him do sit-ups. He said they were uneducated men who took great pleasure in making him feel like a circus clown. I was proud of him for refusing to sign the papers. I think he surprised himself. It was an act of courage which helped replenish his self-esteem. Eventually though he had to succumb. The properties were sold for a pittance of their true value and even most of that money was confiscated. But we no longer cared. Because, at great expense, three transit visas for Cuba had arrived.

My father was wracked with guilt that he was leaving his mother behind. He wouldn't stop talking about it.

'Your mother herself has urged you to go,' my mother kept saying.

We were all sad for a lingering moment leaving the family home for the last time even though it was a ruined shell of its former self. I thought of the leafy shadow pattern of the tree in the square that the moon made tremble over the wall of my bedroom at night. Then an unexpected memory returned to me in the hallway. An afternoon I stole into my parents' bedroom and looped Mother's pearls around my neck and danced in front of the mirror. It was a moment of guilty pleasure. Guilt with pleasure mixed in it always made me feel I had stepped dangerously outside the jurisdiction of my parents. I was trying to feel what it was like to be a grown woman. Now it seems like a dark premonition of the doomed struggle I would be put through to grow into a woman.

The harbour smell, the brine and tar, went deep into my body. The salt air on my face and neck made me skip along the Hamburg dock. It was a long time since my body and mind had been happy together. I had never been on a big boat before. The SS *St Louis* was a luxury liner. My father, who now made more effort to remember me, told me there was a cinema and a pool on board. Almost every passenger on the boat was Jewish. There were lots of children. I dared hope I might make a friend again. I craved to be knowable to someone, to put an end to the feeling of not being good enough. I longed to have high hopes of myself.

We set sail for Cuba, a two-week voyage. On the boat it was a shock to be treated with respect and even affection by the German crew. The captain quickly became a kind of hero to everyone. He didn't hide his contempt for Hitler and had instructed the staff to treat us with courtesy. He even took down the portrait of Hitler during Friday evening prayers. We could do whatever we wanted on the boat. In the evenings my mother and father danced together to the music of a band or watched a film on the large screen. In the day I played in the swimming pool. There were no restrictions. The world seemed sane again. There was a feeling of goodness in my hair and on my skin.

I soon made friends. It was a joy to be accepted again by children of my own age. They helped lift the thick frightening shadows that had swamped my mind. While watching the boys make big splashes by jumping into the water of the pool my new best friend Ella asked me which of the boys I liked best. I told her I liked them all. It was a new experience to discuss the individual qualities of boys. To discover what features attracted me. Sometimes, while we stood at the rail talking about these things, the light turned the sea a beautiful green. At night, when I was lying on my bunk, the creaking of the boat seemed like an extension of the busyness of my mind as it worked out all these new thoughts. Every day I had a new secret I kept from my mother and father.

We were never to set foot on Cuban soil. As a child a lot of information is withheld from you. Your life as you know it differs enormously from what adults believe it to be. They have no knowledge of how far you travel in your mind. As a child you are like a spy working alone in the midst of schemes and plots you have to unravel by covert means. However, I understood why my parents withheld what they knew from me because every additional piece of information I picked up carried a new charge of swirling menace. I learned there had been a large protest in the capital of Cuba. The Cubans didn't want any more Jews in their country. The most popular newspaper carried the headline, *Jews Out*. The Cuban government was constrained to rescind our visas and ordered the boat with all its passengers to return to Germany. A couple tried to commit suicide by jumping overboard. All the lifeboats were lowered into the sea around the moored ship and lights shone down on the ocean because of a rumour that a mass suicide was planned. Ella and I discussed this. I couldn't imagine my parents would want me to kill myself. Even if it meant returning to Germany which had become hell on earth.

I stood by the rail with my mother and father and we looked across at the land we were never to know as the ship's foghorn sounded a plaintive note and we slowly sailed out of the harbour. A heavy atmosphere of tension and fear now permeated the boat. When I looked across from my bunk at the dying light stirring on the porthole I began to think of everything as the last time it might happen. I thought there were already things I had done for the last time without knowing it would be the last time. Like taking Nana out for a walk and thrilling at the sight of the sleeping kittens in the bookstore window.

Ella and I were still picking up and sharing information in our covert fashion. We learned one person had committed suicide by jumping overboard. We tried to summon a memory of her, give her a face. The boat sailed slowly close to the coast of America and we could see the lights of a city. My father thought it was Miami.

'We would be safe there,' he said. 'It's so close we could almost swim there. What an insane world we've brought you into.'

I reminded him of times we had swam together and recalled the taste of a sudden gulp of sea water and we managed to laugh even though the memories seemed as remote as the stars up in the sky.

We learned the captain of the ship was determined not to deliver us back to the Nazis. That his idea was to run the ship aground off the coast of England. For days we seemed to drift along what felt like the edge of the world. Then there was a great celebration when we heard France, Belgium, the Netherlands and England had agreed to take us in. The band played music and mother and father began dancing again. I never learned how it was decided which families went to which countries. The ship docked in Belgium. I had to say goodbye to Ella. It was another of those last time moments. She and her family were going to England. That was where everyone wanted to go. We all wanted to be as far away from Hitler as possible.

We were very poor in Paris. We lived in a two-room apartment in the Le Marais district. I had to sleep on the sofa. We had a stove but no hot water. I had to get used to eating the same things every day. Fortunately, French bread was more exciting to eat than German bread. None of us could speak French. None of us could make ourselves understood. I spent a year away from school while I learned the new language. I found I much preferred it to German. It made me feel more grown up. I tried not to revel in the fact that I was more accomplished at something than my mother, that I possessed a superior knowledge. I would help her out when we went shopping. Father found a number of jobs doing manual work. He was always complaining that his back and arms ached. There were other Jewish refugee families in our building. They all spoke a strange mix of Yiddish, Hebrew, German and French. It was disorientating not to share a common language, like trying to compose a jigsaw with many missing pieces.

Everyone knows what happened in May 1940. Our worst nightmare returned when the red and black Nazi banners appeared on the streets of Paris where they possessed a still more hypnotic sinister swagger. Before long the anti-Jewish laws were enforced. I had to leave school. We were made to wear a yellow star. It made me feel ugly and unclean, like I carried a contagious disease rotting me from within. One day a French policeman stopped us in front of Notre Dame. He demanded to check that our stars were attached properly to our coats. He was currying the favour of all the German soldiers strolling around. I hated that man and his pert waxed moustache.

The French police came for us in the middle of the night. It was like *Kristallnacht* all over again. A violent sundering irruption into our intimate world. Everything my mother and father had worked for once again counting for nothing. Except this time no one was physically harmed. Two policemen stood watching while I got dressed. We were taken in buses to the velodrome. Inside there were already thousands of people. Every loud noise carried a sinister echo, especially when someone began screaming. We were kept there in squalor for days without food or water. Every joint in my body, every thought in my head ached for some small measure of comfort. Once again it was painful to see my father reduced to such a state of helplessness. Then the French police escorted us to Gare d'Austerlitz and I had my first experience of being locked inside a cattle truck. The camp at Darcy was in the middle of the countryside except we were penned in behind barbed wire, monitored by French policemen in watchtowers and raking searchlights. I slept on a wooden bunk with a scattering of itchy straw for a mattress. My mother slept on the bunk below. My father was in the men's part of the camp. Word was we would soon be deported to the east. For a while it felt like we were living inbetween time. Then alarm returned when all the women were ordered to hand over their jewellery. Many threw their wedding rings into the latrines, including my mother. Some were consequently beaten by the French police. We were living in a lawless place now. The next day trucks of German troops arrived. We were all ordered outside. There were two armoured cars with machine guns pointed at us which made my heart beat faster and my mouth go dry. Then the Germans began dragging us children away from our mothers. Women were screaming and scratching and shoving at the cordon of French policemen. The fathers too were beside themselves with disbelief and anger. Shots were fired into the air. The noise stood apart. There was suddenly no telling what might happen next. While we all stood as if frozen everywhere you looked birds took to the air. I exchanged one last look with my mother and father. My father looked dishevelled and distressed like someone fighting to stay above water. The image remained stamped on my retina for days afterwards. All the adults were marched off. We children, about nine hundred of us, were left alone in the camp. The French policemen who guarded us were officious, sticklers for mean detail. Not one of them gave the impression of possessing any kindness or being able to think for himself. Unlike most adults around children they used coarse language. Only the nurses showed us any sympathy. I helped look after the younger children. They were like stories which would never be told. Their faces as if ghosted over. Time dragged by every day as if we had too much of it, when, in reality, so little remained to us. I gave a lot of thought to all the things I would never do again. I realised my life was of no interest to anyone except myself. It was the loneliest thought I had ever had. I grew accustomed to my irregular heartbeats, the nits in my hair, the hunger pains, the headaches and the whistling in my ears. The loose print dress I wore was filthy.

On the platform of the rural train station we had to tell our names to a frowning man at a desk who wrote them down in a large ledger. German soldiers with their snarling dogs and French policemen shoved us inside the cattle truck, nine hundred children without a single adult companion, and bolted the doors. The sadism and depravity of what they were doing was concealed beneath an expression of mild impatience. They knew what was going to happen to us and yet they obeyed orders as if it was just another part of their job and had a practical purpose, as if they were supervising the delivery of mail. I now wonder what these men tell their grandchildren when asked what they did in the war. In the cattle truck I eventually fell asleep. And when I woke up I had stubble on my chin and a wife with her back turned to me in the bed. I was Fabio Lombardi. He came back to me in a great disorientating gust. The first thing I did was to vomit over the edge of the bed. I couldn't help myself. My violent retching woke my wife. I ignored her concern for my wellbeing.

'Where did we spend our honeymoon?'

She looked at me with the irritation I was accustomed to and had learned to overlook. I finally got her to answer my question.

'Yes. Havana. And when we went to America where did we go? I'll tell you where we went. We went to Miami. Now listen to this.'

When I excitedly told my wife the story of Eva she worried for my sanity. That's understandable. Were our roles reversed

I would have thought along the same lines. She asked me with mocking eyes if possessing a vagina had given me any new insights into the nature of the female sex. 'The terrifying vulnerability that comes when you first realise you are attractive to men for example. Or to be treated every day as if you are precariously prone to damage in both physical and moral realms.'

My wife likes to berate me for how little I understand women.

That day I fact-checked as much of my experience as Eva as was possible. Many details of my odyssey were verified by official history. The SS *St Louis* had indeed set sail for Cuba and been turned back. Parisian Jews had been taken to the velodrome and then incarcerated in a camp at Darcy. Eva was telling the truth.

I've now been awake for four consecutive days. As Eva recedes back into the shadows of my mind I have felt constrained to take stock of myself as Fabio. I have acknowledged Fabio could have been a much better man. Fabio is a man full of pent-up frustrations. He is thrifty with empathy. Rarely does he try to understand anyone by putting himself in their place. Yes, I was an envious man. There was always someone more handsome, more talented. I have always regretted that there was no music in me. In a dream world I would be a singer-songwriter. A man up on stage under the lights. Like Luca Carboni or Vasco Rossi. Had that happened I would have married a more beautiful woman than my wife. I feel bad about this element of the fantasy because I am deeply fond of my wife despite how easily irritation comes to her. The first time we ever made love was in the midst of a vineyard in broad daylight. She instigated the experience and I'll always be grateful to her for giving me that memory.

I suppose now is the time to admit that at the last election I voted for the candidate of a right-wing party which wanted to put an end to all the immigrants arriving from Syria and North Africa. I didn't feel strongly about these refugees one way or the other. It was the anger with which he spoke that attracted me. I recognised it. I related to it. It didn't matter what he was angry about. I was angry too. Angry that life had shortchanged me. Anger was the buried monster in me that kept reawakening. I regarded my vote as little more than a harmless gesture of protest. Now I wonder if we are put on this earth to learn lessons. I feel a small measure of comfort that Eva had been a good girl. She had nothing to reproach herself for. Surely, she will be rewarded. Perhaps after the gas Eva will wake up with the bearded face of some desert tribesman who is guided by the stars or a saffron-robed Tibetan monk striking a clear note from a bell high on some snow-clad summit.

The Dance Company

I have extended my boundaries. I have occupied new territory. I have become a pioneer. The further you venture from familiarity the more interesting your thoughts become. It feels like I have walked into a mirror and come out on the other side. The mirror I have obsessively monitored myself in. The mirror I have performed all the grooming imitation games of adolescence in. The mirror I have practiced all my dance moves in. The mirror in which I sought the ideal, but which instead gave back to me all my imperfections, all my faults, all my mistakes. Yes, when after the audition, Mina Haller invited me to join her dance company, it felt like the pitiless judging glass turned to water and I stepped into it and walked out into a new world on the other side. Can you see me? Can you hear me? If only you could see and hear me.

The audition took place in Germany. Everywhere you looked rubble and cranes and scaffolding. Restoration and redevelopment and industry. Now I'm in Prague. There's more respect for the past in Prague. There's mostly shame for the past in Germany. And because you only now exist in the past it feels like you're closer here in Prague. Can you see me? Can you hear me? If only you could see and hear me.

Every morning I walk over the Charles Bridge. In my long tweed coat. The long tweed coat that of all my clothes is most eloquent of how I want to see myself, how I want to be seen. I was wearing it the last time I saw you. The smile you gave me is still the saddest thing I will ever see. Every morning I marvel at the plumes of my breath adrift on the air over the Vlatava river. Yes, I have never felt more alive, more in step with my secret self. I have never felt I belong to a time and place as intimately as I do while crossing the Charles Bridge. There is adventure in the names of the streets and squares. Adventure in the foreign smells. The sense of being in the midst of adventure awakens the child in me and brings you closer. Can you see me? Can you hear me? If only you could see and hear me. Every morning I sit down to a cappuccino in the same bar in Prague's old town. Every morning I pay for my cappuccino with the foreign currency that seems to leave a magic dust on my fingers. Every morning I walk out into the square just before the bells of the astrological clock strike nine. Every morning I walk into the rehearsal studio with a favourite song in my head, a thrilling song in my heart. These feel like moments that have been waiting for me ever since I was born.

Mina still dazzles me. I can't grow accustomed to the sight of her. Her physical presence so powerfully affects me that I am incapable of looking at her with ordinary observation. Every new day the sight of her, like snowfall, brings a new wash of wonder and gratitude. She's about fifty. A little younger than you were when your body began to betray you. There are cat's hairs on her clothes. The only evidence she shares a tactile tenderness with another creature. She has never married. She seems to stand guard over her solitude. She is tall and thin. As thin as you were in the hospice. She has beautiful chiselled features. Shy eyes, a shy mouth. Long black Medusa ringlets. She makes medleyed shapes of her body that enliven me with the excitement of wanting to emulate them. Her body is a transfiguring instrument of grace and power. She remains an otherworldly vision no matter how much I look at her. Yes, the visual fact of her permeates me, floods me. It's like I am in the presence of a hallowed character from history. A rare eminent human being who is of value to humanity. I wish you could meet her. My throat tightens, my face flushes whenever she addresses me personally. The rhythm of my heart will not slow. I hang on her every word. Her every word is scripture. She has become my compass. She guides me through the storms. I cannot bear the thought of misunderstanding her. I cannot bear the thought of disappointing her. Her presence is like a struck tuning fork by which I can evaluate with clarity the measure of truth in every step I take, every shape I make.

The company is outwardly a harmonious ensemble of disparate individuals. But there is rivalry. Everyone wants to be her favourite. Yes, everyone jostles for position. The competitive spirit is masked beneath smiles and acts of generosity. Mina is the recipient of relentless flattery. It's a wonder she isn't spoiled by it. But there's a humility to her. She seems to cast off all vanity, like shaking rainwater out of her hair. The company is like a guild with time-honoured customs, feudal rankings, secret codes. Step by step, I am finding my place.

Now that I'm settling in I have begun to take more note of the female dancers. Not that I'm looking for love. Not that I know of. Not actively anyway. But we're always looking for love, aren't we? Yes, we're always looking to be loved. There are eight girls in the company. Two of whom are especially attractive. A Japanese girl called Miho and an African American called Dinah. Sexual attraction is aspiration in its most elemental form. This though is something I would never be able to say to you. Only now do I realise how shy we were with each other. It's perplexing that mothers and sons should be so shy with each other, don't you think? I suspect all but one of the eight male dancers are gay. I have wondered how long it takes a gay man to tell I'm not gay. One time, with Branko, a Serbian dancer, I had to make it clear.

Every evening all my muscles ache. It makes me feel virtuous when all my muscles ache. I am staying in a hostel. On one of the hills on the outskirts of the city. I have been put into a different hostel from the other members of the company. There wasn't room for all of us where Mina is staying. Only Dinah is also staying at this hostel. Our exile was decided because we are the latecomers to the company, the two most recent additions. I don't mind being alone. I had to get used to it after you went away. I find it relatively easy to make friends, even to give depth to friendships, but essentially, I feel most myself when alone. I think this is because I don't like the burdens of responsibility. Life is less exciting but more manageable when you only have to answer to yourself.

Mina is putting together a new choreography. Every day she makes us improvise on a theme she gives us. 'You were born a thousand years ago,' she says, and her voice deepens when she is fully engaged with what she says. 'How would you move?' Or, 'you are arguing with a lover. Show me your gestures.' We have to do this one by one, alone, in the riveting, in the intimidating spotlight of Mina's gaze. She sits on a wooden chair in front of the stage smoking one cigarette after another.

She singled me out for praise for my performance today. I danced innocence in the face of blame. I was aglow for the rest of the day. Yes, I was walking on air.

But the next day, at coffee break in a bar, Lionel, an Argentinian dancer, made fun of me in front of the entire company. I was waxing lyrical about how much I loved working with Mina. Lionel repeated the way I said 'fabulous' in a mocking tone. Everyone smiled so I smiled too, though I didn't understand the joke. Five minutes later he repeated the way I said 'awesome' in a mocking tone. This time I knew there was malice in Lionel's parroting of what I said. This was confirmed when he mocked me a third time. I asked myself if it might have anything to do with the Falkland Islands. Even though that was ten years ago now. I wanted to tell Lionel I despised everything Margaret Thatcher stood for. Generally, I have found to be English abroad meets with favour. It's the first time I've felt disliked because of my nationality. It occurred to me that everyone in the company belongs to nations who have fought each other in wars within recent memory. Mina herself is German, Miho is Japanese, Hunter is American, Alessandra is Italian, Marie-Claude is French. Miho doesn't hold Dinah accountable for the destruction of Hiroshima. Dinah doesn't hold Hunter, the white American boy, accountable for the contemptuous way blacks have been treated by whites in America. No, if we're going to bear grudges for what our nations or races have done to other nations, other races in history we would all have nothing but bloodthirsty hatred to offer each other.

Lionel now mocks me at every opportunity. Though never in front of Mina. No, in front of Mina he is charm and humility personified. He is determined to make my life miserable. I don't understand why he dislikes me so obsessively. I believe I'm essentially a likeable person. It's a belief that's at the heart of my sense of self. If I lose that belief all my edges begin to blur and I become a stranger to myself. I've asked myself if perhaps I've become too pleased with myself. I can't bear the sight of him now. Can't bear the sight of his navy-blue velvet jacket and tight-fitting red cords, his cravat knotted high on his neck. His bushy eyebrows, fleshy lips and thin silvery scar on his forehead. His jaunty way of walking into rooms.

I have thought of letting everyone know I am Jewish. As a way of distancing myself from what Great Britain did in the Falkland Isles. As a way of disassociating myself from war criminality, of aligning myself with the persecuted. Grandfather, you know, is no longer talking to me. No, he was appalled I was prepared to live in Germany. Become a student of a German. Contribute to the German economy. (We're only in Prague for a month at the behest of some

Czech art council; then we return to Ulm where Mina has her permanent base.) It's the fear of causing Mina embarrassment that prevents me telling everyone I'm Jewish. I can't help remembering the one time I made it known to a German I was Jewish. It was to a girl called Hanna. Her face changed colour. Her body trembled. It pained me to witness how defenceless she became against the shame she felt. Her feeling had deeper roots than she could control or explain and rocked her entire being.

We're working on a section of a new choreography of Mina's that calls for joyful abandon. We all have to run about in figures of eight throwing buckets of water at each other. The problem for me is that Lionel has made me feel so miserable and tense that I find it difficult to access any other emotions. It's like Lionel has control of the jukebox of my mind. I no longer choose the songs. I have never before in my life detested anyone with such ungovernable visceral intensity. It's an emotion which bullies and bends me out of shape.

Yesterday I saw Lionel sitting in a corner writing in a notebook. Evidently, he keeps some kind of diary. Branko teased him about it. Lionel said writing things down was a good way to improve his English. Branko asked if he wrote things about him. Lionel said he wrote things about everyone. I have decided I have to read his diary. I need to find out why he dislikes me so intensely. That's how unhinged his dislike of me has caused me to become. I have begun keeping an eagle-eye on his shoulder bag. It magnetises my attention now more than Mina does.

Yesterday his bag was sitting close to the door. Taunting me. Daring me. I could perhaps deftly pick it up unnoticed and carry it into the bathroom. I want to find my name in his secret book. Discover what words he uses to describe me. I need to know what I am doing wrong. There is something amiss in me I need to correct. I walked towards his bag. I tried not to hurry. Despite the urgent beat of my heart. I tried to appear nonchalant. But I felt the eyes of the entire studio were on me. I felt myself inflating, becoming larger than life, lighter than air. Grotesque. I was within six feet of his bag. It was taunting me. Daring me. I squeezed my hands. I rubbed my eyes. I was within three feet of his bag. My palms were sweating. My heart was thumping. I was larger than life. Grotesque. I was within a foot of his bag. *Now is the moment.* Sweat iced my back. Black panic flooded into my head. Like there was a big bang. All my stars collapsing. My pathfinding stars. I walked past his bag without picking it up. No, I didn't have the courage. In the bathroom I splashed water over my face. My face which I barely recognised in the mirror. For a moment the fingerprinted glass reflected back an ugly stranger.

When he mocked me today I began trembling. I wanted to hit him. My body prepared itself for violence. I was on the verge of grappling with him. I heard you telling me I was being over-sensitive. I heard you telling me to get a grip of myself. But I keep imagining now a physical fight between us. Trying to work out how it might pan out, if I could win it. The last time I had a fight I was about eleven. I remember I gave a decent account of myself, except when the fight was over I began to cry. I didn't understand why I was crying, why tears were dampening my cheeks, but it was humiliating to stand there in front of my peers with tears on my face.

My dancing is suffering. My timing is all off. My focus is all out of synch. I can't get the rhythm into my feet. My body keeps betraying me. Every day my body betrays me because my mind is distracted, my mind is muddied. And I'm finding it difficult to sleep. Last night I stood by my window watching Dinah doing tai chi down in the courtyard under the moon. I decided to go down and talk to her. I decided to confide in her. But when I went down into the courtyard she had gone.

As if I had hallucinated the beautiful vision of Dinah doing tai chi under the moon.

In bed I recalled again the fight in the school playground. Except another, more urgent memory superimposed itself. It was the memory of a boy in my class. A boy I had given no thought to for years. His name was Rueben and he had darker skin than everyone else in our class. He had no friends. He was given a hard time by the classroom bullies. One afternoon the classroom bullies cornered him in the playground. They knocked him down and then they picked him up by his arms and legs. They carried him to the large rubbish bins and they dumped him inside one of them. I didn't participate in this act, but I did nothing to put an end to it. I raised no objection. It's probable I felt no objection. It's probable I even laughed along with everyone else who stood by watching. Rueben never returned to school after that day. Only now do I possess the emotional sophistication to understand the torment he must have endured, to sympathise with his plight. Only now do I feel an urgent need to apologise to Rueben. To tell him how sorry I am that I didn't offer him any support. To tell him how sorry I am for all the things I have said and done in my life that I didn't mean.

The next day Mina took me aside. I saw Lionel glance over at us as she walked me to the far end of the studio. I saw the devious interest in his hateful eyes. Mina sat me down. She lit a cigarette. Her long black corkscrew hair was tied back into a pony tail. I saw her through smoke as if she was smouldering. 'It doesn't seem to be working out for you here,' she said. She was uncomfortable. She fidgeted in the chair. She took deep draughts of her cigarette. Like she wanted to disappear inside the smoke. She made me uncomfortable. I thought I might cry. Like I did in the school playground. 'You don't seem happy with us,' she said. She took another deep hit of her cigarette. 'So I think maybe it's best for all of us if we part company,' she said. I could tell she thought I had no enthusiasm for her work. That I didn't respect her work. But I said nothing. I didn't tell her nothing could be further from the truth. I had to let the misunderstanding go. I had to allow this grotesque misrepresentation of my distracted state of mind pass without contradiction. Because it was too humiliating to tell her the truth.

I left Prague the next day. An outcast now. I didn't see Lionel again. At least I was spared the sight of him revelling in his victory. I walked to the station with my bag. I boarded a train for Paris. I felt Rueben was sitting opposite me on the train. Sitting there with all the muck from the rubbish bin clinging to his school uniform. I never expected to meet Rueben again and especially not to be on such intimate terms with him. Rueben had become my companion. United as we are in our shunned isolation. Baited and bullied until we cracked. Baited and bullied until we bled. You once told me we all become angels in the end. You were in bed at the hospice. Towards the end. I sometimes wrote the things you said on my hands when I returned home. 'We all become angels in the end,' you said, and your smile only lasted a second. Rueben has become an angel, an avenging angel. I leant my head against the greasy window. The rattling window. I was glad you couldn't see me.

The Accident

The wind gusting with such force that on the open road the car swayed as if it might take flight. This wild unforeseen weather. Where had it come from? Climate change, he says aloud, even though he is alone in the hire car. No trace of climate change in my life, he thinks and adjusts the rear-view mirror so as to exchange a sympathetic look with the reflection of his face for a moment. But it feels good to be in Italy again. Italy makes him feel lighter on his feet. It is a source of regret that he has never been brave enough to spend more of his life in Italy. Italy feels like my spiritual home, he says aloud, not bothering to elaborate to himself what he means. He is driving from Rome to Florence, taking quieter roads so as to see more scenery. He has treated himself to a night in Florence. Then he will fly back to England, to his marriage and job. My job, he says. I suppose it could be worse. He recalls walking through the Forum, the gleaming oracle of all those broken stones. The statues of the virgins were all missing their heads, he says. It's something he will tell his wife. Not that she will take much interest. How glad he is that the sales conference is over and done with. It reminded him of sitting in assembly at school. The impatience to be somewhere else, anywhere else. He now finds himself trying to remember the names and faces of some of his class companions. He is recalling the face of a boy known as Mac when his world changes.

The oncoming black car as he takes a bend monstrously fills his entire vision. A mayhem of adrenalin turns him into a stranger to himself. A shrill noise emerges from his mouth he has never before heard his vocal chords produce. He swerves, but too late. The impact and hollowing crunch of metal on metal, the shattering of the windscreen floods a black tide behind his eyes. He is thrown forward. As if he might be propelled hundreds of yards across the rural landscape. Instead the violent clasp of the seat belt sucks all the breath from his lungs and brands a burn onto his chest. He sits still for a moment, trying to get his breath back, trying to get his bearings back. He looks over his shoulder at the car he has hit, at the damage he has done. He was driving on the wrong side of the road, he realises. The faces from his schooldays had distracted him. He thanks a god he doesn't believe in when he sees a woman emerge from the car, apparently unhurt. He takes a series of deeper breaths, prepares himself for the mortified apologies he will now have to make.

She stands for a moment looking at her damaged car. Then she looks over at him. There is no anger in her. If anything, she imparts a self-effacing shyness. As if what she is most accustomed in life are private moments. She holds to her breast what looks like a violin case. He goes through the pantomime of apologising, of bringing down upon his own shoulders all the blame. But his attention is constantly struck by a disconcerting familiarity about the woman's face. It's as if a crowd has parted to reveal her standing in a spotlight.

They exchange personal details. He fingers the tie he has taken off and balled into his trouser pocket. He keeps assuring her he will make it clear to her insurance company that all responsibility for the accident is his. They discuss the physical repercussions of the crash. Neither of them considers themselves hurt in any way that requires attention. They share a disinclination to make a fuss of their health. He tells her he hasn't seen a doctor since he was a child. He will remember it as the first time he took her into his confidence, told her an intimate truth about himself.

Neither of their cars will start. She calls a garage. He listens closely to her speak in Italian, her native tongue. It's like she is casting beautiful spells out into the air.

They sit down on the grass verge by the side of the road, waiting for the tow-trucks to arrive. For a moment she sits with her head thrown back. He can feel the eagerness with which her body drinks in the sensual wellbeing imparted by the warm sunshine in his own body. The sunlight they share is like a conduit into her body. Or perhaps he's being ridiculous, as his wife often maintains. He glances at the arch of her back in this gesture of surrender. He can't think of anything to say except how good it feels to be alive. He knows she is feeling this too. Then he catches her smiling at the two mangled cars and the skid marks on the tarmac. He smiles too. He has an image of them as two birds perched on a high wire. So remote do they seem from the world around them.

He learns she is married with two children and is due to perform a recording session in Rome the next day. She is from another world, out of his league, he thinks, wrenching up a blade of grass and twirling it between his fingers. Please don't ask me what I do for a living, he thinks A sales rep for Barilla UK. Was that really the best I could have done? Her name is Francesca. He takes her name to the most private part of his mind. He says it to himself and it echoes as if his mind has become the interior of a beautiful old church. He keeps stealing glances at her beautiful hands. The mystery of her hands. The history of her hands. He is mortified when the first of the two trucks arrive. The act of separation is a banality of pleasantries on the surface, but he experiences it as a momentous sundering.

He feels bereft when she leaves him alone by the side of the road. He didn't, he knows, give a very compelling account of himself. She made him feel he is still an untold story. He calls his wife and tells her what has happened. He paces up and down at the side of the road. But he barely listens to what she is saying. The only thing he wants to talk about is this woman. He wonders how much space he has forged for himself in her thoughts. She's probably already forgotten me, he thinks. He feels she has moved him closer to the essence of life and his wife is now pulling him away from this important place he has discovered within himself.

He has to wait almost an hour for his tow-truck to arrive. He shares the passenger seat with a gruff man who talks across him to the driver, a younger man. But though he is of no more interest to them than an insect they can't alter his feeling of having acquired a new relevance in the world. He doesn't know where they are taking him. It's the next phase of the upheaval from his familiar life. After twenty minutes they pull into a garage at the foot of a hill. He signs papers. He only understands about half of what he is being told in broken English. He looks up at the medieval town perched on the hilltop.

His first impression when, out of breath, he walks into the medieval piazza of the hilltop town is of a place where everyone is enamoured with their lives. Children are playing. Women are animated by what they say. Old men gesticulate as if their hands are puzzling out problems.

She is sitting at a table on the terrace of a bar in the medieval piazza. She smiles over at him. His body wants to break into a dance. This beautiful place has restored her to his life. He joins her at the table.

'I've never been here. It's nice, isn't it?'

'Beautiful,' he says. It thrills him to say the word beautiful to her.

'I've decided to spend the night here,' she says.

'Me too,' he lies. In truth he was resigned to catching a bus to the train station down at the foot of the hills.

He orders a glass of prosecco. He would like to tell her he

likes the sound of her voice. Everything she says interests him. Her manner of expressing herself strikes him as authentic. Her hands fluttering in the air, making shapes for emphasis. That they nearly died together has created a strange easy intimacy. It's as if she's impressed by the fact that he nearly killed her. As if this has given him some kind of hypnotic power in her eyes. She creates a space for him he flows into and fills. It is effortless. As if they are singing along to a prewritten score together. He cannot stop looking at her. His eyes will not accustom themselves to the sight of her. He has been married for nineteen years and has never been unfaithful to his wife. But this woman called Francesca produces a swell in him, like being lifted and buffeted by a succession of waves.

They have dinner together on the terrace of a trattoria. He will remember it as the most magical evening of his life. The church bells ringing out among the ghost lights of the piazza, the scent of laurels and the pollen of the lime trees sweetening the warm air. It all feeds the nest of intimacy that develops between them. He has the feeling she sees something in him his wife has never given him credit for. There arrives a moment, a wondrous moment, when he believes she has consented to sleep with him. It's like a new probing softer light in her eyes. Then the idea strikes him as pure fantasy on his part.

She tells him one of the pieces of music she most enjoys playing is by an English composer.

'*The Lark Ascending* by Vaughn Williams. You must know it well.'

He nods and smiles. He tries to hear the piece of music in his mind. But he can't for the life of him find the music in his memory. He is adrift in a moment of shameful ignorance. There is too much he should know but does not know. This is what she makes him feel. The waiter arrives with bill. He insists on paying.

As they are crossing the piazza she tells him there is footage of her playing the Vaughan Williams composition on YouTube. The self-effacing shyness of her uppermost again. But this will become the pretext that allows him entry into her hotel room. He will never see the room he booked in the same hotel. She will tell him it's the first time she has betrayed her husband. Everything she says makes him feel special.

He returns to England with a feeling his life has been both enriched and ruined. He understands this paradox is possible because he has a double life now. The world in which his body has to function has become a sham. That his wife detects no change in him disappoints him. It seems to imply she takes very little interest in him, that her understanding of him is superficial and functional. Fidelity was a gift he gave his wife, a gift he has now taken back. It surprises him that he feels so little guilt. Only occasionally when their shared history is apparent in a look she gives him does a brief unsettling pang arrive.

He watches the footage of Francesca playing *The Lark Ascending* every day. When he wakes it's what he most looks forward to. She is wearing a black sequinned dress. The music she plays moves through her body like a fluid she struggles at times to contain. Her eyes are mostly closed in concentration but now and again they flicker open for a moment and he recognises her as the woman he made moan and laugh. The first time he watched the film the wonder of her restored image and the sorcery of the music moved him to tears. He marvelled that those same fingers dancing over the violin's strings had chosen to explore all the contours of his naked body. That he had been a magnet to someone so gifted was an accomplishment he wanted to be recognised by the world. Except she always takes him back. Back to a moment which is isolated from the rest of his life. That one night has made the rest of his life seem unfocused. He can't really explain it to himself. It wasn't that Francesca had been more passionate or accomplished at love-making than his wife. It was simply that she made him feel he belonged more intimately to his life. She moved him closer to the essence of himself. He has never known such intimacy with anyone else. The creation of intimacy begins to strike him as the most important accomplishment of which we are capable. The measure of intimacy achieved ought to be the touchstone of all experience. It's what Francesca does when she plays her instrument, creates an intimacy between the listener and the music in which life is transfigured.

He begins picking fights with his wife. He makes her walk on eggshells. His abiding and chaffing feeling is that she misrepresents him. She bends him grotesquely out of shape, she disrupts the tides of his being. And that he does the same with her.

Seven years after the accident they get divorced. He tries to tell his daughter about Francesca. She refuses to listen, she becomes angry with him, more angry than he has ever seen her. She tells him he is living in a delusion. It is more disheartening for a man to be misunderstood by a woman than by other men. But he sometimes finds he agrees with her.

He often tries to picture the grass verge on the roadside between Rome and Florence as it would be now. All trace of the moment he shared with Francesca effaced. He marvels that it still exists out there in the world. The same is true of the hotel room – number 17. All trace of the beauty he created with Francesca effaced. Sometimes he thinks of going back there, to the place in the world where his life had both begun and ended. But he knows it would not make any more sense of what remains to him the most bewilderingly meaningful experience of his life. The one thing it left him he can understand is the music. It is the music that remains and authenticates what he feels.

The Patsy

You haven't a clue who I am. You can't place me. I could be your worst enemy. I could be your best friend. Why not say something? Whatever comes to mind. You've never once said anything memorable to me. I mean in the way of imparted wisdom. You always kept your thoughts to yourself. When you looked at me you seemed to be thinking of someone else, someone worthier of your attention. You compelled me to remain silent. It was usually how we communicated. Coded silence. We were like etched hoarfrost on a black window to each other. That said, I always felt you were passing judgement. It was what you did in your leisure time. Your silence was like a trap you set for those around you. You compelled me to keep everything about myself secret. I don't feel anything I do is meaningful unless it's secret. You haven't changed as much as Mother thinks. Here we are wandering aimlessly down this path, past flowers neither of us know the names of and still I feel you are setting a trap, still I feel you are using your silence as a weapon.

I create and keep secrets for a living now. I'm not allowed to talk about my work. That's always been easy for me. And yet today, something about the way your eyes widen when you look up at those trees shivering in the breeze makes me want you to look at me with the same puzzled concentration. I want to shock you into seeing me.

The thing is, when all's said and done, your secrets never had any glamour or danger. They were mean scrawny things.

My secrets, on the other hand, would get me killed if I leaked them. One thing I do for a living is to read through the files of prison inmates. Juvenile offenders especially. I look for individuals that meet the criteria to become a sleeping asset. The kind of person with confused ideas, the kind of person who will never get back on track. We can always find a use for people who have come irrevocably off the tracks. They're the easiest people in the world to incriminate. Because they're never any the wiser. They never know their left foot from their right foot. It's important that they're not very likeable. That they're incapable of arousing too much sympathy. The media always has to be taken into account. Or the renegade parts of it we have no control over. I also look for someone who wrestles with political ideas. There's nothing so effective as a half-baked political idea for generating anger and, as we know, anger is the underlying motive for almost every violent crime. Once we've found a suitable character we will learn the nature of his every vanity, the hidden root of everything he does and says, what he dreams of, what he's frightened of, what he eats, how he uses social media, what music makes him want to dance, what fantasies he uses to escape the monotony of his dead-end life. Then our sleeping asset can be fed into the plot without him ever realising there is a plot. Not a week of his life will now go by without him getting some fateful nudge from one of our guys. All the inestimable resources of the agency are now available to make sure he's incriminated in a plot. A plot perhaps yet to be formalised. He doesn't know it, but he now has virtually no free will at all. His handler will be teasing out of him virtually his every decision from now on. None of my chosen guys have ever been called upon for operations. Until now. And you wouldn't believe me if I told you who is in the crosshairs. A high-profile do-gooder. The kind of person you always hated. The kind of person who believes in social equality. Social equality is the last thing the people I work for want. Someone who is trying to bring to public knowledge what has to remain covert and hidden to continue being lucrative, to continue bringing the money in. I've got a hunch the world is soon going to know about my sleeping asset. I've got a hunch he will soon enter the history books. Not a bad fate, all said and done. I'll even tell you his name. His name is Joey Frost.

'Something's eating away at you, Joey, isn't it? I can feel it. And it bothers me that you don't trust me enough to share it. I mean, how long have we known each other now?'

Joey still can't believe this beautiful girl continues to seek him out. Her thick long wavy hair has many glinting tints of red in it in the afternoon light. There are lacy transparent patterns in the tights she wears. Like a secret coded message he can't work out no matter how hard he stares at them. She smells like midnight in fantasy land. He can't help feeling there must be some trick involved. Because he knows he isn't worthy of the excitement she has brought into his life. He is careful not to say much to her. The less he says the less chance there is of disappointing her and sending her away. He met her in a bookstore. She had smiled at him. Then he watched her brazenly slip a book into her bag. Next thing he knew she had taken his arm and hurried him to the exit. An alarm went off and she urged him to run. They ran together, the urgency of it separating him and her from the rest of the world. It was like a moment from someone else's life.

'I get why you don't want to share your secrets. I don't like sharing mine either. To feel you are carrying a secret keeps you apart from all the mundane hullaballoo around you, doesn't it? I have this hunch you've spent some time in prison. Possession of marijuana, was it? Or something more daring? I have this hunch you still feel locked up. They've let you out, but you still feel you're inside. No one ever knows any full story, do they? And because of that we all feel only half known. Let's try to know each other better than that. Sit over there in the armchair. The truth is, I'd like to feel you inside me, Joey. But at the moment this isn't possible. Because I too have my secrets. But I'm going to make an effort to trust you. I'm going to take off my clothes, Joey. All my clothes except my panties. I'm going to do this so you can appreciate how deeply I'm taking you into my trust. You can look but you can't touch. I'm not ready for touch yet. You see, I've suffered abuse, Joey. I was gang-raped when I was fifteen. My older sister refused the advances of this boy. As revenge he and two of his friends abducted me in a van while I was walking home from school. My sister felt so bad she got addicted to crack cocaine and died of a seizure. They say it was an accidental death, but I feel sure she killed herself because she felt so guilty on my behalf. She loved me. I was the only person she truly felt attached to in the world. Those three boys were never convicted for their crime. Would you help me take vengeance on those three boys? Come to the rifle range with me tomorrow. We can practice becoming hotshots. Humour me. I probably won't kill them. But then again I might do. Who knows what we will end up doing. That's the mystery that keeps us interested in our lives, isn't it? Every night I picture myself standing outside the house where those three boys live, waiting for one of them to appear at the window. I take aim and there's the shattering of glass and a quick flash of red spray.'

'How many times have you been to the rifle range with him?'
    'I don't know. About seven.'
    'And you always make sure he's noticed?'
    'I got him to aim at the guy next door's target like you said. The man threw a fit at him.'

'How's his marksmanship?'

'Surprisingly not bad. I get the feeling it's one of very few things he's ever done that he's been quite good at.'

'I've seen he's been posting lots of pictures of her on his Twitter page.'

'He's got three followers. He's virtually invisible. What does it matter what he posts?'

'It will become part of his secret history. How did you get him to keep posting pictures of her?'

'I told him to post a picture of her every time he's thinking about me. I told him she's my idol.'

'You could make a career for yourself in this line of work.'

'No thanks. But I wish I didn't enjoy it quite so much.'

'It's empowering, isn't it? To manipulate a narrative. Do you like him?'

'Not particularly. I'd like to say he has a kind heart, but I don't think he does. He has this private smile that gives me the creeps. Most of the time he doesn't know what his face is doing. He accepts everything he's told. He barely has a word to say for himself. What are your plans for him?'

'Wait and see. You play your role and all your mother's problems disappear.'

'How much longer?'

'At the beginning of next month, you tell him you're finally ready to sleep with him. You give him the money and tell him to book a room in the Plaza Hotel on Thursday the 7th of May. You arrange to meet him there at six. You go there at five and you take the rifle with you. You leave the rifle on the bed and leave.'

There is a burning cramp in Joey's stomach when he opens the door to the hotel room. Sometimes he has the frightening feeling that his mind is going to suddenly change the way it works. He's never been in a hotel room before. It echoes back his movements. There's a bundle on the bed. He unwraps it. It is the rifle she gave him the money to buy for her. He has come to like the feel of a rifle in his hands. He sits on the bed, curling his fingers around the trigger. Taking aim at the painting of a peaceful lakeside scene hanging over the sideboard on the mustard wall.

Outside in the square some kind of rally is taking place. He stands by the window, resting his weight on one hip, holding the rifle loosely at his side. He looks down at all the people gathered in front of a makeshift stage with footlights and a PA system. He looks for her in the crowd. He has been standing by the window for an hour now and she still hasn't arrived. It doesn't surprise him. He always knew she was too good to be true.

It all went according to plan. The high-profile do-gooder has been permanently silenced. There's more than enough evidence to convict Joey Frost as the lone assassin. There will be anomalies of course. We like the anomalies. They hint at how much power we have. And everyone wants their creative work to be known. That's human nature. If the secret services in many countries around the world want to get rid of some powerful opposing voice they just kill him. Or her. They hardly bother with subterfuge. But we have to sustain the illusion we live in a country where free speech is a prime value and the criminal justice system is respected to the letter of the law. So an entire bogus narrative has to be constructed. His handler has vanished into thin air. She exists now merely as a figment of his over-excitable imagination.

Except I have a confession to make. It would have all gone to plan if it had actually been carried out. But I went rogue. I did not have the backing of the agency. I wanted to see if it was possible to create a completely bogus narrative to explain a history. You see I can't help believing we all construe bogus narratives to explain our history. And to do this we all need a patsy to take at least some of the blame. You are my patsy. It's you I want convicted to take the blame for what is amiss in my life. You who have prevented me from being the better man I always hoped to become.

Byron and Shelley (Brits abroad)

The girl in the flouncy tattered lime green dress and lace petticoats is wearing a crusty black wig of curls and stands on an iron trunk in front of a marble equestrian monument. She is holding a red umbrella and has not twitched a muscle for fifteen minutes. When a young boy steps forward to touch her, she sticks out her tongue at him and everyone laughs. In the piazza with its sentinel pine trees bent back by sea winds, a crowd of about fifteen people have gathered around her.

Jake Cookson, who earlier busked here, is transfixed. He is wearing a ruffled white fencing shirt, ripped jeans and a red velvet jacket. He has small silver hoops in both ears. By his side is a guitar in its case and a small amplifier. He is sitting on the sea wall holding the paperback which, in part, drew him to this place - *There was a sea fog, in which Shelley's boat was soon after enveloped, and we saw nothing more of her.*

The girl in the green ball gown from another century steps down from the trunk and receives a round of applause. A tall bearded man with white dust in his uncombed hair walks over to Jake.

'Are you one of the yacht people?' His accent is American. His voice grave and accusatory. Having taken an initiative he now seems at a loss as to what to do next. His right hand is clenched into a fist as though holding captive something precious he is fearful of losing.

'Yacht people? Who are the yacht people?' says Jake, fingering the coral beads on his neck.

'You don't know Isabella? You look like you'd know Isabella.'

'Put like that I wish I did know Isabella. But I've only just arrived here.'

'You're not a suspect then?'

'A suspect?'

'The police think there may be a murderer on the loose.'

'I've got no blood on my hands. I've just been sitting here reading about the death of Shelley.'

'And keeping a close eye on Erin,' he says, nodding over his shoulder towards the girl got up as a china doll.

'You think she might be my next victim?' smiles Jake.

'She models for me. I'm a sculptor. Sometimes I let her sleep in my studio. She attracts dangerous men. Men whose sexuality has come awry. She completely vanishes into these performances of hers. There are men that truly believe she is a doll. Something in her performance compels them to take her at face value. Because she makes believe to the public that she has no interiority, no female plumbing, she attracts all kinds of twisted male fetishes.'

'Dolls I suppose do not answer back.'

'My name is Magnus Almond.'

'Jake Cookson,' says Jake.

For such a big-boned austere man the sculptor's hand-shake is surprisingly feckless.

Jake has hardly spoken to anyone since arriving in Italy three days ago. Yesterday he spent the night in Pisa where he had run through his set of Oasis, Verve and Suede songs and earned himself only sixteen euros. His home tonight is a tent in the nearby camp site.

Before long, Erin, the painted doll, shuffles over to them. She has a studied walk, part of her act, swinging her arms loosely at her side, barely lifting her feet off the ground. Without saying a word, she points impishly to her large trunk which is sitting in the middle of the piazza. She is never, it seems, out of character.

'Why don't you carry Erin's trunk for her?' says Magnus. 'I warn you, it's heavy. I'll get us a table at a bar on the wharf.'

Stepping over the tarred landing ropes and discarded fishing nets Jake heaves the trunk down the wharf. This is not how he likes to see himself, bent double and red in the face carrying some girl's luggage about. He averts his eyes from those of the African street sellers, feeling that he has become a figure of fun to them. Up ahead Erin every so often breaks into a quick loose-limbed geisha shuffle as if wound up like a clockwork toy.

Magnus has secured a table outside a bar further down the wharf. Erin, hitching up her skirts and petticoats, sits down cross-legged on the ground and begins counting all her silver and bronze coins. Under her tarnished frills she is wearing army boots. Jake has still not heard her speak. Magnus quickly dispatches two glasses of red house wine. He tells Jake that he had once been a Catholic priest.

'In some respects, I still am,' he says with a meaningful arch of his unruly eyebrows.

It is not difficult to imagine Magnus alone with a candle and a black book in bare rooms with high ceilings.

'What led you to take up sculpture?' Jake asks, rolling a cigarette.

'My belief in the urgent and eternal primacy of the creative form.' He speaks with an undertone of aggression as if sceptical of Jake's ability to sustain attention.

'People don't care about artistic form anymore,' Magnus continues. 'The modern world is far more interested in gratification than inspiration. Shall I tell you what I respect in life? I respect anything that has a regenerative power. Beauty has that power. What was it Shelley said? Poetry lifts the veil of the hidden beauty of the world. Poetry has form.'

'Didn't he have a house here?'

'There it is, across the bay. The white building. I live in Tellaro. Do you know where that is?'

'No.'

'It's further down the coast,' he says, pointing up at the ruined castle high on its summit. 'Once upon a time it was the most idyllic place on the planet. That was before Rufus Woodburn and the yacht people arrived.'

'The mysterious yacht people,' says Jake. Erin is now rummaging about in her iron trunk. Jake notices all kinds of oddities - a pair of puppets, a variety of vintage lace undergarments, candles, handmade notebooks, miniature antique books and what she now pulls out - a set of watercolours and brushes.

'Rufus Woodburn is one of the yacht people. He's just bought an apartment opposite mine - which isn't mine at all because I only rent it. Of course it wasn't good enough for Rufus Woodburn *as it stood*. He had to improve it; he had to add a panoramic roof terrace. So I have to put up with builders waking me up at the crack of dawn with their damn tools of destruction. And if it's not the builders it's the music and orgasmic squealing from his yacht which is often moored nearby. Rufus Woodburn is the perfect indictment of the modern world - brash, discordant, attention-seeking noise.'

'You don't like the modern world?'

'It forces me to be cynical, which is not my nature. That's what I don't like. However, I make an exception of Isabella. She's a sweet girl. I was teaching her to sculpt before she went missing. Of course what will probably happen now is I'll be arrested for murdering her. What proof do I have that I didn't kill the girl? I'll tell you. The only proof I have that I didn't abduct, rape or murder her resides in my own memory. Once again, I'm entirely reliant on my memory for my innocence. Do you know it's often only our memory which stands between us and a complete moral collapse? Now there's an interesting thought. But, of course, there's no such thing as an experience memory doesn't edit and alter.'

'So this Isabella has gone missing?'

'Three nights ago. She didn't return home. She's renting a place in Fiascherino. Near where DH Lawrence once lived.'

'Is there any English writer who didn't live here?'

Red in the face, Magnus now excuses himself. Jake watches his large frame disappear unsteadily down the steps which lead into the dark bar and its English pub bric-a-brac and wood panelling. Meanwhile Erin has been quickly producing a watercolour sketch of Jake.

'Let's see your picture of me.' Jake's voice is lustily ironic; a rakish smile plays around his mouth. Her picture is a clever cartoon-like image of him playing his guitar with emphasis paid to his red velvet jacket and shock of swept back hair.

'I'm going to stick it in my journal. Sometimes I paint pictures instead of writing.'

'You're American,' he says.

'That's not how I think of myself. I'm lots of other things before I'm that.'

Jake catches sight of a crooked tooth in her mouth. 'Are you and Magnus lovers?'

She giggles and frantically shakes her head from side to side. 'Magnus has never had sex.'

'I don't believe you.'

'It's true. He told me.'

'No wonder he drinks like a fish. Some people you know believe our sexual and creative energies run through the same channels and have the same source. In other words, the more sex we have the less creative we are.'

'That's probably what Magnus thinks. Do you think that too?'

'I'm a romantic scoundrel. I believe whatever is necessary

to milk out the most sensation from every moment. I'm always spilling myself. Always leaving behind stains.'

She screws up her face in distaste, clamps her hands to her ears and shakes her head back and forth, giggling.

'How do you spell scoundrel?' she asks.

He spells out scoundrel and she paints the letters in red watercolour on the back of her picture of him.

'My friend Radek would like you. He's a vampire. He wasn't born a vampire. He's become one by willing it. And dental surgery. He doesn't bite though. He uses a syringe. And he doesn't take anyone's blood by force. Also he doesn't drink anyone's blood that has bad energy. I like your guitar.'

'It belonged to a friend of mine who committed suicide. He stabbed himself in the heart with a kitchen knife.'

He gets no sympathy from her. Inwardly he apologises to his dead friend. He tells himself to stop using Alex's death to make himself more worthy of interest. He watches her tug off her time-worn black wig to reveal a shaved head. He is struck by her beauty, its wild creature blend of vulnerability and resistance. 'I think I'm going to take a walk on my own,' she says. As if controlled by a puppet master she twitches and stutters up to her feet and then once more eases into her rapid doll walk. Jake is mesmerised by the mechanical grace of her movement.

Later Jake accompanies the odd couple to the end of the wharf where they halt beside a moored fishing boat.

'The *Ariadne*,' says Magnus, giving the old wooden vessel a hearty kick with his boot.

Jake breathes in the erotic smell of seaweed and brine and watches the man jump aboard and sway awkwardly for a moment. He passes Erin's extravagant trunk to Magnus and then helps Erin herself to climb in. She sits down in the stern and Magnus begins to push the oars against the black tide. For a while Jake watches as the darkness of the sea and sky seem to expand around the boat. Only the large white yacht and its trailing fairy lights, further out at sea, undermines the exalted solitude of the *Ariadne*. As Jake watches the receding boat diminish in size it somehow grows in stature.

Across the curve of the bay Jake turns to look again at Shelley's white house, which gleams faintly in the midst of a crescent of smudged lights. The smell of the sea in his nostrils makes him think of lost friends, ex-lovers. Of things he never said that he should have said, of things he never did but should have done. He walks back in a wistful mood towards the town of Lerici. The sound of the sea is now like the faint rustling of sheets. Along the seafront beneath the pine trees is a carousel which is covered for the night in green tarpaulin. As he approaches he hears a scratchy muffled rendition of a romantic eighteenth-century piano sonata coming from inside. Streetlamps stretch his shadow over the paving stones. He exchanges a smile with two African street sellers sitting on the wall in front of their ebony figurines and primitive wooden masks before lifting the cover and disclosing a gash of light from within the carousel. He pushes his guitar and amplifier through and then ducks inside. It is lit up by a handful of prayer candles. A pale boy with buoyant hair and blueberry stained lips is sitting astride a porcelain pony holding a bottle of red wine. The scratchy music is provided by an antique HMV gramophone.

'Hello. Felix Chantley at your service,' says the young man who, despite the warm May weather is wearing a tweed coat. He speaks in an affected effeminate drawl, prolonging every syllable for all it is worth. He is friendly and aloof at the same time. He dismounts and makes a show of hobbling towards Jake.

'I recognise you,' says Jake. 'You played Byron in that film last year.'

'Indeed. That was Byron's limp as described by Trelawny that I just appropriated.'

Jake produces his paperback copy of Trelawny's memoirs of Shelley and Byron from his pocket. 'A man after my own heart,' he says.

'I don't suppose,' says Felix climbing back onto the painted pony, 'you know anything about the rumpus.'

'What rumpus?'

'An English girl has *disintegrated* into fairy dust. Under *pertly* suspicious circumstances. The carabinieri as we speak are ferreting into the matter. You're not by any chance one of the yacht people?'

'That's what everyone here asks me. I've just met a rather farfetched American sculptor called Magnus who kept talking about the yacht people.'

'Oh, he's probably the murderer. Not poor Ivan. And I expect the delectable Erin will be his next victim.'

'What are you doing here?' asks Jake, also climbing onto a porcelain pony.

'Looking for a new lease of life? What does one do anywhere? And trying to escape from the British press.'

'I'm becoming more and more intrigued by this murder mystery. What do you think, is the romantically mysterious Isabella alive or dead?'

'Apparently Ivan was ordered to the police station last night. He's writing a biography of Shelley. He rather looks like a dark-haired Shelley. He walks about with his clothes kind of hanging off him and idealises girls. Makes impossible demands of them. He idealised Isabella. He would have made a more convincing Shelley than the neanderthal who played him in the film. He did sit-ups and pelvic thrusts on the set. I can't abide men whose self-esteem resides in their pectorals. I was tempted to let him drown when we did the scene on Lake Geneva. I haven't seen Ivan for a few days. The last I heard he was furious because Isabella jumped on the back of Massimo's vespa and left him standing alone. Massimo is a waiter who looks like Mephistopheles – he has piercing blue eyes and a goatee beard.'

'So, Ivan was jealous of her antics with Mephistopheles the waiter and has bumped her off?'

'Ivan wouldn't hurt a fly. He hardly seems to inhabit his body at all. Though he is jealous. Actually, I'm pathologically jealous, too,' says Felix after finishing the wine in his glass. 'Relationships bring out the worst in me. I always have to have the last word and my last word has a habit of being inappropriate. Since *Don Juan* everyone seems to expect me to be Byron...'

'That sounds rather entertaining to me.'

'Oh there's nothing I enjoy more than pretending to be Byron.'

'You sleep around a lot then?'

'Heavens, not at all. Too much physical effort involved. Carrying a dictionary from one end of my room to the other often leaves me winded. I could quite happily live without sex.'

'So you're not like Byron at all?'

'To my mind Byron didn't like sex; it was something he compulsively did to nurture his dislike of himself. Sex with women was his cynicism; sex with boys was his guilt and shame.'

At three in the morning Jake and Felix are sitting in a moored wooden boat with a bottle of wine. They both have wet trousers from wading knee-deep into the sea.

'The great object of life,' said Felix, 'is sensation - to feel that we exist - even though in pain - it is this craving void which drives us to gaming - to battle - to travel - to intemperate but keenly felt pursuits whose principal attraction is the agitation inseparable from their accomplishment.'

'Byron?'

'I like to claim his words as my own.'

'The romantic poets. Why is the idea of an early grave so damned attractive?' says Jake, about to light another cigarette.

'I get the impression Jason is in Italy to sow some wild oats,' says Lady Lydia Wentworth. She is holding a chewed chicken wing. Grease glistens on her top lip. She perches forward on a thin-legged chair adorned with capricious arabesques and whorls. Her green staring eyes, abetted in their devilry by an arching eyebrow, tunnel into Jake with disarming divination. Over the disused fireplace a portrait of her as a sultry wide-eyed siren brutally makes plain how much damage the years have done to his aunt's face. There is no trace in the painting of the furrows of cynical asperity around her mouth; only her finely chiselled high cheekbones have retained their hieratic grace. 'Or has that expression gone out of coinage? You see, we are very much a world unto ourselves here.'

'A world unto ourselves,' grins her son Hugh, slumping down further on the sofa. Every time he moves, which owing to the bulk of his frame, isn't very often, a drift of dust rises from the stained gold cushions. By his side is a plate smeared with a red and yellow haemorrhage of sauces which Lady Lydia sometimes uses as an ashtray.

'Tell me the truth,' she says, 'don't you find England simply ghastly nowadays. It is the worst.'

'The worst,' repeats Hugh.

'I certainly...' begins Jake, watching ash topple from the cigarette she holds in her trembling hand into her lap.

'But I expect you, Jason, enjoy London. The drugs and nightclubs. If I were young again I would not have children. One receives little gratitude for the sacrifices one makes. Of course Hugh here is largely inconsequential, but my daughters are just waiting for me to die. Between you and me, I've cut them out of my will. But tell me about your own prospects. One hears so little family news in our Italian bower. I rather think though, now I come to think of it, news did reach us about some scandal involving one of Katherine's sons.'

'That was me. But my name is Jake, not Jason.'

'I'm so glad to hear it. Wasn't there an electrician and a snooker table involved?'

'An electrician and a snooker table,' says Hugh with the ghost of a snigger.

'You mean when my father caught me having sex with the man who came to set up a new alarm system in the house? Unfortunately for me that snooker table is my father's pride and joy. I put that down to youthful high spirits on my part,' says Jake, glancing up at the drapery of abandoned spider webs hanging from the ceiling.

'And now you've been cut off? I did warn my sister not to marry that ghastly man. There was something of the stray dog about him. Always sniffing about under tables so to speak. My sister always did have a weak spot for maimed animals though. She once brought a wounded pigeon home and then cried all night and told tales when I gave it to the cat.'

'My father...'

'But before you go on, I would like to ask you something. What did you think of Filiberto, the gardener? You met him as you arrived. Did you find him rather sinister? You see it's Hugh's contention that he's probably an axe murderer. A girl has been murdered, you know. I haven't told you, have I, Hugh? Filiberto was doing his disco dancing in front of the mirror again. I went to ask him about the parsley.'

'About the parsley,' echoes Hugh knowingly as if his mother is speaking in a private code.

'He had the music up so loud he didn't hear me enter. He was gyrating in front of the mirror wearing nothing but pink underpants. This is what he was doing.' Lady Lydia staggers unsteadily to her feet and thrusts her pelvis back and forth and makes erratic mating gestures with her arms. 'Oh, he was absolutely eating himself up in the mirror – 'I am irresistible,' he was telling himself, 'I am the gold at the end of the rainbow.' Of course when I was young, men weren't so narcissistic.' She draws Jake into her orbit with a pointed facetious look. 'Things though have to change, I suppose. One just wishes it wasn't always for the worse.'

Hugh is now ostentatiously taking no notice of his mother. An embarrassed frown serrated his forehead while his mother made an exhibition of herself. A sheen of perspiration waxes his pink face as he begins playing a game on his mobile phone. The acoustics of the eighteenth-century drawing room echo the retching of hollow staccato bleeps and bips. The concentration on his face is admirable in a way. It was probably with a similar level of concentration that the theory of relativity was formulated.

'What did he do when he realised he was being watched?' asks Jake over the soundtrack of the space attack.

'Perhaps he had known I was there all the time?' After stubbing out her cigarette in the carnage of ketchup and mustard and lighting another one she says, 'Wouldn't that rather confirm my suspicions? He is rather sinister. I once watched him chop wood and I thought then how lovingly he handled the axe. Are you winning, Hugh?' she asks with unconcealed disdain.

'You can't win, mother, not really,' says Hugh, still frantically punching keys and staring wildly at the glowing screen cupped in his hand. 'You can only score points.'

'Well, don't ask me to play. The cynicism of such games appals me. When I was a child we invented our own worlds - worlds where high endeavour ensured glory and triumph. Children ought to feel on top of things when they're playing. Just think of the damage you might be doing to your character, Hugh. Games like that might lead you to believe that nothing's worth the effort.'

'Like you, you mean, mother.'

'Why don't you play with him, Jason? I'm sure Hugh would like that even though he's too shy to say.'

'Actually, Jason is called Jake,' says Hugh, censoriously. 'He's already told you that twice.'

'I'd prefer to have another drink,' says Jake.

'Yes, let's have another drink. I think Joan, my secretary will be arriving soon. Oh well, it can't be helped. She's a dreadful woman. Always trying to get her money's worth. I don't mind so much that she's cheating me; it's her conversation I can't stand. Aren't you dead yet, Hugh?'

'You get three lives.'

'Thank heavens that is not the case in nature,' she says pouring herself another glass of gin. She begins pacing by the window without attending to Jake's empty glass. 'Technology does tell such appalling lies. I've never understood even the attraction of the telephone. To my mind the telephone just increases the amount of nonsense we talk in our lives. I suspect it taps into a yearning people have to respond to a foreseen emancipation or emergency. What's your relationship with technology, Jason? For or against?'

'I don't think it answers to our deepest needs,' he says flippantly.

'This, I imagine, is a wonderful place for a young man wishing to play at being Shelley. I sometimes wish Hugh would play more at being Shelley.'

'Who is Shelley when he's at home?' says Hugh who, downcast, has finished playing his game and now hauls his monolithic bulk from the sofa in wincing incremental stages.

'He was the prototype for romantic young men like Jason here. He took exception to just about everything his parents believed in, didn't he? One of our ancestors was besotted by him, you know. I've got all her diaries upstairs somewhere. Where are Cynthia's diaries, Hugh? I hope you haven't used them to pin your butterflies in. Hugh collects butterflies. Don't ask me why. Why *do* you collect butterflies, Hugh? Why don't you write poetry like Jason here.'

'I write songs, not poetry,' says Jake, following Hugh's exit from the drawing room with relief. 'I'm a musician. The thing is, Aunt Lydia, I don't have any money to record my songs.'

'I believe we have an old cassette machine lying around here somewhere. Perhaps you would like to borrow that? I'll ask Hugh if he knows where it is. Huuuugghh,' she calls out in a hoarse whisper.

'Actually, what I meant was I need to hire a recording studio.'

'Is that wise at your age?'

'I'm twenty-four.'

'I had Hugh when I was twenty-four but then there weren't so many options for women in those days. Not that all this newfound freedom has done my daughters much good. One of them has a faddish eating disorder and the other stabs herself with syringes and screwdrivers. But it's so nice of you to come and see us, Jason.'

'What I was wondering is, well, I don't suppose you'd be willing to loan me some money, as a sort of investment maybe.'

'You want me to be your patron?' She stares at him as if he has made an indecent proposal. Bemusement makes her appear momentarily younger.

'That would be rather ideal,' says Jake uncertainly. There is a smell of singed hair as, lighting another cigarette, the flame of his aunt's lighter leaps too high.

'You see, you are like Shelley. He had ideals, at least when it suited him.'

'I'm not really sure I have ideals. I don't want to change the world.'

'No, Hugh doesn't seem very interested in anything

along those lines either. Young men seem to be at rather a loss nowadays. None of you seem to have much drive. I'm so glad I'm a woman. Of course Hugh was too fat to go into the army but I can't see anything wrong with you physically. Don't you find though that there's something marvellously forgiving about fat? Hugh never has an unkind word to say about anyone. Can I ask you a personal question?'

'I don't see why not.'

'Do you think your mother is to blame for you being homosexual?'

'I'm not,' Jake smiles. 'I gave it a try once or twice. That's all.'

'But you do, you know, give that impression to an untrained eye. Do you really think it's all a question of genes? I have my doubts. Virginia Houghton's son Quentin is homosexual and I think Virginia was responsible. She couldn't abide her husband and shared a bed with poor Quentin until he was eight. That is surely not healthy. The idea of sleeping with Hugh is, well, simply repulsive. I was just saying, dear, that the idea of sleeping with you is repulsive.'

Hugh, re-entering the room with a huge plate of micro-waved oven chips and a red stain around his puckered mouth, smiles as if he has received a compliment.

The studio whose walls show the shapes of its white stones had once been a boathouse. A black drape covers the only window, cloistering it from the outside world. Jake has his back turned to Magnus when he pulls down and steps out of his shorts. He turns around, fully naked, not sure whether to rage or laugh at this latest episode in the narrative of his life. Magnus gives his armature more hammer blows. He is wearing a grubby cream-coloured apron. Jake lifts the visor of the suit of armour standing in the corner of the studio. Outside a phone begins emitting an anorexic squeaking of Beethoven's fifth symphony. Magnus pauses in his hammering to express his contempt.

'Any ideas for the pose you want?'

'Are you familiar with Donatello's David?'

The saucy narcissistic rent boy offering his wares, you mean, Jake is about to say. Instead he nods.

'Well, a kind of variation of that.'

Jake mounts the model stand where he has to submit to the humiliation of a litany of instructions. 'Can you rest more of your weight on your left foot and splay your fingers more widely on your hip?' Ironic that he is being depicted as a homosexual since this is the unforgiving view of him his family harbours. That one moment of reckless rebellion has stamped on him an identity that no revision on his part can apparently alter.

A pose is finally settled on. Every two minutes Magnus issues a new imperious command. Jake feels his beady analytical blue eyes wandering over his nakedness like a hungry insect. He understands the reluctance of primitives to yield up their image. Magnus slaps another mass of wet clay onto the armature and kneads it into the required form with his long spatula fingers.

At midday Felix arrives at the studio with a young man whose dark fringe flops over his eyes. Jake has been allowed to put back on his clothes before they enter.

'I thought you were under arrest,' says Magnus to Ivan.

'Let me go after two hours of interrogation,' says Ivan, rapping his knuckles on the suit of medieval armour. 'It was unnerving though to be scrutinised as if I might be capable of murder.'

'First degree *omocidio*,' says Felix.

'She's been missing now for four days,' says Magnus. 'I spoke to her housemate Grace yesterday. She's heard nothing.

Her phone is dead. Have you spoken to any of the yacht people?'

'The disappearance of Isabella is probably some new prank they're playing. They do tend to get bored very easily,' says Ivan. He exchanges a secret society look with Felix who is sitting on a splintered workbench on which are arrayed various rusting metal tools. Behind him on the walls of rough-hewn local stone hang two eighteenth century duelling pistols. Like the suit of armour, Magnus picked them up cheaply in a local market but has a superstitious fear of keeping them in his home.

'I wouldn't be surprised if she's punishing you,' Felix says to Ivan.

'Punishing me for what?'

'Idealising her.'

'How's the Shelley book coming along?' asks Magnus, squinting shut his right eye and tilting his head birdlike on its long sinewy neck to study his emerging figurine of a naked male.

'Not exactly firing on all cylinders. Shelley once said, when composition begins inspiration is already on the decline, which, to my mind, is a case of hitting the nail squarely on the head. I suspect it doesn't help that I'm presently trying to get to grips with Godwin.'

'What do you make of old Godwin?' asks Magnus. 'I've not actually read any of his work.'

'I'm reading *Political Justice*.'

'Not a very sexy title,' says Felix.

'Not particularly sexy reading either,' says Ivan. 'Men who think they have all the answers generally don't ask very interesting questions.'

'I always found Shelley's atheism tiresome,' says Magnus. 'He once referred to Christ as a malignant soul.'

'I think his atheism was largely an argument he had with his dad.'

'Oh, one would much rather have dinner with Byron,' says Felix.

'Everything Byron said was ladled with irony,' says Magnus, 'which is why he's more attractive to us in our age than Shelley. But irony is often nothing but our pride wanting always to be wise before the event. It's a kind of emotional bunker. One's faith should always be a moving current. But I take it you've read that rather beautiful translation Shelley did of Dante's sonnet to Guido Cavalcanti? How does it start?' muses Magnus, stopping in his tracks and looking up towards the vaulted brick ceiling.

Guido, I would that Lapo, thou and I,
Led by some strong enchantment, might ascend
A magic ship....

'That's quite a prophecy. The three men in a boat theme seems to be a recurring motif in literature. Do they always meet a sticky end? There were three men in Shelley's boat when it capsized. Wasn't there a story that Shelley angrily impeded one of the other men from lowering the sail? Sailing at full mast in a storm amounts to suicide.'

'Shelley once said that everything a man writes, says or does contains an allegorical idea of his own future life,' says Ivan. 'There's actually a rather eerie prophecy in *Julian and Maddalo...*'

'The poem about Shelley's conversations with Byron in Venice. We used some of that in the film,' says Felix. He jumps up from the bench and pacing up and down and raising a shroud of white dust recites the lines he knows by heart: 'O ho! You talk as in years past. Tis strange men change not. You were ever still among Christ's flock a perilous infidel, a wolf for the meek lambs - if you can't swim beware of providence.'

'I can't swim,' says Ivan.

'Seeing as you're writing a biography of Shelley,' says Jake, 'you might be interested to know that one of my ancestors knew him. My aunt has this woman's journals in her house.

She lives nearby.' This is a lie. His ancestor admired Shelley; she did not know him. He has lied, he realises, because he wants to ingratiate himself further into Felix and Ivan's world. He likes the look of them. Their company makes him more optimistic about himself. They are like the gang he has always longed for but never found. The tribe who wear the same body paint as he does. He wishes they were musicians. They would make a fabulous eye-catching spectacle together in a band.

'Do you think she'd be willing to let me read them?'

'No. But we could steal them.'

'Things are finally livening up around here,' says Felix. 'Can we wear balaclavas and climb a ladder?'

'I don't see why not,' says Jake.

'Is your aunt Lady Wentworth?'

Jake nods.

'She's my landlady. You might ask her first before breaking into her house,' says Magnus, who loathes the woman and is secretly exhilarated by the idea of these three young men breaking into her house. 'That, you know, would be a criminal act.'

'I was thinking the other day how it's about time I broke the law again,' says Felix.

Alone, Magnus goes home for lunch. On the cracked marble stairs of his building the stench of damp is nauseating. Current audibly hums through the exposed tangle of electrical wires shoddily attached to the wall. His apartment is rudimentary. It smells of plumbing. There are no rugs on the stone floors, no decorations on the cracked stuccoed white walls. The blistered green shutters are fastened shut against the dazzle of the sea's reflected glare. Every room hosts orderly queues of unsold bronzes and plaster casts. Magnus hasn't sold a sculpture since 1984. He dusts them every Thursday evening.

He eats the same thing for lunch every day (ravioli with a sauce of tomato, garlic, basil and pecorino cheese), relishing operations at the scored wooden chopping board, the slicing of garlic into wafer thin segments, the smell of basil on his fingers. He rinses the dishes with lavish spumes of detergent under a steaming hot tap and bleaches the sink and sponges down the table while the coffee is percolating. The gurgle and euphoric mounting spurt from within the aluminium pot is one of the sounds he most relishes hearing. When he sits down with his cup of coffee he feels he has escaped to the higher and safer place in his mind.

Magnus admits to himself he is upset that Ivan and Felix didn't invite him to lunch, that they never invite him out to dinner though perhaps, as the senior adult it devolves upon him to make the first move? He removes the bluebells from the glass jar on the table. It strikes him as uncharacteristically negligent that he hasn't done this earlier. They are emitting a stench of decay. Isabella brought them to the studio for him before she disappeared. Their rotting stalks ooze a brown slime over his fingers as he dumps them in the trash. They remind him of the income he is losing as a result of her disappearance. The small amount Isabella has been paying him for tuition has become an integral part of his budget. There is a piece of paper on the table on which he has neatly itemised the month's expenditure (he has no money coming in; it is all going out). Once upon a time numbers had been a comfort to him. He enjoyed adding, subtracting and multiplying them. They obeyed laws he could understand. Recently though they have begun to let him down. Sixty-one, he says aloud, looking at his speckled hands. Sixty-one is his age. He still feels himself suspended between acts. He is still waiting for the emergence of a more decisive design. He has learned only a tiny portion of the things he wanted to learn, seen very little of all that he expected to see as a young student. And now, he often thinks, the only new frontier that awaits him is death. Now and again, when he is being austerely truthful with himself, he suspects Ivan and Felix view him as a figure of fun. It is true he is stuck in his ways. His habits, like his clothes, have undergone little change in thirty years. His life has been an attempt to pare down his dependencies to the barest minimum. Irritation quickly prickles his skin when anyone threatens to disrupt his routines.

He goes into his bedroom. There are more sculptures here, arrayed on shelves, jostling on the floor, surrounding his single bed and tidy bedside table – plaster casts of feet and hands, busts of models whose names he has forgotten, copies of Roman and Greek copies. There is a brittle crack in his joints as he cagily folds his body down into a kneeling position beside the illuminated glass tank and its microcosm of a woodland habitat.

'I started a new figure sculpture today,' he informs his two pet iguanas. 'A very good-looking boy called Jake.'

Magnus often wonders what his two reptiles see when they look at him. He knows, deep down in his blood, that it bears little resemblance to what he sees when he stares into a mirror. There is a kind of occult knowledge in their fixed gaze that sometimes makes him feel uneasy. A sense also that, were they a lot larger, they would take pleasure in eating him. He can feel their eyes upon him even when his back is turned. 'Lunchtime soon. Are you both hungry?' he asks.

The iguanas, Castor and Pollux, don't flinch.

Then the hammering and drilling starts up again from the building across the narrow alley.

'So auntie didn't come up with any cash?' says Felix, sitting back languidly and holding a cigarette at arm's length. He is pleased with his self-assured good-looking new friend and enjoys showing him off to the waiters whose approbation is important to Felix. Equally he is showing off his privileged status and complicity with the waiters to Jake. They are sitting amidst bougainvillea, jasmine and myrtle on the terrace of Osteria dei Bardi, a restaurant in the hills between Tellaro and Fiascherino. The afterglow of the sunset is still in the sky. The three tall waiters, deftly juggling the hand-painted plates and carafes of wine, waltz in figures of eight around the ten or so tables. Now and again they stand sharing a joke by the entrance.

'She almost ate me alive. She kept referring to me as Jason.'

'Abandoned by his Argonauts but still on the trail of the Golden Fleece?'

'Something like that. And you should see her son. Hughsie. He's so fat he'd sink a boat. I don't think I ever realised before today just how cruel women can be when they come adrift from their better feelings. I felt like a dartboard while she was talking to me.'

As Felix is opening the menu he knows by heart his attention is summoned by the approach of a stranger clearly intent on introducing himself. The intruder is wearing red linen trousers and white trainers, a pair of expensive sunglasses sit on top of his greying groomed curly hair. He strides over to the table with the virile exuberance of someone advertising a health product in a commercial.

'Sorry to interrupt,' he says, 'and I'm sure this happens to you all the time, but I just have to tell you how much I admired your performance as Byron.'

'Thank you very much,' says Felix who is still only half drunk.

'No, I mean it. You brought Byron to life in just the way I've always imagined him. Do you know what I mean? I actually think that was my favourite film last year.'

Felix smiles awkwardly and lifts his wine glass to his lips.

'Actually, I believe you know a cousin of mine - Laura Pilhurst-Atkins.'

'Can't say she rings any bells.'

'She's a good friend of Annabel Huntingdon. Oh, but I haven't introduced myself. Rufus Woodburn. Here, let me give you my card. I meant what I said,' persists Rufus, resting his hand on the back of Felix's chair. '*Don Juan* was my favourite film last year. In fact it was partly due to the scenes in Italy that I decided to buy an apartment here in Tellaro. You might have seen it – it's down there, near the church. Some of the locals aren't terribly keen on my proposed roof terrace. It was a devil getting planning permission. We're having a party on the yacht tonight. We'd love to have you as our guest of honour. Why don't you come and join us for a drink when you've finished your meal? We're inside.' He nods over his shoulder towards the open front of the restaurant where, against a red wall beneath the vaulted brick ceiling, can be seen a table whose occupants have lustrous blonde hair, carelessly expensive clothes and a studied indifference to what is going on elsewhere.

Felix pulls a face for Jake's benefit as Rufus Woodburn returns from whence he has come with his air of entitlement and ease.

'Let's see the card,' says Jake. Felix hands it across the table to him. 'Global Solutions,' he reads out. 'Why don't we go to this party? I'm curious about these yacht people.'

Felix frowns, then takes note of the flitting liquid green lights of the fireflies among the myrtle leaves.

'He give you his card?' grins the tall crop-haired waiter called Vanni. He produces a backwash of bristling energy as he arrives at their table and stands towering over them with his hands on his hips.

Felix smiles. He comes to this restaurant almost every night and not only is given generous discounts by Marco, the owner, but has struck up a friendship with the three waiters - Massimo, Niccola and Vanni. Generally they talk about football and one Sunday the three waiters took Felix to see Spezia play. Felix stood in the *curva ferrovia* jostled on all sides by the team's belligerent black and white-emblazoned supporters known as the *ultras*. He excused himself when, after the game, Vanni suggested they go in search of a ruck with Pisa supporters.

'I think it is Rufus who has killed Isabella,' says Vanni in a conspiratorial whisper laden with irony.

'Why do you say that?'

'One night he come here with her and she is very drunk. Usually she is always with Ivan. Ivan is *molto simpatico*.' Vanni again drops his voice to a whisper and speaks through cupped hands. 'But Ivan do not come here now since Massimo and Isabella, you know.' He whistles and knots his hands together. 'Ivan is like a *Siciliano*, very jealous. He not like it that Isabella go with Massimo on his vespa. Massimo do not know because once Ivan tell Massimo that they only friends and not lovers. *Comunque*, she not even kiss Massimo; she only tease him. But the next time we see Isabella she is with this *stronzo*,' he concludes nodding over his shoulder towards the table inside the restaurant.

'What's a *stronzo*?' Jake asks.

'A dickhead,' supplies Felix.

Jake smiles appreciatively up at Vanni. A car passes by, spilling out a thudding soundtrack of drum and bass. It might be a spacecraft for the attention it seeks. There follows a moment's silence among the diners on the terrace, as if everyone has to convince themselves all over again that the heart of the evening is here and not somewhere else.

'*Allora*, what do I bring you?' Vanni asks, resting his chin on his fist in a mockery of rapt attention.

'More wine,' says Felix.

'*Grande sei!*' says Vanni, clenching both fists and raising his stubbled chin to the heavens.

'They worship you here,' says Jake.

'I inadvertently entertain them when I'm drunk,' says Felix, examining his nails. 'I've passed out about three times and slept here more than once. Apparently I also entered the freezer one night.'

Nine people, smelling of alcohol, sit weighing down the launch. As a preliminary to casting off everyone waded into the Mediterranean and a great deal of raucous giggling, shouting, splashing and playacting ensued. Shutters flew open in a house near the pink church up on the rock and an angry Italian man told them to shut up and called them *maledetti inglesi*. The *maledetti inglesi* responded by laughing louder still. Jake was inspired to call out Magnus' name. Then remembering how Magnus had dropped a gas canister on his foot earlier and Felix had coined a new name for the sculptor – 'Swellfoot the Tyrant,' after the play Shelley wrote – Jake yelled out, 'Swellfoot the Tyrant.' The chant, erroneously deciphered, is picked up by one of the girls. 'Small feet are tiresome,' she calls out. One of the males, a brusque stentorian-voiced army type wearing a white England shirt, informs everyone that the length of a man's penis corresponds to the size of his feet. He takes off a large shoe and waves it proudly in the air at the green-shuttered houses perched haphazardly on the rock.

The boat begins slicing its way through the black water towards the fairy lights of the white yacht in the near distance. Small blue pills are passed around as they clear the rocks and the few lights of the fishing village. Jake takes a swig from the wine bottle and swallows two without asking what they are. Felix declines. Rufus has a girl sitting in his lap and clasps two other girls on either side around the waist. All three girls are wearing short denim skirts and tiny tops which reveal tanned midriffs and glinting studs of silver. Jake can smell perfume on female skin. It lures him into visualising its source. The neck, of course – that is where a woman lays the first ambush.

'Have you noticed how adverts nowadays are trying to turn birds into blokes?' asks the army guy.

Felix makes no effort to appear interested. The man, the girth of him, his slingshot diction, makes him feel peevish. Not that he is bothered what Felix might think of him. It is as if he is hauling himself up a rope ladder and all his attention and vigour is concentrated on the task at hand.

'Birds don't behave like blokes though, do they,' he goes on. 'Unless they're fucking stupid. I mean, when have you ever seen a glamorous sober girl pull a strange man by the tie and thrust his head down into her cleavage? You might see some fat drunk slag wearing pink flannelled sportswear do it but you're not going to see a girl with a platinum credit card in her purse do it. Girls are nothing like blokes. If you asked ten blokes if they wanted a no-strings-attached blow job from a girl at least nine of them would be up for it, if you asked ten girls if they wanted some random bloke to go down on them nine would say no. That there is the difference between birds and blokes. Tell me I'm wrong. Girls have to be drunk to act like men. But that isn't what TV is trying to tell us, is it?'

'Probably not,' says Felix mumbling the words with no trace of his former ironic hauteur. He feels this spokesman for male integrity is sucking blood from his neck.

A blue and silver dance of photons from a camera momentarily disorientates Felix when he clambers up onto the deck of the yacht. Jake strikes up conversation with a good looking blonde boy who sits in a deckchair skimming through a magazine.

'Where does he get his money from?'

'Rufus?'

'More flesh,' bellows out the army type. 'Get your titties out!'

'He invests other people's money. Sometimes on art. Usually on the Dow Jones. He made half a million pounds today and then got some pranic healing, whatever the fuck that is, from his personal guru – the fat guy with the beard.'

'I wondered where he fits in. But I thought all the money came from a tea consortium.'

'Yeah right. Not even the English drink that much tea. He's also got a five-star Michelin chef on his pay roll. Either he's got the night off or he's down below preparing canapés. Our host is dead chuffed your actor friend has graced us with his presence. No doubt he's already twittered and tweeted it.'

'I don't use social media.'

'Wise man. A strange thing happened yesterday. We took the yacht further up the coast. Thought we'd explore some of the other bays. Near the Cinque Terre we spied this secluded bay with lots of tents on the ridge above the beach. Seemed like some kind of festival was taking place. There were fire eaters and jugglers. A few of us got into the launch to investigate. Next thing we know this kind of mutant pirate craft is coming out to meet us. It was a war party of vagrant unwashed males. We were told to fuck off. As we were leaving we caught sight of this girl waving distress signals at us. Rufus thinks it was Isabella Castlereagh, the girl who's gone missing. Apparently, it's some weird cult who have set up camp there. The bay is owned by the state railways. There's a disused railway line running through it. You can only get to this bay by sea or through a tunnel in the rocks that is about half a mile long.'

Jake is excited to tell Felix this news. He goes in search of him. Down below deck, in a pungent inner chamber, a boy and a girl are watching film footage on a laptop. There are clothes and towels underfoot, a trail of gossamer lingerie. On the screen two women are standing by the side of a donkey. The less attractive one kneels down and begins examining the animal's undercarriage. She says something and laughs. There is no evidence on her face she is about to do anything out of the ordinary. Now and again the donkey strains to see what is going on beneath and behind it. The animal's erect penis looks like a gnarled tree branch. It is very long, strangely brittle, uncannily crooked. The girl has taken hold of it and is pulling it sideways. She gives it an experimental lick. Much as someone would take their first taste of something they had been told was a local delicacy. She holds it with a dainty tenderness. Her tongue probes in an experimental reverential fashion. She closes her lips on the head. Soon a discharge of white fluid begins leaking out. There is no jet propulsion, no contraction or spasm of muscles. The seminal fluid just leaks out in a continuous dribble. Jake notices the girl is careful not to swallow any. It is Jake's habit when watching pornography to replace any male actor with himself. He thus now finds himself, like Bottom, turned into a donkey.

'How much do you think those girls got paid for humiliating one of God's creatures?' he asks his two companions. They ignore him. He wonders if it's the chemicals he swallowed that are responsible for the flood of sympathy he feels for the donkey.

When, a waste of hours later, Felix and Jake are about to climb down into the launch a kind of raffle has begun on deck to decide who would be sleeping with whom.

'I want to sleep with you,' says a girl peering down at Felix as he drunkenly descends the ladder.

'None of those people will have sex,' says Jake when they are in the launch skimming towards shore.

'You sound bitter,' says Felix.

'They try to turn it into a game. Sex isn't a game.'

'What is it then?'

'Sex is nature's heart of darkness,' says Jake. 'The haunted house where all our ghosts are awakened. Every sexual encounter raises up a ghost, ends with a haunting.'

'That might explain why I avoid them,' said Felix.

Back on the mainland, they wander along the coast road, passing a bottle of wine back and forth. Darkness has dwindled to mist. The air has begun to brighten, and the natural world is stirring into its secret arrangements.

They reach the piazza at Tellaro where the coast road ends. The village has been built into the rock and is a maze of sloping arched alleys forking off at surprising angles, spiralling up to the church or down to the sea. No street is much wider than a corridor. The houses tumble crookedly, playfully into each other like drunken friends. The dusty pastel colours of the facades are like the otherworldly pigments of early Renaissance frescoes or the smudges of paint on Minoan pottery.

They sit down on one of the large slabs of rock in the small cove. The thin stretch of beach below is strewn with the feathers of sea birds and crushed seashells. Waves, plunging in and out of hidden crevices below, fling spray in cascades within inches of their feet.

When they hear footsteps they both instinctively duck down behind a giant jutting rock. Magnus appears outside the pink church and then begins descending the steps towards the sea. He is talking to himself. There is the sense of vehement veins pushing against his flesh. He holds an electric drill. They watch as he clambers into his boat and rows out of the bay. He appears admirably at one with his boat under the high moon. Jake doubts if he himself has ever provided anyone with such a poetic image.

'What's he up to?'

'Looks like he's just thrown something overboard.'

Indeed, out at sea, there is a gentle splash.

When Jake and Magnus are on their way to a bar for the morning coffee break, descending steps through an archway and a tunnel of rose-pink houses, the sculptor is accosted by three builders. One of them, a wiry little individual who looks like an angry garden gnome, begins shouting and gesticulating at Magnus. Almost immediately shutters begin opening in the vicinity and women appear at windows - heavy-set women in overly laundered clothes whose features are set into grimaces. They lean out into the sea air with their arms resting on the sills. One or two shabby cats are also keeping an eye on the proceedings. The altercation takes place outside an abandoned palazzo of rough stone with two empty niches and a crown of whorls and arabesques. Magnus towers over the three circling men whose overalls are smeared in white paste and who have left a foxtrot of white footprints on the paving stones. The chief spokesman of the builders is waving bunched fingers under Magnus' nose. His face is gorged with rising blood. Magnus' Italian sounds comical even to Jake who cannot speak the language. The words he uses are longer than the ones the builders resort to. Some have four syllables and sound like they belong in an epic poem. A word that repeatedly comes up is *trapano* – which, Jake is later to learn, is the Italian for drill. The builders are accusing Magnus of stealing their drill.

'*Sei un straniero di merda*,' the foreman yells. He has thrown his shoulders back and the buttons on his shirt look like they might ping off.

'*Smettila di sprecare il mio tempo*,' Magnus says. '*Sei un italiano di una vulgarità unprecedente*.' Magnus shoves him aside and marches forward. The foreman springs after him. There is a scuffle, a few punches are thrown and then Magnus, groaning and cursing, is lying on the ground in the foetus position. His trouser hem has rucked up to reveal a stretch of his naked leg. The hairless skin as milky and forbiddingly white as a corpse.

His assailant leans down towards him and delivers up his

final insult, the verbal equivalent of a scalping. There is some muttering from the female gargoyles above. The impression is that they approve of the punishment meted out to the aloof foreigner.

The three builders turn their attention to Jake. The spokesman still twitches with the menace of an electrified fence. Jake raises his eyebrows, a gesture designed to disown any affiliation with the wounded man on the ground. The man shoves him aside. Jake is left with a grubby unflattering idea of himself.

Later he walks along the coast road. Lizards dart off into the undergrowth or hide in cracks in the walls at the fall of his shadow. Heat rises up through the soles of his feet from the scorched tarmac. The flowering oleanders everywhere scent the air with asphyxiating sensual sweetness. He waits on a deserted stretch of the coast road near his campsite for Ivan and Felix to arrive in the hired car. The plan is to rescue Isabella from the cult.

'What we're doing here is disrupting and aborting routine,' says the short wiry man whose flesh is tanned to creased hide. He is speaking to a group of ten or so individuals sprawled out on a grass ledge above the sea. 'We're going to take a vital step towards erasing the ego, deleting personal history. In this way you will recuperate resources of energy you've wasted on merchandising self-conceits. Energy you've squandered on false promises and gratuitous sexual liaisons. Within the temenos of your box you will call on death as your guide and ally. Death is not the negation of life but the negation of the ego. Remember, only effort that isn't fearful is productive. What you have to do tonight, when you're inside the box of living wood you have made, is practice the breathing technique I taught you and inhale back into being the energy you have wasted on those experiences. Suck it back into your bloodstream by making of yourselves an energy magnet. Making an energy magnet of the self, I call this step in the recapitulation and recovery process.'

Isabella sits down beside her brother, apart from the group. Behind them is a congregation of grubby tents.

'These fools are going to spend the night in coffins calling back into their bodies all the energy they have dispersed into the world, if you can swallow that. Recapitulation. It works on the drowning man principle - you have to visualise all the decisive events of your life and then through a breathing exercise reclaim all the energy they took from you. You start off with your sex life.'

'Ben, let's get out of here. Please?'

'I'm not sure what you're supposed to do with all this recuperated energy once you've reclaimed it. He's still a bit vague on that point. Unless I wasn't listening at some point. To have energy in excess is little more than the prerequisite for boredom. That's what people use to wreck council estates.'

'Are you listening to me?'

'Just a few more days, okay. It's not like you're a prisoner.'

'That's exactly what it's like.'

'You can leave whenever you want.'

'A seven-mile hike over the hills or a half hour walk alone through a dark tunnel with rats and human shit everywhere. And anyone could follow me into that tunnel. You're supposed to be my brother.'

'Half-brother.'

'Whatever. And Radek's got my bag with all my things in it. I've been wearing the same clothes for a week now.'

'Radek's only playing. He'll give it back if you ask.'

'I have asked. He said he'll give it back if I give him some blood.'

'Give him some blood then. I did. It doesn't hurt.'

'He's not a vampire.'

'He wasn't born a vampire. He says personality is fate and personality is forged by acts of will. He's forged the personality of a vampire. You've got to admit it's pretty cool.'

'Someone who had dental surgery to make his teeth pointed and lives in an orange tent?'

'Why did you fuck him then?'

'Because I was off my head and you led me into his den. I don't remember much of what happened that night and I don't want to.'

'Looks like your friend, Cressie wants a chat.'

Cressie is signalling to Isabella from a ledge above the ragged circle of tents. Isabella files her way through the quarrelsome map of polyester playhomes and plastic sheeting, lifting her feet over the cat's cradles of guy ropes. They are soiled, stale smelling things, these tents, and the candid glimpses they grant of threadbare inner life depress her. It's like a place with a memory of war. There's a baby's stroller on its side. Playing cards are scattered in the grass, among airing sleeping bags and discarded food packaging and Isabella notes the leering face of a joker. Beyond the camp she has learned to tread carefully as there is human excrement among the stones and grass.

Cressie is waiting for her on the promontory. She has a tight hard-fought smile that begs charity and a penchant for elasticated clothes made of synthetic fibres.

'God, you have to be so secretive in this place,' she says. Down below, the salt tide sucks at the ancient rocks and the wind blows about the voices of a few people on the beach, splashing in the sea. 'Okay. I'm not going to tell you what it cost me to get this phone. Your friend is coming tonight. With the actor Felix Chantley. Let's go somewhere no one can see us.'

They clamber down to a hollow in the rocks. Here Isabella sends a text to Grace, her flatmate.

'Why don't you come too?'

Cressie puts her hand inside her top and vigorously scratches her shoulder. 'I'm just not ready. I know this will sound stupid to you, but I do feel I'm learning stuff about myself here. I just wish for once I could make myself indispensable to someone.'

Isabella gives her a hug. 'I think it might do you good to get back to civilisation. You've been here two months.'

'I suppose I'm kind of in love with Radek. I always know when he's looking at me. I feel my skin go pale. He's talking to your brother and looking at us now. Will you tell Ben you're leaving tonight?'

'No. I don't trust him.'

'Can you believe I'm going to spend the night inside the box I made? I'm quite proud of myself for making that box. Actually, you should warn your friend because we've got to take our boxes to the tunnel and stay inside them there. We don't want the car running into any of us.'

'Good point.' Isabella takes the cheap phone and begins punching in another text message.

'Here comes Radek.'

Isabella panics. Her fingers tingle and go jittery. She sends the message without finishing it and then inadvertently presses a key that makes the phone's dashboard momentarily glow.

'You know phones are strictly forbidden,' says Radek, showing his two sharpened canine teeth in the wide grin with which he greets them. He is wearing a black hat perched rakishly on the back of his head. His eyebrows are slender pencil lines arced up in a perennial expression of devious amusement. 'So what are you two beauties plotting?'

'I want my bag back.'

Delicately, he pushes back strands of his dyed long black hair from his chiselled mannequin face and then lays his hand with its long curved fingernails on Isabella's shoulder. He says something in a mesmeric ancient-sounding language she doesn't understand. He can speak about five languages, all as if they are his own. His green eyes glitter like a jewel held up to light.

'Vampire language?' says Isabella.

His black t-shirt has *I Fuck Nuns* blazoned on it.

'I'm disappointed you're not going to spend the night in a coffin.'

The ring tone of Cressie's phone discharges its summons into the air. It sounds shrill, loaded with urgency.

'Aren't you going to answer it?' asks Radek, with an air of being the custodian of occult knowledge.

'It's my ex-boyfriend,' Cressie says. 'I don't want to talk to him anymore.'

The ring tone ceases and the phone begins to speak. 'Hi. If you wanna leave a message, I'll get back to you.' There is some static, some scuffling. 'This is Grace. Don't really understand this message. People in the tunnel? Are you okay? We'll be there in about three hours to get you out. Lots of love.'

'You've got visitors coming?' says Radek, his skirmishing green eyes bright with exciting new knowledge.

'Such a shame we're not in a four-horse closed-carriage. It feels like we should be,' says Felix. 'But nevertheless this might be the most exciting thing I've done since climbing up from a gondola to the window of a palazzo by the Grand Canal just before the part in the film when I had to seduce an eighteen year old Italian heiress.'

'If that film's anything to go by, Byron spent a lot of his time climbing in and out of windows,' says Ivan. 'Women will always love a man who climbs in through their window, even though, as a general rule, they can't help marrying a man who waits patiently outside their front door.'

'I think it was his favourite occupation. His way of granting the irritation of sexual compulsion an entertaining sideshow.'

Ivan is driving with Felix beside him. Jake and Grace, Isabella's flatmate, are in the backseat. The roads they travel grow increasingly more deserted. For a while the sea is at their side, black glass with sliding discs of lustre. Then there are lemon trees, oleander shrubs, terraced olive groves, grey stone walls, long meadow grass, white shingled beds of streams, orange tiled rooftops, hairpin twists in the tarmac, dips and curves on the planet's surface. The headlights tunnel into the blackness, stirring into life ghostly visions of what lies ahead, like phantasmagoria in a crystal ball. It is so quiet and still you can sense how ancient the earth is, how paltry is your share in its history. Ivan wonders why this feeling is quietly exhilarating instead of depressing. He can sense the dew on the land, feeding roots, renewing virginity; it is a feeling on his skin, like rubbing a handful of earth between his palms.

Felix has a map on his lap and makes fun of his inability to read it. He and Ivan become a double act, flashing back and forth repartee, showing off for Grace, dramatising themselves as males no woman would be able to feel sorry for.

The night is a flourish of enlivening scents when, lost, they park the car. They need to stretch their legs, take their bearings. There is an untidy row of green shuttered pink houses set back from the road, nestled into the fold of the hills. A shine of white stones studs the wooded slope on which a primeval smoke seems to lift the surface detail off of the appearance of things.

'I don't think we're irremediably lost,' says Ivan after studying the map.

They sit down on the wall overlooking the ocean down below. The waves embroider the shingled beach with a ragged silvered stitching; the percussive assent they make as they break and the lamentation as they withdraw over the pebbles seems to come from a distance in time as well as space.

'Once upon a time people navigated by the stars,' says Ivan. 'I wouldn't have a clue how to do that.'

'Nor me,' said Grace. 'I wish I knew more about the stars.'

'Everything forms one kind of map or another. Compiling a biography is a form of mapmaking,' says Ivan, looking out to sea.

'The most uncanny moment in Byron's life, retrospectively speaking, was when, as a youngster, the boat he was on sailed past Missolonghi. He wrote of his impression of it so it must have had some personal impact on him. Little did he know he was catching the first glimpse of the place where, fifteen years later, he would die. It was as if it was waiting for him, winking at him almost. Already on his map.'

The entrance to the rock is further along the coast road. There is no signpost and they almost miss it. A steep bumpy dirt track leads down onto a tiled pathway which is only just wide enough for the car. When they enter the arched gash in the rock an uncomfortable silence makes itself felt inside the car. The temperature suddenly drops. Ivan leans forward in his seat and keeps an attentive eye on the sightline the headlights forge through the disturbed darkness. The visible world has tapered to a claustrophobic luminous shaft. Now and again a jolt rocks the vehicle as the front wheels bump over a slab of loose stone. Ivan has to drive very slowly. He has an uncomfortable feeling, as though they are violating some sacred precinct. A memory ambushes him of when, as a schoolboy, he had picked up a porn magazine he found in a park and taken it home. The idea that he had been watched in the act plagued him and blackened his mood for days afterwards. He felt he had been supernaturally seen. He feels like that now.

'Somewhere on the planet, right now,' he says to clear his mind of its unholy chill, 'native women are gathering beans and thrashing them in a village made of mud and straw.'

Felix looks askance at him.

'Somewhere an old woman is recalling how it felt to take off her ball gown and stand naked by an open window in the light of the moon,' Ivan persists.

'I'm not playing this game.'

'Perhaps you should try that number again?' Ivan says, catching Grace's eye in the rear view mirror.

Grace does as she's told. 'Phone's still turned off.'

Ivan slams his foot down on the brake. 'What the hell is that? A wooden box. There's a line of wooden boxes. They look like coffins.'

'The vampire army,' says Felix.

'Aren't vampires supposed to sleep during the day?'

'Perhaps they're having a power nap,' says Jake.

Ivan shuts off the headlights and stops the car. Darkness absorbs them, seeming to ooze forth like a sentient presence.

'What shall we do?' asks Grace.

'Looks like we'll have to walk the rest of the way.'

'Hells' bells,' complains Felix. 'No one said anything about walking.'

'I'm going to have to reverse all the way back through this bloody tunnel. Let's hope we don't have to make a quick getaway.'

'This should be going out live on television,' says Felix.

They get out of the car. An underworld chill lifts off the rock. It smells like the beginning of time in here, like life before civilisation. The shutting of the car doors echoes with the fury of a thunderclap.

'Hello. Hell-lowwww.'

The voice comes from inside one of the boxes. Grace lets out a scream and clasps hold of Ivan. Her body is hot and jostled with need.

'Who's there?' whimpers a disembodied female voice.

'Let me be love,' says Ivan leaning over the box. It's what he wants Isabella to hear when he talks to her, talks on and on.

The exit is barricaded against vehicles - planks of wood and dead branches are laid over a series of oil drums. There are some lights about two hundred yards away, picking out a caravanserai of canvas dwellings.

Isabella comes jogging towards them across the stony bedewed grass. Ivan has never seen her run before: she looks ungainly, as though her ankles are loosely tied together. She hugs Grace. The embrace she gives Ivan has a reluctant undertow to it. *She loves me, she loves me not.* He watches an unmoored light shoot across the dark sky.

'Let's get out of here.'

'Someone's coming.'

'Shit. It's Radek.'

'The vampire?' asks Felix.

'Yep.'

'Thank heavens for that. For a moment I thought we had come all this way for nothing.'

Radek walks with elegant assurance, with the confidence of earning from his audience a large measure of aesthetic approbation. There are painted red and black stripes under his eyes, as if he is on the warpath. He hands Isabella her bag.

'Forgive me,' he says, but not as though he means it.

'Everything you do is for show.'

'A man after my own heart,' says Felix.

Radek turns to Felix. He clasps him to his breast and presses his mouth to his neck.

'Steady on!'

The vampire presses a hand to Felix's heart.

'Thump thump thump,' he says, smiling boldly into Felix's eyes.

'What a wonderful showpiece you would be at dinner parties,' Felix says, recovering his dignity.

'I'll take that as a compliment, Lord Byron. And Isabella, let's stay in touch. OK? Perhaps I'll pay you a visit one night,' he says and shows his fangs.

Magnus runs his finger over the wound on the Madonna's cheek. In places the innards of the image, made of wax, plaster, canvas and vegetable fibres, show through macabre gashes in the painted surface. The three hundred-year-old papier-mâché sculpture has been entrusted to him for restoration. In less than a month the almost life-size female icon will be required for the annual festival in which she is escorted out to sea by a procession of candlelit boats.

He sits down in front of her and stares with something resembling uneasy love at her face. He finds himself think-ing back to his training as a priest. Many details now elude him, but he does remember the day, kneeling before the altar, his hands had been anointed and bound in the consecrated cloths and the fear and awe of realising he was now spiritually authorised to change bread and wine into the flesh and blood of Jesus Christ. 'Thou art a priest forever after the order of Melchizedek,' he says out loud. He was able to dispense saving grace - what a farce that had turned out to be. He had quickly felt himself unworthy of his new status. The last year of his training, during which he had been prepared for preaching and absolving sin, had been spent trying to conceal his mis-givings from his superiors.

He leaves behind large incomplete footprints in the white dust as he walks over to the shelf and picks up his sculpture of Jake. It weighs more than he expected. He places it on a wooden tripod and unfurls its protective sheath of wet plastic sheeting. He then sprays it with water. Jake is late yet again. He feels his face heat up with indignation. He begins complaining aloud to himself. It further annoys him that he is too shy to openly remonstrate with his model. 'You never speak up for yourself,' he says aloud. There are two people in his head. Like a child and an adult. The child acts, the adult comments and cajoles.

Jake arrives wet, wearing headphones. First one song and then another whipped up such an exhilarating pulse in his blood that he sat on the rocks watching the continuum of vanishing circles the rain made on the sea. He feels a bit sorry for Magnus when he arrives, for the fact that he is old and set in his ways and a stranger to the headrush of loud anthemic music on headphones. He walks up to the Madonna.

'Wow,' he exclaims. He is about to touch her brightly painted face but changes his mind. 'Actually, she gives me the creeps a bit. You can almost feel the presence on her of the world that made her. You know, witch hunts, plagues, superstition, filth, short life expectancy. That kind of stuff.'

'I find her beautiful,' says Magnus, glad of the opportunity to disagree with his model. Does he really find her beautiful though? There is something of the primitive totem about her, an occult spookiness. Jake isn't wrong to be a bit wary of her.

Magnus sprays his clay figurine with more water and lavishes it with few tender caresses while Jake removes his clothes. He is wearing lime green boxer shorts today, Magnus sees, and his hair and clothes smell of the rain. When Jake is naked and has got into pose on the low box, Magnus stands against the far wall and trains his squinting eyes on him.

'We rescued Isabella,' Jake says to alleviate the unpleasant self-consciousness that Magnus' appraising stare is inducing in him.

'So I heard. Much ado about nothing it would appear. Do you think you could look more to your left? Keep your head in the same position but move your eyes?'

Jake does as he is told. His neck muscles complain at the elaborate contortion.

Soon there is a mounting commotion outside, a metallic rattling and scraping on stone. The warped wooden door of the studio jars against the stone floor before flying open and thunder-clapping against the wall. An antique green lawn mower appears, like an exhibit from Jake's childhood. It is followed by a man in overalls frowning with exasperation whom Magnus does not recognise. The man, registering the Madonna and the naked Jake, crosses himself with an expression of alarm. Magnus curses him in Italian. Lady Lydia Wentworth then steps over the threshold. She has frosted blue powder on her eyelids.

'I'm most awfully sorry for bursting in unannounced, Mr Ormond,' she says, with the barest minimum of sincerity. The thick slapdash smudges beneath her cucumber green eyes, pencilled in as if with charcoal, have the effect of widening them into an expression of avid attention. There is a mineral hardness, a pinioning relentlessness about their staring quality. 'Oh dear, and I see you were busy. Jason is my nephew, Mr Ormond. However, be that as it may, you have my word I shall not whisper a word of what I've seen to his family. I've never been one to take notice of the vices of others even when they are utterly incomprehensible to me. However, I cannot say the same for this Italian labourer. In all likelihood he's a gossip like the rest of his race.'

Magnus, all six feet-two of him, has the frozen tongue-tied air of a schoolboy caught in some shameful act.

'The reason for my frightfully rude intrusion, Mr Ormond, is my lawnmower.'

Jake, not bothering to dress himself, grins.

'It's not, you see, working. And I can't make this Italian man understand a word of English. Naturally I thought of you.'

'Why did you think of me, Lady Wentworth?'

'Why, because of your profession of course. You're an

odd-job man. An artisan. Isn't it the purpose of artisans to fix things? To restore the flailing and decaying to some state resembling their original pristine condition.'

'I'm a sculptor, not a mechanic, Lady Wentworth.'

Ivan stands up and faces the sea. Far out on its dark expanse the moon trembles. He takes a bow. 'Let us recollect our sensations as children,' he says crisply and loudly. He holds aloft a bottle of red wine. Not far from his feet waves dribble ribbons of foam over a barren tract of shingle.

'The memory of good is ever grim,' contributes Felix. He is sitting on the shingle and has just set fire to a torn page of a magazine. A flurry of blue and yellow flames shoots up the edge of the printed page and billow out black smoke and a confetti of orange sparks.

'We less habitually,' slurs Ivan, 'distinguished ourselves from all that we saw and felt. Of course the question then arises,' he says, turning to Felix, 'why grow up at all?'

'Why indeed?' asks Felix watching the last of the fiery points extinguish themselves amongst the pulp of black cinders. 'What anyway is there to grow into?'

'Any feeling with virtue in it?'

'Only action has virtue in it. And I should know.'

'Why should you know?'

'Because action is what I'm incapable of unless I'm pretending to be someone else.'

'Like Byron?'

'Acting is a piece of cake. Not to have to stand by the things you do. One reaps all the benefits without suffering any consequences. Although maybe there have been consequences. Perhaps Byron is now more real to me than I am to myself.'

Ivan wades into the sea up to his knees and then turns around to face Felix. 'Of course I, you know, live too intensely in my own imaginings,' he says. Struck at the back of the knees by the surging tide he sways and extends out his arms as if balancing on a tightrope.

'What are you going to do next?' calls out Felix.

'I was hoping *that* might be decided by higher powers. Here I am yielding myself up to the medium of water,' he says with a wide grin. 'I don't feel very safe. I can't swim, you know. When I was a little boy I used to fill up a sink and dare myself to put my head under the water. I never could.'

'Art thou afeard to be the same in thine own act and valour as thou art in desire?'

'Why linger,' booms out Ivan, 'why turn back, why shrink, my heart? But look, it says in that magazine that a romance is flourishing between Felix Chantley, the Byronic actor and Isabella Castlereagh, the beautiful daughter of Lord Clive Castlereagh in the idyllic bay of Lerici.'

'I thought,' says Felix after drinking more wine from the bottle, 'we'd burnt that page.'

'There's even a photo.'

'Got a stiff talking to from my publicist today.'

'I think Isabella loves me, but she doesn't know it.'

'Her mind refuses the events of her body? That sounds more like me, and you, come to think of it. The only thing I seem to learn from women is how little I have grown up...'

'Let us recollect our sensations as children,' intones Ivan. He holds in his hand a soggy wad of banknotes he has extracted from his trouser pockets.

'I do believe, for the first time in living memory, that you are drunker than I am.'

'There will come a time when all this will become merely a dream,' says Ivan, water dripping from his clothes as he staggers back to join Felix on the beach. He roots inside his jacket pocket and pulls out a small notebook. Listen to this,' he commands. 'But first of all, I need some light.' He holds the incriminating page of the magazine over his lighter. The flames gather around the photo of Felix and Isabella, dart over it until the image blackens and wrinkles and finally disintegrates into a crisp pyre of glittering ashes. Meanwhile Ivan reads aloud from his notebook: 'Do you not remember, Shelley, when first you read the third canto of Childe Harold to me? One evening after returning from Diodati. It was in our little room at Chapuis. The lake was before us and the mighty Jura. More fire,' demands Ivan as his light source fades and dies. Felix lights another page of the magazine and Ivan continues to read, 'That time is past, and this will also pass, when I may weep to read these words, and again moralise on the flight of time. I think of our excursions on the lake. How we saw him - Byron,' he says, glancing significantly at Felix, '- when he came down to us, or welcomed our arrival with a good-humoured smile. How vividly does each verse of his poem recall some scene of this kind to my memory! This time soon will also be a recollection. We may see him again, and again enjoy his society; but the time will also arrive when that which is now an anticipation will be only in the memory. Death will at length come and in the last moment all will be a dream.' Ivan finishes off the wine from the bottle and gets to his feet. 'You do know, of course, that we shall have to fight a duel.'

'I think we should fight a duel now,' says Felix as another withdrawing wave rakes through the shoals of shell fragment and pebbles on the beach.

It is four o'clock in the morning and they have the world to themselves. On the slowly brightening air drifts a scent of refreshed stone, moistened soil, newly aroused pollen. The footsteps of the two drunk young men ring out cleanly in the sloping stone alleys of Tellaro where red geraniums and green shutters are beginning to regain their bolder pigments. Magnus' studio is half way down an aisle perched above the rocks and sea; fishing boats hang upside down from the roof of the stone gallery. There is a strong smell of cats and salted stone. Ivan tries the door to the studio, but it is locked.

'I think we will have to break the window.'

They both stand facing their spectral reflections in the small square of black glass. Ivan, sick of the sight of himself, presses his nose to the pane. He then takes three paces back and, fishing his phone from his sodden pocket, tells Felix to stand back. He is about to throw his missile when spluttering spasms of laughter suddenly rack his body and screw up his face into a mask. He looks at Felix and he too starts to laugh. It is with great difficulty - one word emerging through heaving sobs every thirty seconds or so - that Ivan explains the source of his laughter. He pictured Magnus, tiny, as if glimpsed through a keyhole, spying on them as he was about to hurl his phone.

The shattering glass leaves an immense fraught silence in its wake. Ivan inserts his hand in the jagged breach and carelessly draws blood from his wrist before undoing the clasp and opening the broken window. Conversing in exaggerated whispers they both climb drunkenly into Magnus' studio. An immediate blast of cold desolate air rises up from the flagstones and sends a shiver through Ivan's wet body. The smell of damp plaster and stone and a nimbus of trapped dust makes itself felt in his lungs. When Felix flicks on the light the sight of the female effigy startles him back onto his heels. She is strapped to an easel with copper wire. 'What's that smell?' says Ivan while unbinding the damsel. 'Smells like prehistory.'

'What are you doing with her?'

Ivan has gathered up the papier-mâché statue in his arms. He dances in a circle over the shards of shattered glass with his new bride before falling over with her.

Felix meanwhile removes the tarnished copper hued helmet and visor from the suit of the armour standing by the broken window. He tries it on for size. It has two long oblong slits for eyes.

'Need some help here,' he says, holding the breastplate with its leather straps to his chest.

Ivan struggles with the rivets and straps. When it is secured the weight of the metal topples Felix forward.

'Can't be bothered with the leg armour,' he says.

Ivan, even in his drunken state, has a feeling of being under close observation. He swivels round and sees the source of his unease over in the far corner of the studio. Two iguanas are staring at him from inside a glass tank. An unflinching intense stare that has some ancient sorcery in it. Ivan frowns. They are like two pieces of delicately carved inorganic matter with seeing eyes. He crawls on all fours towards them, doing his best to return their eerily piercing voodoo stare. 'Do you think I can't see you?' he says. Neither of the reptiles twitches a nerve. He removes the wooden lid. 'Give you boys, or girls, a bit of air,' he says. He turns around to look up at Felix in the suit of armour and bursts out laughing.

'You've damaged one of the Madonna's arms,' says Felix from behind his visor.

'You're not going to turn superstitious on me I hope?' says Ivan. 'Anyway, Magnus will be able to put her back together. Isn't that what he's being paid for?'

Without replying Felix unhooks the pistols from the wall. Ivan, watching him about to inspect the guns, says, 'No. We're not to know if they're loaded or not.'

Ivan follows Felix in his medieval armour through the window. The noise they make sets a dog barking, soon joined by another. Ivan remembers the iguanas when they reach the end of the alley and that he hasn't replaced the lid of their tank, but he is too drunk to care enough to clamber back in through the broken window.

They follow the twisting walkway which skirts the village.

Pale light twitches along the line where the sky meets the sea. Down below chasms in the rocks suck in the advancing waves and spit them out with a low elegiac sigh.

'Not really fair though, is it, this duel?' says Ivan, smirking at the sight of Felix in his crusade armour.

'Fair? Is that what you expect? Anyway, can't be bothered to take it off now.'

'Okay. We stand back to back, walk ten paces and then turn and fire,' says Ivan.

Now and again, breaking the vast silence, a gull utters a plaintive cry or unseen smaller birds twitter inland where foliage can be felt to stir with the aroused expectation of sunlight. A pale pink shimmer of light, followed by a more diffused yellow glow smudges the lower tract of grey sky. The hills to their left have turned an almost transparent dark blue. Behind them the gold ochre and pink facades of the houses on the rock take on a transfiguring ghostly hue as a restless silver flame licks at the horizon.

Felix and Ivan stand back to back, both holding their pistols at their side. Ivan issues the command and, counting aloud, they begin striding in opposite directions. Ivan watches a lone boat out at sea become a stark silhouette as the glow in the eastern sky intensifies. Sobering up suddenly it occurs to him for the first time that maybe the pistols are loaded. He looks down at the weapon which hangs heavily from his hand. It looks too ornately pretty to be dangerous.

'Eight,' calls out Felix. 'Nine,' he replies in a hoarse strained tone. They turn to face each other and raise their pistols. The triggers make a vacant toy-like clicking noise.

'I deem myself unsatisfied,' says Felix.

'I deem myself unsatisfied too,' says Ivan, as a sundering molten-gold line burns over the sea and is followed by the glowing rim of the rising sun.

When Magnus arrives at his vandalised studio the next morning his shoulders collapse and a heave of unprecedented emotion catches in his throat. He sees everything through a blurring gauze. He kneels down, all his joints creaking, in order to identify whether it is Castor or Pollux that lays life-lessly chewed and bloodied on the floor. The severed arm of the Madonna too is lying on the floor amongst splinters of broken glass. He sits down on the wooden stool and doesn't move until Jake enters the studio.

'I won't be able to work on you today. She needs my help,' he says, nodding towards the Madonna.

'What the hell happened?'

'Obviously I've made an enemy. Perhaps those builders.'

'They killed one of the iguanas?'

'That was probably a cat. Guess which one it was.'

'What do you mean?'

'Castor or Pollux?'

'My Greek mythology isn't up to scratch. I don't know who they are.'

'Twins, but by different fathers. Pollux was immortal; Castor wasn't. At first, I thought it was Pollux that was dead, but it isn't; it's Castor.'

'I'm really sorry, Magnus,' Jake says. He feels an instinct to put an arm around the older man and in imagination performs the gesture, but something rigid and antiseptic in Magnus repels the physical accomplishment of the act.

'Do you think you can do me a favour? I owe your aunt two months in backdated rent which I've just about been able to scrape together. Perhaps you could give it to her?'

'No problem.'

Magnus pulls out a blank envelope from the inside pocket of his jacket and hands it to Jake.

Later Jake plays guitar in the piazza while Erin stands in her puppet doll pose beside him. She is wearing a blonde wig tonight and a dishevelled cherry-red taffeta dress. The darkening sky has emptied the square. Jake licks the brine from his chapped lips. There is a sundering thunderclap which momentarily makes him less brave than he would like to believe. The sky is black with here and there an elusive spark of deliquescent silver. A splintering flash of lightning makes the streetlights flicker and momentarily brightens the unripe oranges on the trees along the promenade. The wind sends litter scuttling over the stones of the piazza. Erin raises her head and opens her mouth to the rain which now falls in torrents. Then a white taxi pulls up beside her. Rufus Woodburn is in the back seat. He opens the door for her. Jake, uninvited, gets in too.

The windscreen wipers sluice a monotonous stream of rainwater and the inside of the car smells of the mustiness the rain has drawn from Erin's second-hand clothes and wig. The man drives recklessly around the narrow blind corners and Jake, compelled inwards into acknowledging his internal organs, their precocious and precarious reproductive procedures, fights down graphic visions of himself mutilated and leaking fluids in a wreckage of twisted metal.

The car pulls up alongside a froth of dripping bougainvillea up in the hills. Sodden purple petals are strewn over three expensive cars parked in an alcove. Jake notices a used condom on the gravel while Rufus Woodburn bellows his name into an entry-phone. An electric gate creaks open in laboured instalments. They descend steep twisting steps between pungent pine and fig trees. Despite the rain two girls he recognises from the yacht are swimming in the pool. They stand up in the shallow end to wave at Rufus. Jake follows Rufus into the sanitised white glare of a large sitting room. Isabella, Grace, the banker type and three Italian men are draped over various sofas and chairs around a large round glass table.

'This is Erin,' Rufus says. 'She's going to perform her act for us on the boat the night of the fireworks.'

Isabella gets up and kisses Jake on either cheek. The brush of her breasts against his chest makes him momentarily wish they were alone together somewhere else. He then has to assure himself he owes Ivan little loyalty.

Rufus suggests a game of cards is in order. 'Vingt-et-un? Come and sit on my lap, Erin. I want you to bring me luck.' Erin giggles and does as she is told. Erin, he realises, never passes moral judgement. She accepts every new moment with a child's benevolent trust. The rain has highlighted several stains on her dress.

All the men play cards. A man called Enzo is banker. He is wearing a tight purple sequinned t-shirt. Mandarin script is tattooed on his left wrist.

Jake loses three hands in a row and then wins a little of his money back in the fourth game. He is conscious of showing off for Isabella. For him she is the electromagnetic force in the room. He tries to imagine what kind of underwear she is wearing. How expansive or economical would be the shapes she made of her body when making love.

'Twist,' he says. Enzo purses his lips and delicately hands him a card as if it contains an erotic proposition. It is the jack of diamonds. 'Bust,' Jake says and loses another thirty euros. He has now lost a hundred and twenty euros – his emergency fund. He catches Isabella's eye. She tucks in her chin and makes a timid display of sympathising with him. There is an acrid dry taste in his mouth, as if he has eaten burnt toast. He pours himself another shot of grappa.

'Why don't we up the stakes?' says Rufus. '*Più alto!*' he says to the three Italian men.

Jake knows he is going to lose. There is some kind of cosmic force in him attracting and kindling negative energy. He feels it as a stiffness in his joints and an overly sensitive sensation on the tips of his fingers. The more he loses, the more stubbornly he fights the conviction that he will go on losing. He is dealt an eight and a seven.

'Twist,' he says. He pulls out the envelope Magnus has given him, tears it open and extracts a fifty-euro note which he flings down on the sticky table. He is dealt a two of hearts. One of the topless girls in the pool, dressed now, is standing behind him and he is struck by the cruelty of her perfume.

Jake has now lost some of Magnus' money. He tries to inwardly laugh off the act of unpardonable irresponsibility but an image of the bearded sculptor as a kind of persecuted saint swims up to the surface of his mind. He recalls vividly the image of Magnus earlier crying for his dead pet, his jumble of private sorrows and chaffing defeats a felt presence in his bloodshot eyes. Jake clasps his hands tightly together. He has to win Magnus' money back. He has to revoke the contingency of facing Magnus with this shameful story.

'I shall have to keep you by my side more often,' Rufus says to Erin. He lights an oversized cigar and Erin momentarily dissolves behind plumes of pungent smoke. She flaps about her hands in a playful hysteria of distaste.

'I'm going to be Jake's lucky charm,' says the girl whose perfume is at odds with all his better feelings. She wriggles into his lap and he feels the greedy warmth of her body seep into his loins. The other girls look at him with a kind of vicarious relish. They egg each other on, these girls, in their eagerness for promiscuous anecdotes. Were he to sleep with this girl on his lap tonight he, as subject matter, would be torn to pieces with cruel hilarity over tomorrow morning's cappuccino and chocolate pastry. Or this is Jake's reading of the situation.

'If I were you I might think about calling it a day,' says Rufus Woodburn. He sits back in his chair and re-lights his cigar.

'Five hundred euros,' says Jake, peeling off notes from Magnus' bundle.

Rufus is banker. Jake gets the ten of diamonds and the five of clubs. 'Twist,' he says. It is the king of hearts.

'One more game,' says Jake. He is surprised his voice doesn't sound more constricted.

'Look, I don't want any more of your money. You're simply not at the races tonight.'

'Five hundred euros.'

Rufus Woodburn looks around at the girls. They don't seem to have anything else to keep them entertained. The corners of his mouth twitch with a sudden inspiration.

'I tell you what, I'll wager all the money I've won from you against your guitar.'

'I've still got seven hundred euros. I'm not betting my fucking guitar.'

'That's my offer. Take it or leave it.'

'That guitar belonged to his best friend who's dead,' says Erin.

'Is that my fault?' says Rufus.

Jake loses his guitar.

'Look, I don't want your damn guitar. I was just trying to make you see sense.'

'It's yours. You won it. Take the fucking thing.'

'I said I don't want it.'

'You don't want it. Alright.' Jake lifts the guitar by the neck and smashes it down on the table. The neck crumples and a string snaps loose. It pings through the air and its stray edge strikes one of the Italians on the cheek. The man takes a smear of blood on his fingertip and looks at it with a frown of amazement. '*Pezzo di merda*,' he hisses at Jake. He grabs hold of Jake's hair, pulling him to his feet, and brings his knee up into Jake's groin. Jake collapses to the floor. Surrounded by beautiful girls he clutches at his outraged genitals and waits in a convulsion of nausea for some kind of bodily kindness to return.

Before any further scuffle can take place, he is forcibly ejected from the house with his broken guitar.

Jake borrows some momentary counterfeit radiance from the stars as he walks along the coastal road. He feels a connection between his solitary form and their expiring glitter. There is always a protection of sorts in the present moment if only it would never end. A futile longing to never have to step beyond this minute of time brings the consciousness of danger closer. Already in the sky there is a thin film of light which sends a chill through him. That, he knows, is tomorrow. And tomorrow does not bear thinking about. He tries to imagine telling Magnus he has lost his rent money and inwardly flinches as if a dentist's drill has touched an unaesthetised nerve. It is equally as inconceivable to explain the situation to his aunt.

Held aloft, the Madonna restored by Magnus, is carried from the pink church along the winding alleys of Tellaro through which washes the low lament of the sea. When the procession reaches the small harbour the papier-mâché virgin bride is reverently arranged in the stern of a boat lit by lamps. The sea too is astir with hundreds of fretted golden flames. A flotilla of small boats waits to follow the Madonna. Jake sees the tall figure of Magnus resting on the oars in his boat. Seated on a slab of rock below the church he, Ivan and Felix watch the gathering of boats ease their way out to sea.

The first firework screeches up into the night sky and ejaculates a harvest of coloured rain over the bay. The thunderous retort scatters birds from their nests. A series of rockets serpentine overhead, looking, with their busy swimming white tails, like intrepid cartoon sperms. Then an ethereal net of red and green radiance drifts down towards the lights on the sea. Cheers and applause meet each new explosion, every new choreography of unearthly aching colour. A succession of sonic booms burrow into the air. Another burst of fiery confetti, of spinning glittering incoherence, fans out over the sky above the candlelit procession of boats and the village on its rock and then expires, dissolves back into nothingness. The fireworks create the illusion that some kind of crescendo is imminent. A dead cindered rocket lands near the rock on which they sit. Then it is over and again it is the fireflies that perforate the darkness with their flitting signal lights

The nightclub, at the bottom of a long flight of concrete steps on the water's edge, is guarded by two men in suits.

Through a flotsam of sliding coloured discs Ivan sees Isabella. She, Grace and an entourage from the yacht are shuffling about on the dance floor. They are reflected in the club's fake chrome pipes and mirrored walls.

An hour later, having understood he and Isabella are still at war, Ivan is sitting at the same table littered with empty glasses. He watches her and Grace stroll arm in arm on pointed heels across the dance floor. She holds a cocktail of a transparent fuscia colour. He feels she is advertising to all and sundry her indifference to anything he might think. He sits with Felix and Jake watching other men doing what he seemingly is incapable of doing - providing unexacting fun, turning a blind eye to all but the bright bounded sheen of the moment.

'The heartless parasites of present cheer,' quotes Felix with a curling lip.

Isabella later begins dancing ostentatiously close to where Ivan sits. Like everyone else, she appears less trustworthy under the flashing strobe lights. Isabella dances as if she disbelieves in herself. Her movements are like a wary circling of a forbidden zone. Nearby, Rufus Woodburn shuffles from foot to foot in his virgin-white loafers.

Ivan is standing on the terrace when the launch cuts through the black water towards the dull gleam of the white yacht in the near distance. After the flashing strobes inside the club the slowly dying flames of all the candles on the water are like a defence of poetry. He sees Isabella on board and there is an eagerness in him to feel disappointed in her, betrayed by her.

At four in the morning Ivan, Felix and Jake make their way down to the harbour at Tellaro.

'I just want you to remember that though plunging irrevocably into the amorous deep I cannot and will not swim,' shouts Ivan as he wades fully dressed into the water. Seaweed floating like discarded votary wreaths clings to his legs. There is sand between his teeth and toes.

'Can't remember anything,' calls out Jake.

'The heart is like the sky, a part of heaven,' says Felix as a wave thumps against his knees.

'Here she is, the *Ariadne*.'

'Perhaps we ought to ask Magnus' permission? Maaaaaagnusssss,' yells out Jake hoarsely several times in succession. His voice, echoing over the sea, up into the sky, is a lonely primitive affront to the timeless poise into which the entire night has settled. They all look up towards the green shuttered houses perched on the rock. There is no stir of movement. The stone buildings mirror the dark privacy of the hillside. Lamplight in whose glow the occasional spinning bat can be seen strike out vivid patches of pink or yellow ochre stucco. Jake yells out Magnus' name again; it sounds like an eerie curse this time. Ivan tells him to shut up. 'Magnus must feel like he's summoned us as agents of retribution. We killed his iguana, you've gambled away his rent money.'

'Magnus' problem is, he's been talking to no one but himself for too long.'

Felix heaves himself up into the *Ariadne*. He positions

himself at the helm, standing motionless like a figurehead. Jake takes hold of the oars while Ivan sits on the cross-slats in the stern.

'Let's ram Rufus Woodburn,' says Felix with a wide sweeping gesture of his arm. 'Full stern ahead.'

Magnus wakes up with a start. There is a disturbance in his field of vision, as if a vase is about to topple from a shelf. A fluster of blind groping and he manages to turn on the bedside light and blinks and scowls at its overweening brightness. There are four fat mosquitoes on the white stucco wall by his bed. They have a gloating satiated air. Magnus stealthily swivels, arranges his body into combat position. He moves his extended palm slowly towards them. With an aggressive grunt he slaps his hand hard against the wall. An eggshell crack appears in the white stucco. A mosquito buzzes in his ear before flitting off. Magnus, taking the provocation personally, jumps out of bed and gives chase, repeatedly clapping his hands in mid-air as he strides furiously across the room. His calf then cramps up and he lets out a howl of distress. He hops on one foot for a bit, moaning pitifully. The mosquito pages him again. He swipes at it and the cramp in his leg takes a sharper bite of muscle. He crumples up on the tiled floor, a figure of fun for any watching ghost or angel.

Cagily he eventually moves again, like an injured player swapping places with a substitute. He hobbles into the kitchen, past the queue of bronzed and plaster figures. Dressed in his grey and pink striped pyjamas which, having shrunk in countless washes, disclose his raw red wrists and pearl white ankles. When troubled his habit is to eat. If his hands smell of rucola, basil or a well-matured pecorino cheese he is more apt to feel at peace with his world. He opens his fridge and takes out some olives and sun-dried tomatoes, both of which are wrapped in oil-stained grease paper. He sits down at the kitchen table under the autopsy blaze of a bare light bulb. Salt and oil from the piece of focaccia bread he breaks up with his hands come off on his long blunt fingers. Not for the first time today he wonders why Jake did not turn up to model earlier. For Magnus there always has to be a rational explanation. He came up with the idea that Jake is ill. However, he later caught sight of him on the rocks while the fireworks were going off. For a moment their eyes had met – long enough for Magnus to sense that Jake had been embarrassed. He fought off the suspicion that Jake's discomfort had something to do with the rent money with which he has entrusted him.

After washing up the utensils he has used he takes down from the shelves his copy of the collected works of Shelley and climbs back into bed. Shelley, he knows, advocated love as the supreme quest in a man's life. But, admonishes a defensive voice in Magnus' head, in deed Shelley had spent his life fleeing from a host of imagined enemies and identifying himself with beauty in the form of pretty young girls. Magnus opens the book critically. He is prepared to find nothing exemplary in Shelley's stanzas; only the self-pleasuring posturings of youthful rebellion. Heaping all three pillows under his head he lies on his back with his knees raised. His naked feet make contact with stray grains of sand between the sheets. A smear of blood on the white wall behind his head where he crushed a mosquito still bears the trace of the insect's spindly legs. He decides against the over-long *Alastor* and instead, in his deep cavernous voice, he reads aloud from *The Sensitive Plant*. Soon his head is swarming not with the ethereal emblems of ideal beauty he expected but shrill discomforting images of corruption and decay - monstrous undergrowths, mildew, mould, leprous scums, knotted water snakes and clanking manacles.

Hardly has he drifted back into sleep when Magnus is

awoken again. A dream in which he was idling in an abandoned cave while in the distance someone called out his name was by degrees making its way from the back to the front of his mind when he realised someone really was calling out his name. He goes to his dining room window.

At first he sees only the now familiar white yacht with its circus lights and restless silhouettes of revellers. Then, among the dying flames of the bobbing candles scattered over the sea, he spies the lone wooden boat. He goes to fetch his binoculars that are usually reserved for the pleasure of observing birds. He brings the vessel into focus and sees it is his boat. Blood throbs in his wrists; he feels a dull tingling contraction under his left arm. His inclination, his secret hope is to blame Rufus Woodburn for the brazen theft of his vessel. He is dismayed to realise the three boys in the *Ariadne* are Ivan, Felix and Jake. Haphazardly they are rowing out towards the yacht's stern. Magnus focuses his binoculars on the helm of the yacht. Two girls he identifies as Isabella and Grace are sitting at the controls. They appear to be laughing uproariously. He sweeps his binoculars over the deck of the yacht. It is bereft of human activity.

Magnus suddenly succumbs to a visceral presentiment. His anger dissolves into an ache of concern. He thinks of shouting out a warning, but he is timid of making any kind of spectacle of himself. He paces the dining room whose open window lets in the cloying smell of nearby wisteria. He hears the yacht's engine emit a low forewarning rumble. Once more he brings the two girls at the helm into focus.

The *Ariadne* meanwhile has eased closer to the large boat's stern. He watches Felix get to his feet and just as quickly fall back down. Now and again he hears one of the boys' voices and wonders why apparently no one on the yacht can hear them too. To his horror the yacht then begins moving backwards. The two girls, he sees, are laughing at their incompetence. There is a confusion of shrill and discordant shouts and the distant thump of the collision. Magnus drops his binoculars and observes the scene with his naked eye. It seems somehow more a staged spectacle than a real event. The deck of the slowly reversing yacht yields up a number of running figures. He stares into the curdling black sea by the yacht's side in time to see his splintered wooden boat sucked down in a chasm of parting water. The yacht grinds to a halt and its occupants are now leaning over the rails on the deck, shouting and scanning the water.

A head appears above the water and a yellow life belt is thrown down. Through his binoculars Magnus recognises Jake as he climbs up onto the yacht's deck. A girl then shouts and everyone races over to the far deck. Someone on the boat jumps into the sea. Magnus has to wait in order to find out what is happening. He paces up and down muttering things aloud to himself. Finally there is a flurry of activity on the yacht. Magnus watches as Felix is hauled to safety. A figure plunges down out of sight beneath the surface of the water. Several times he reappears, drawing deep intakes of air into his lungs.

Unbidden, unwanted, a lurid image of Ivan's dead body as it might eventually be washed ashore sickens Magnus. As he looks up at the stars he feels a primitive cry hollow out a void within him. He feels unsteady, irresolute, as if he is caught in a gale and his hair is lawlessly flapping and his clothes ballooning out behind him.

A stunned mournful silence emanates now from the insolent yacht. The black ungovernable sea flickers with dancing filaments, flaking moon debris. Magnus sits down on the cold stone floor and wraps his arms around his raised knees. Another unsolicited image, more comforting, more familiar in its elegiac misted beauty rises up in his mind's eye. Isabella, looking more than ever like a Pre-Raphaelite muse, kneels down beside a gravestone and lays there a loose bouquet of wildflowers. Magnus welcomes the hot tears that arrive as his being simultaneously goes out in kinship to the sorrowing young woman and acknowledges its own failure to inspire love. He makes the sign of the cross on the night air.

On the thin crescent of beach the sea pebbles shine moist and clean like semi-precious stones. The distant lighthouse blazes an irregular golden star into the black space across the bay. When he closes the window, Magnus sees his bloodless face in a puddle of light on the dark glass and behind it the grim frozen expression of one of his sculptures.

The Fence

'Does god like foxes more than people?'

'Why do you ask that?'

'I want to know if I like god or not.'

'He might not answer your prayers if he thinks you don't like him.'

'Dad says god lost the plot a long time ago. What does plot mean?'

Her daughter saying dad with fondness opens up an ugliness of irritation and jealousy in her.

'It's like a plan. It means if god once had a plan he's forgotten what it is.'

'You forget things all the time.'

'I know. I'm a scatterbrain.'

'Why do you make me say prayers?'

'Because you look so beautiful with your hands clasped and your eyes closed.'

Mother and daughter are standing side by side in front of the glass-paned kitchen door. Watching the three fox cubs frolic in the tall grass at the far end of the garden. Pink blossom is falling from the tree she ought to know the name of. Regret and reproach, despite the sheer surprising joy her daughter so often provides her with, are interruptions she has to face more and more often nowadays.

'I don't like the colour pink. Do you like pink? I think it's a deceitful colour.'

'What does deceitful mean.'

'To tell fibs.'

'You tell fibs. You tell fibs to dad and make me take your side.'

'They aren't so much fibs as secrets. We like sharing secrets, don't we?'

She looks at the weeds between the paving stones of the patio and the broken sections of a rotted drainage pipe. Another reproach levelled at her.

'What would happen if I went out into the garden?'

'The fox cubs would run away.'

'Why?'

'Because you'd frighten them.'

'I don't like that. How could I tell them I'm not frightening?'

'You'd have to learn fox language.'

Later that afternoon she opens her front door to her neighbour, Mr Sharp. He wears a smile, but not a smile that puts her at ease. It's like a flag of the respectability he prides himself on possessing. There is nothing personal about his smile. He obsessively mows his garden lawn several times a week. She knows he disapproves of her wild garden. As if it's some kind of indication of moral laxity. The reason why she has no husband. He asks her how she is, compliments her on her daughter's beauty and then, as if his entire speech has been painstakingly scripted, comes to the point. 'I've come to speak to you about the fence at the back of your garden. It needs two new panels. Your responsibility, I'm afraid. At the moment it's a gateway for every fox in the neighbourhood. I've even seen cubs. Anyway, I've just blocked the gap so at least the foxes won't be able to get through anymore.'

She nods and smiles. She tells him she will do as he asks. He believes he is a good and kind man. She can sense this. But what he insists on and demands in return is respectability. And she can't help putting on an air of respectability for him. She is furious with herself for not speaking her mind after she shuts the door. Why didn't she tell him she and her daughter like the foxes? Ask him what harm they do? She enacts in her mind everything she should have said and then feels still more displeased with herself.

She is still ashamed of her timidity after she has put her daughter to bed with a story and settled herself on the sofa with a glass of wine to watch the result of the Brexit referendum. Her dream is to one day return to Florence where she studied sculpture for three years and make her home there. She met her husband in Florence. Initially he held little attraction for her. She agreed to have dinner with him because he was so insistent but mostly because she wanted to repay the hurt Eddie had inflicted on her. She and Eddie had been in the midst of a feud. Their relationship, forever a kindling factor during her stay in Italy, was a circling dance around each other, during which they rarely touched and were always fully clothed. Like two stars sharing a complimentary orbit to touch would produce a catastrophe. Or so she maintained. To his protests. They repeated the same dance over and over again. It always had a beauty. Like something outside of time. Like a secret pact they shared with the moonlight and the church bells and the old stones of Florence. But there was a border she would never allow him to cross. When he spoke to her she could never quite work out if it was her body that listened to him while her mind fought him or her mind that listened to him while her body fought him. Just as she could never work out if it was something he possessed or something he lacked that frightened her. Then Eddie began sleeping with her flatmate. She was betrayed on two fronts. She found herself wanting to unsing every song she had sang, unsay every beautiful thing she had said. It was then, bristling with anger, with a desire to cause pain, add to the ugliness, she went out to dinner with her future husband. She heard on the grapevine that Eddie later took credit for her daughter. He told someone that without him she would never have married her husband. It made her laugh because it's probably true, but it also annoyed her because it reminded her of how he always had to have the last word. Sometimes she wonders what it says about her that the most decisive coupling she has undertaken in her life was determined by a third party. The truth though is that she has never been able to drop her guard with any man. Only with her daughter is she free of inhibition. Only with her daughter can she enter into the secret cadence of her being. She has danced the can-can with full-hearted abandon for her daughter. She cannot conceive of a scenario in which she would dance the can-can for any of the men she has known.

One night she and her husband had argued bitterly and there was an overwrought silence in the car. As they crossed Battersea Bridge at two in the morning she saw Eddie walking alone under the string of lights in his winter coat. There was something mystical about being able to see him without his knowledge. As if either he or she were a ghost. He looked impoverished, defenceless, as if he was offering himself up to calamity or crime. She asked herself if she'd rather go home with Eddie at this moment than continue the life of constant petty bickering with her husband. But she knew Eddie would have no home, not in the conventional sense. He had no aptitude for creating a home. She realised this was something she had always known about him. He was like a country with an unstable government. She felt strangely exonerated as the car left Eddie behind on the bridge over the moving water and entered the King's Road. Looking out at a group of party revellers on the kerbside she apologised to her husband for her bad mood.

But she is haunted by the alternative braver life she might be living. She would have to tear through the corseting fabric of custom and then take a decisive step to find it. She has never torn through that fabric. No doubt that's what frightened her about Eddie. He would have compelled her to live in this alternate world which both attracts and alarms her. Her intention to return to Florence one day has become the imaginative manifestation of this desire to step into a brave new world.

The result of the referendum disgusts her. Never has she felt so ashamed of her national flag. Her dream of returning to Florence, she knows, has now lost much of its feasibility. There is a heaviness in her limbs when she lifts herself off the sofa. She goes to the bathroom. She looks at her face in the mirror. Her face looks the same as it always does. There is no trace of the ugliness she feels has taken hold of her. She returns to the living room. On the television there is footage of the celebrations at the Leave headquarters. The trumpeting triumph on people's faces is incomprehensible to her. More and more people are beginning to behave like characters in TV commercials. She knows Mr Sharp was all for leaving the EU, like all the other small-minded people in her country. He would be lost without his fences. They are like the model of everything he believes in.

Her heart begins to canter when she makes the decision. Restoring the foxes' access to her garden by removing whatever barrier Mr Sharp had placed by his fence belongs to the alternate world she has always avoided. She makes up her mind the time has come to act. It's the first time she has contemplated committing a criminal act as an adult. She puts on a hooded jacket and hides as much of her face as she can in case she encounters a local dog walker or jogger. Then more menacing images of the night outside flash up before her. A deranged madman. A gang of hooded delinquents high on crack cocaine. She has to brace herself to step outside, under the moon and stars. Her footsteps are slow and uncertain. There is a scent of blossoms she ought to know the name of. She finds she can't escape the feeling that she is being watched.

It occurs to her that the world is now on film all the time. She sees grainy footage of herself meddling with her neighbour's fence. As she is half way up the front garden path an ambulance speeds past, its lights momentarily dyeing the leaves of the plane tree at the end of her garden a shrieking chemical shade of blue. The moon seems brighter when the emergency vehicle disappears. She stands for a while gazing up at it. It doesn't comfort her. It makes her feel small and shaky. When she looks down the sight of her shadow shocks her. She can't recall the last time she stood staring at her shadow. It then dissolves into the darkness, but its hidden presence remains as a marauding ghost in her mind. She suddenly feels what she is planning to do belongs to a current of madness in her. And that she is putting the cherished life she shares with her daughter at risk. She turns around and returns to her home, again wondering what the name of that blossom is.

Centre-stage

He has climbed back into the reality the old photograph depicts. He has his ghost arm around her ghost waist and the ghost kiss is only a moment away. She was his induction into the mysteries of a naked female soul. Almost thirty years have passed since he last saw her. Would they even recognise each other now?

'I guess I'm about to find out,' he says to himself.

It was a song he is ashamed of liking which brought her back to the forefront of his mind. This song is like a guilty secret he would never admit to anyone.

Once upon a time his identity had been founded on championing the right music. Teenage years were all about finding the tribe to which you belonged. All about finding your look, your war shirt. Because you had to escape the roundabouts, the one-way streets, the carparks, the chainwire fences of suburban daily life. He was always then looking for the real thing. And it was music that pointed the way, rebel music. The song that sprung open a casket and released into the atmosphere the scent of the girl he hasn't seen for thirty years is not rebel music. It is a bland American FM song he first heard while been driven along a freeway towards the Country Club Plaza in Kansas City. It was a song he had heard again while sitting on the bed of his hotel there as he prepared himself for the most momentous encounter of his life. This is the thing about songs. They are shooting stars that can take you back in time. And it is because of this song that he is now gazing out at sunlit clouds on a transatlantic flight. On his way to see the girl the song reminds him of. Of course she will no longer be a girl. The last time he saw her was the watershed year of his life.

When, thirty years ago, the letter arrived from Kansas City telling Ivor she was getting married, the band he sang in was beginning to attract the interest of several record companies. There had been an inspired week when he and Tom wrote four new songs, all of them pulsing and aglitter with a memorable hook. They had several gigs lined up, one of which was at The Venue at New Cross where a plethora of A&R men would attend and pass judgement. The news in the letter made him feel overwhelmed, helpless. He didn't like this feeling. This feeling of being dumped back into the audience, a passive spectator.

He was both sheepish and defiant when he confronted Tom. 'I've got to go to America for a couple of weeks.'

'Why? When?'

'Tomorrow.'

Tom looked at him as if he was either playing a prank or had lost his mind. He had to lock horns with his friend. He had to subject his amorous resolution to the threat of mockery.

'Leah's getting married. In three weeks. I've got to stop her.'

He didn't like saying Leah's name to Tom. Though he had never overtly voiced the suspicion to himself he sensed there was a joke attached to it in Tom's mind. This was evident now. Though he sometimes could not resist speaking of her and she featured persistently in the lyrics he wrote he had always sought to play down the importance of Leah to Tom. Tom admired his independence of spirit. Tom's idea of him was an important part of his sense of self. He was careful not to subject it to alteration.

He met Leah when working in a record shop in Soho. It

was her last day in London. She had looked at him as though she recognised him. They talked for no more than five minutes but exchanged addresses. She gave him the piece of red ribbon she wore in her hair. The first time he understood how much spirit power there can be in objects. However, he didn't give her much thought until a letter arrived. Soon the letters, ever fatter in their well-travelled envelopes, were what he most looked forward to. Her handwriting as evocative of magical distant lands as ancient script inked on papyrus. Writing ever longer and more frequent letters he became more accomplished at harnessing the beauty and power of sequencing words. He learned language is a means of moving us away from the darkness within, towards light. He became prolific at writing lyrics for songs. He had a blue notebook he carried around with him. He sat at a desk composing on a typewriter. It was an image of himself he liked, an image of himself he thought ought to be painted for posterity. Leah began to perfume her letters. The scent became the most secret thing in his world. That she had a boyfriend and believed in an afterworld where punishment was meted out caused him little concern.

He and Tom had known each other since schooldays. They made music together in his bedroom. It was the most intimate thing he had ever done. The first time Tom coaxed him to sing the words of 'Metal Guru' while he strummed the chords he felt more naked than he did in the bath. Soon they began trying to compose their own songs. Often he could sense the presence of a song at the far end of a darkness before he heard it. And the finding of it entailed a kind of vision quest, like the Lakota believed. He came to believe everyone has a distinctive song within waiting to be sung. The song within was how we made our truth heard. His task was to find his own song and compose a number of variations around its basic framework. He was aware of the power of songs to console or beautify you in amorous paint or dress you in your war coat. How a song can make a room seem as big as the world. How a song can make you feel there is magic in your life. He and Tom performed autopsies on their favourite tunes, stripping them down to basic components, as if there was a scientific formula to writing songs which produce a fiery blazing arc through darkness.

'A great song is a memorial to a moment in time.'

'No. A great song *is* a moment in time.'

'Already a memory before it's over.'

He obsessively modelled his voice on David Bowie's. Spent all his free time singing along to the songs on Hunky Dory, Ziggy Stardust and Aladdin Sane. He listened closely to black soul singers, how they seemed to sing from the heart. He spent all his time emulating other voices. The next challenge he set himself was to add some memorable distinctive kink of his own to his singing voice. He came up with a trick of almost overstraining his vocal reach.

Just before he went to America he and Tom had begun to take exception to each other in small matters. Ever since Tom had started going out with Karen. Karen didn't like him. It was the first time in his life he had experienced such open hostility. It baffled him. It polluted what had always been the clean sparkling air he and Tom inhaled together. It whittled away at his self-esteem. He was glad every time Tom betrayed her by snogging a female fan in a carpark, something he couldn't resist doing frequently though he never went further. Often when he looked at Karen he had the image in his mind of Tom betraying her as if he might make her receive it on some otherworldly wavelength and give back to her some of the discomfort she caused him.

Tom stopped short of ridiculing his motive for suddenly taking off for America. But it cost him an effort. Ivor left with the nagging suspicion that they weren't as good friends as he liked to believe. That maybe Tom made fun of him behind his back.

He caught a flight to Chicago the next day, then a connecting flight to St Louis and then sat on a Greyhound bus for five hours. He felt he had brought his entire life onto that greasy shuddering bus. He kept marvelling at the oblivion of Leah. Here he was edging across the planet towards her and she didn't have a clue. He enjoyed the power this feeling gave him of being the stage director. He gave no thought to the possible consequences of what he was doing. It was like he was carried along by the game fever of childhood make-believe. It was the gesture itself he was fixated on, as if it existed outside of time and carried no responsibilities. His role in life was to be on the stage under lights, not part of an audience in the dark.

Leah worked in a large elegant department store in the Country Club Plaza. The Country Club Plaza seemed like a fantasy world. A film set with all its ornate fountains and pristine themed Spanish architecture. When he caught sight of the store where she worked he felt like he did before going on stage. The same mix of terror and excitement. The creaturely quivering in his limbs. The momentous hush of expectation in the air. The heat was suitably exotic. It increased the glow he felt on his skin. Inside the store he made his way past people for whom the day was ordinary. Leah worked in the women's lingerie section. He felt he was moving through the store on an escalator. His legs had that same weightless feeling. When their eyes met she was holding a black pair of lace panties. She stared at him as if he might disappear at any moment. He had begun to pride himself on his way with words but when he spoke he found he had nothing but inanities to fall back on. It took a while for both of them to return to some semblance of their everyday selves. And then she kept saying her boyfriend's name. He didn't want to hear that.

They kissed for the first time in a park by a lake the

following day. He was flooded with a bounty of generosity. He felt love for the entire world. He extolled Tom and the other members of the band to her. She kept bringing up Ted, her fiancé. She told him Ted took good care of her. That she had grown up with a lop-sided swing in her garden that her father had never been able to fix and believed this was why it was always her who was chosen to play unhinged females in drama classes at school. The implication was that he himself would not be able to take good care of her, like Ted. He had difficulty refuting this argument.

'Why should you need someone to take care of you?'

Ted appeared in the restaurant where they were having dinner three evenings later. He looked with his long pony-tailed hair and cowboy outfit more American than anything Ivor had yet seen in America. Plates and glasses were broken in the fracas that took place. All eyes were upon their table. Afterwards he made fun to himself of his yearning to always be centrestage. Ted, evidently, was a violent man. He pulled Leah out of the restaurant by her hair. Ivor's neck was bruised where Ted had squeezed it in his ugly hands.

When, defeated, he returned to London three weeks later Tom told him he was no longer the band's singer. They had replaced him.

'What do you mean you've replaced me?'

'You abandoned us, Ivor. You made your choice. At a vital crossroads in our career.'

'You're joking, right?'

'I'm sorry, Ivor. We had to play that gig. Karen's cousin stepped in. Actually he blew us all away. I don't know how to say this, but his voice suits us better than yours does. And the record company wants him. You ought to start up your own band. You're a brilliant singer. That's what I'd do.'

A month later he smuggled himself into one of their gigs at The Marquee in Wardour Street, feeling like an illegal immigrant. He stood at the back of the packed club determined to convince himself the new vocalist, singing his words, was a poor substitute. But there were no consolations to be found that night. There was an irresistible energy to the songs that made his body want to move despite himself. They were riding the crest of the wave. They were unstoppable now, invincible, bulletproof. They were going to be big. He could sense it in every bludgeoning chord; he could sense it in the fervent tribal atmosphere inside the club.

In the following years all virtue went out of Ivor. Or that's how it felt. He was riddled with resentment, jealousy, bitterness and hatred as the band went from success to success. Their first single charted and they appeared on Top of the Pops. There they were on television, where he most wanted to be. Instead he was signing on for unemployment benefit every fortnight. Their first album was the most hyped record of the year and they appeared on the front covers of the music papers. There were images of them on almost every London street. Except his face was missing. He felt his face had been erased from its rightful place in the world, just as all his words had been rewritten.

He moved from Notting Hill to Lavender Hill and then from Seven Sisters to Lewisham. He worked in a music store. Putting products into bags and ringing up purchases on the till. He said 'Thank you' countless times every day. It was what he most often said. 'Thank you' and 'Goodbye'. Whenever someone bought a Lover Spit CD his hands trembled as he packaged it and accepted payment. It became a kind of phobia.

The faces he encountered every day appeared increasingly nondescript. Tom meanwhile was ever more ensconced in the world of beautiful people. His most passionate hope during this time was that some calamity would befall Tom. Karen had long since been jettisoned. There were late night photos of Tom with mini-skirted models. He knew some pleasure when several years later a rumour reached him that Tom was addicted to crack cocaine and too paranoid to leave his home in daylight. Meanwhile all his attempts to form a new band failed. He no longer met musicians. He could not find a new tribe. Every new person he met seemed like a tourist in his life. Someone struggling to locate themselves on a map, to understand the currency, to speak the language. Neither could he find a replacement for Leah. Anyway, it was clear to him now that love, romantic love, didn't bring the changes hoped for. This was the secret everyone carried in their hearts. Love, once found, could not be recharged when its batteries died. He stopped writing songs. He had nothing to say. His acoustic guitar was filmed in dust. His blue notebook had got lost. His typewriter sat on top of the wardrobe. He stopped listening to music. Except when a new Lover Spit album came out. Then he knew a passionate longing to find evidence that their music had lost its glamour, lost its vitality. Instead they embarked on another world tour and were met by screaming girls at airports. The singer told an interviewer that had he kept every pair of panties thrown onto the stage he would need to rent a garage in which to store them. Another experience denied him. He realised Tom's decision to sling him out of the band had deprived him of sexual union with probably at least a hundred women from all parts of the world. The beautiful naked bodies of these women haunted him, the intimate knowledge of them he had been denied.

When, a couple of years ago, Tom was all over social media after a woman accused him of sexually abusing her when she was fifteen he found he barely cared anymore.

He found Leah on Facebook. Not long after his fiftieth birthday. She was lax with her privacy settings and he was able to stalk her undetected. It was the only thing he looked forward to doing most days. There were photos of her as a young woman on her page, but not a single photo of her in middle-age. A post on her profile page revealed she was now single and the manager of a bar in Kansas City. Then, while watching a film, he heard the song. It was the soundtrack while a lonely man drove through a desert. The song which made the past live again. The song which, unwanted, unworthy, was part of the soundtrack of his own life.

On the plane he thinks about history. His own history. It astounds him how little experience he has accumulated since being thrown out of the band, how few worthy or heartening memories he has made, as if he has been living the same wrong day with minor variables over and over again. He thinks about all the unwritten songs somewhere inside him. The songs he and Tom would have composed together. Then he thinks of himself as an unwritten song. It occurs to him he ought to hate Leah. She now seems like some hallucinogenic drug he had swallowed that had fatally impaired his judgement, derailed him from the life he was meant to live. He plays with a fantasy of buying a gun, walking into the bar where she works and shooting her. He has to hide his grin from the suited woman sitting beside him. He wonders what it is, if anything, he now wants from Leah. Certainly it isn't romance. He's had enough of that. Some evidence perhaps that his gesture wasn't as wrong-headedly self-destructive as it now seems. Some evidence that it was a gift he gave to her that she has benefitted from.

When he is again standing in the Country Club Plaza, the last place he had truly been happy in, expecting to at least catch a surviving spark of the euphoria and enchantment he had known arriving here as a young man, he is struck by how much less of himself he possesses now. It's like he is standing in a graveyard. A big part of the love one feels for any place is in the missing of it. Now that he is back in its midst he is inclined to hate the place, as if it was part of the malfeasant spell that tricked him out of his intended fate. When last here he felt he stood out from the crowd. No one takes much notice of him today. He is making up the numbers. He buys a sandwich and eats it by the side of the fountain he and Leah had stood beside the day he arrived to stop her from getting married. As it turned out he had succeeded only in causing her marriage to Ted to be postponed for six months.

He smokes a cigarette in a red splash of neon outside the bar. It has begun to rain. The drops before his eyes dyed crimson. Fear, as usual, is trying to find a foothold. Trying to make him change his mind.

Everything is a kaleidoscopic blur when he crosses the threshold. It takes several deep breaths to calm his heart and focus his eyes. There are no more than fifteen people inside. He sees at least three candidates who might be a greatly changed Leah. He wonders how dramatically time can sully an image. Of course he himself has lost his hair. It's a humiliation that alienates him from his favoured idea of himself every new day. Then she appears from a backroom. His recognition of her carries no charge of uplifting emotion. He finds her neither attractive nor unattractive. All the old glory has been utterly effaced from her presence. She is like just another nobody person crossing his path. It is incomprehensible to him that he is looking at the individual responsible for cutting his life in two. His instinct is to hide his face, make a run for it. He realises he no longer has any desire to step onto a stage. But then their eyes meet. He senses he is a puzzle to her, a momentary glitch in the continuity of the functioning of her mind, but she quickly shrugs off whatever thought it was he inspired and returns to her duties behind the bar.

The Guard

'I rarely paused to give thanks. That's my regret. We don't fully appreciate people until they can no longer hear us. The human condition poses so many paradoxes of this kind. It's important to recognise kindness in others. Remember that.'

He beats his cane on the cobbles as he walks. She has hold of his brittle hand. It's like a small helpless creature she is protecting. She wonders if it's because he can't see her that he talks to her as if she is an adult. She closes her eyes, to experience the world her grandfather now lives in and marvels how he manages to locate himself in the dizzying blackness.

'Let me give you some advice. Every day you should do at least one thing that frightens you. Do we have a deal?'

'Okay,' she says.

'I know exactly where we are. Half way across Ponte Sisto. I can hear the tide of the Tiber and smell the river mud. This is where I asked your grandmother to marry me. My heart was in my mouth. I had never before dared to want anything so much. And I was sure she would laugh and say no. I wish I could remember what she was wearing. It was often the buttons on her clothes that caught my eye. They were like threshold guardians. But you're too young to understand that.' His smile is like a gift he gives her. 'Earlier that week we had been to the zoo. We both marvelled at a giraffe. It was like beholding a divine vision. We had to throw back our shoulders to see the height of her. Her legs were a marvel of both extreme vulnerability and extreme power. And she had the most gentle eyes. It was a cruelty she was held captive like that, far from her native terrain. It was something your grandmother and I could agree on. Sometimes I think of that giraffe and I can't help thanking her, because it was her that moved our hearts closer together.'

Within six months of his wife dying Grandfather went blind. He said it was appropriate the world vanished for him when she departed. Appropriate that he was left with only the pictures in his own mind. When he lost the use of his eyes he became like an otherworldly being to Chaya. A much deeper aura of mystery enveloped him. Chaya was twelve when she took it upon herself to become her grandfather's eyes. She got to know all his secret signals, all his nervous gestures. She learned from him the currents of love. It physically pained her to ever see him in difficulty.

Soon after her grandfather went blind, her father disappeared. They all woke up one morning to find he was no longer in the apartment. He had taken no bag with him. Though at the time the fascist government denied Jews many liberties they didn't do them physical harm. However, her father was convinced sooner or later violence would arrive. The Nazis terrified him. The Nazis turned him into a shell of himself. Chaya could never find him when she looked in his eyes. His body was fished out of the Tiber within a week of his disappearance. No one wanted to believe he had ended his own life. Not even her grandfather could make sense of the tragedy for Chaya.

It was not long after her grandfather told her about the giraffe that the men entered the apartment at five in the morning. The impatient contempt with which these men treated her grandfather was her first experience of holding hatred in her heart. A throbbing hard-shelled, sharp-edged monster of attrition in her small thin body she could not give expression to nor appease. She, her grandfather, her mother and her five year old brother were arrested.

They were taken to a camp in northern Italy where the men and women were separated. She only got to talk to her grandfather over a wire fence for half an hour every day. Overseen by Italian men in uniforms. A kind teenage boy with unruly dark hair led her grandfather to where she and her mother waited for him behind the cruel wire fence. In the camp he appeared still more frail and ancient, like a storyteller in a bedtime book. She described to him the visible world they now lived in. She collected details of the life in the camp the minute she awoke. Detail became a kind of treasure trail to her. And everything she described heightened her intimacy with the world around her.

'There was a young woman today who washed her hair in the rainwater. I want to do that one day.'

She always felt her body perform an elegant ghost dance when she got her grandfather to smile.

The white ribbon in her hair grew a little grubbier day by day.

Then they were taken to a train station in trucks. She was reunited with her grandfather in the cattle truck where the world shrank to a pressing blackness for her too. The detail of life here was not something she had words for even if she had wanted to describe it to her grandfather. The various fleeting smells of shoe leather, damp wool, hair oil, sweating socks, body odour, shampoo soon vanished behind by the overwhelming stench of vomit, urine and excrement. She could no longer find the familiar protective smell of her grandfather. It became hard to concentrate on anything except the dizzying nausea, the racking thirst, the monotony of the hammering wheels beneath her. She became intensely aware of her feet inside her shoes. She wriggled her toes to join up her body, keep alive her connection with it. The worst thing of all was to return to the horror after brief escapes into sleep. One time she dreamed of eating a peach, the sweet juice running over her gums and lips. The truth of her surroundings had never seemed so heartless and cruel when she was abruptly woken up.

When the door was finally unbolted and opened, blinding surgical light flooded into her eyes like a physical presence. It was unlike any experience of light she had ever known. It was light that wanted to harm her, to erase her. Outside dogs snarled and barked. Men yelled in a guttural foreign language. Every shouted word an inflicted cruelty. Women began sobbing. She held on tightly to her grandfather's hand. She explained to him they had to walk down a wooden ramp. She squinted through the searing light and saw the grains in the wood of the ramp so intently did she study it for pitfalls. Twice her grandfather almost tripped, almost stumbled, almost fell. On the platform a man in a uniform tried to wrestle her away from her grandfather. Shouting in a language she didn't understand. 'My grandfather is blind and I have to look after him,' she said. The guard tore her hand from her grandfather's hand and shoved her grandfather so hard he fell to the ground. She caught sight of him sprawled out on the concrete before the confusion of the place forced her to avert her eyes. The desire to help her grandfather to his feet was an urgent pulse in her young body but the guard blocked her way. She stared up into his face, this man who had humiliated her grandfather. The clenched teeth, the lazy left eye, the plump mole on his chin. It became a face she could never erase from her memory, a contemptuous ugly hateful face. The last image she had of her grandfather was of him sprawled in an undignified heap on the ground in the stark white light. In the chaos she also lost sight of her mother. Smoke drifted through the white light. She was all alone in this place of stark terror.

What is hell?

It is a place of dreadful and endless torment.

It was a girl called Irene who told her what they burned in the chimneys. She conveyed the information in hand signals because they didn't speak the same language. Irene was contemptuous of Chaya's naivety. It angered her as if it was an affront to her own understanding of the world. Eventually they improvised a mutant language they could share and formed an alliance of sorts. They shared what scraps of additional food they found. There were times when Chaya was the more resilient of the two. She lived intensely in her body. It never stopped complaining, never stopped making impossible demands. Her mind was as if evacuated. She once dreamed of her grandfather's giraffe. That such a magical creature could be roaming around in the same world in which she lived was beyond her comprehension. But not even in sleep did she escape the camp. She knew where she was and the horror she would have to face the following day even while sleeping, even while dreaming. She never understood why she was spared the gas. She thought it might have had something to do with the confusion caused by her grandfather's fall to the ground. She came to believe her grandfather had saved her life. She was ashamed how rarely she felt it was a life worth saving.

Chaya was the only member of her family to survive the Nazis. She was fifteen when the camp was liberated. The first time she saw herself in a mirror after the war she no longer recognised her face. She felt irremediably removed from everything around her. She looked for menace, for cruelty on people's faces. She was shuttled from one place to another, one country to another. Finally she arrived back in Rome where a kindly old couple did their best to provide her with a home. Rome though was like a theatre after the audience has left and the lights have been extinguished. There was no indication life would continue.

When she was nineteen she moved to Florence and got a

job as a waitress. For a long time she felt unable to trust herself. Her mind would darken and she would begin to sweat. She felt she didn't know how she would act from one moment to the next. She might begin screaming, she might begin smashing plates. Madness was a tide in her body, a whisper in her ear. People expected of her a recognisable normality. But she saw the world as a place of insanity and herself as grotesque. The horrors in her head swarmed out at night like sewer rats. There was no way of holding them back. She was careful never to reveal the tattoo on her arm. To keep her guilt and grotesqueness concealed. It meant she was never able to swim. Something she yearned to do. It meant she met with coldness any amorous advances from boys. She felt they would be horrified if they knew the contents of her mind.

She began to enjoy her job in the restaurant. It became a safe hiding place. She began to gain confidence in her ability to pass as a normal functioning human being. She was conscientious at work. It mattered to her that the restaurant thrived. She liked to see Marco, the owner, happy. She took pleasure when the takings were good. Her favourite part of every evening was when the metal grille was pulled down at the end of the night and, in candlelight, the staff all sat down to a meal of their own. Marco sometimes talked to her of his growing interest in Buddhism. She liked the idea of karma. That the Nazis and especially that one guard might return to the world as hunted rodents. But she knew it was critical to her precarious wellbeing to always keep in check her hatred. Which meant rarely thinking about what happened at Auschwitz. The war was sometimes discussed. Everyone had a story of improbable personal survival. Marco told her he owed his life to a kitten.

'I was on my way to a meeting. I was a member of a resistance group. The *Partito d'Azione*. I saw the kitten in Piazza d'Azeglio. Huddled beneath shrubbery. She was in a pitiful state. So instead of going directly to the meeting, I took her home. By the time I arrived within sight of the building where the meeting was taking place the secret police were already there. We had an informer in our ranks. I watched my friends escorted out to a van. They were all tortured at Villa Triste. Only one survived.'

Chaya dreaded all talk of the war. That was when her mind darkened and she began to sweat. She made out she spent the war in Rome. Made out her parents and grandfather were still alive. She told no one she had been in the camp at Auschwitz. She never recalled her experiences there, but neither could she forget them. They were like a dirty throbbing serum in her blood. Only Marco guessed she was hiding something. She had been on the verge of confiding in him one night when the chef suddenly broke out in barrelling laughter at the other end of the table and the moment was lost.

On her nights off she went to the cinema. There was something about sitting in the dark with strangers which offered comfort. It affirmed how she felt about her life. And it was a relief to escape into narratives which bore no resemblance to her own. She discovered the plots of films often began by punishing virtue but always ended by punishing vice. Only occasionally though did the untruth of this narrative bother her.

She saw the guard again one afternoon when she was sitting outside the church of San Miniato high above the city. She knew it was him immediately by the intensity with which she was suddenly breathing. Her inflamed blood stung her face. He was alone and entered the church. She followed him in. Her heart was pounding in her throat with an urgency which made her dizzy. She felt herself both stealthy assassin and helpless little girl. She watched him take the holy water and cross himself. She stood staring at his hunched shoulders, oblivious to the map of star signs on the marble paving stones beneath her feet.

She followed him along the right aisle, down the steps into the crypt where several people were praying before the altar. He sat down amidst the slender columns, under the honeycomb vaulting with all the prayer candles flickering shadows over the walls. She wondered if he was praying for forgiveness. And if so, whether or not he would feel it was granted. The Benedictine monks of the monastery began chanting from somewhere below. Music as weightless and evanescent as the flight of a newly metamorphosed butterfly. For a moment her thoughts turned to her grandfather, her mother, her little brother, until it seemed that the translucent echoing chant of the monks was a requiem for them.

She followed him out of the church. This was a decision she didn't have to think about but that frightened her. It made her unknown to herself, as if she had little inking of what dark acts she was capable of. She recalled her grandfather's advice to do at least one thing every day that frightened her. She hadn't followed his mantra. There had been too much fear to overcome in the camp. She had already had a lifetime's fill of battling fear. She noticed now that his clothes were worn and inexpensive. And was aware of a loneliness in him. There was a brief whisper of satisfaction that he was not, apparently, thriving. He now began descending the steps down to San Niccolò, where the Stations of the Cross were marked. Twenty yards behind, keeping close to the ivied wall of the rose garden, she still felt herself both stealthy assassin and helpless little girl. Her heart was still thumping in her throat with an urgency she didn't understand. What was it her heart expected her to do? She walked down the steep steps with a feeling that her grandfather was watching her, waiting for her to do the obvious thing. But she had no idea what this obvious thing was. Even though she felt she was in the midst of an inevitable moment. The moment that had been awaiting her ever since the murder of her family. She looked at her watch. She only had twenty minutes before she had to open the restaurant. Today was a special day. Marco had entrusted her with the keys to the restaurant for the first time. It was her job to let in the chef and his two assistants. Marco had to meet his wife and two children from whom he was separated. To let Marco down was among the worse things she could imagine in her present life. She had to make a decision quickly. What was she going to do? How confront this man with the crime he had committed?

She followed him over Ponte alle Grazie. He looked down at a white swan gliding on the moving tide of the river. And then she followed him into Piazza della Signoria. He paid little attention to the statues as if he had seen them once and had no need to look at them again. There was a bounce to his walk now as he crossed the piazza. As if in the midst of so many Renaissance wonders his body had been excited by an inspiration. He entered a bar. She looked at her watch again. He soon emerged with a lemon yellow and mulberry red ice cream. Their eyes might have met had he not been so fully concentrated on savouring the treat he had granted himself. She was angered he allowed himself this pleasure. She wanted to snatch the cone from his hand and throw it to the ground. It made her ugly to herself how deeply into her being he was able to feed resentment, that he was able to make himself a resident deep down at the heart of her.

It was now she had the idea of showing him the tattoo on her arm. The idea brought forth dampness under her armpits, produced a tremor in her legs. But it was the only way she could think of to get him to own the shame of what he did. She continued following him down the crowded street. His pace had become more leisurely now that his attention was lavished on his ice cream. She had to hope he would eventually enter a quiet street. She did not want to make a spectacle of herself in front of an audience. But he kept to the busy streets. As if he purposefully made sure he was never alone with himself. When they were in the vicinity of the station of Santa Maria Novella the activity of the thickened crowd grew more urgent. She almost lost sight of him. Then she spotted him disappearing into a cheap hotel.

She agonised what to do. She was already ten minutes late in opening the restaurant. She reasoned she could return to the hotel tomorrow. But then the idea of him leaving Florence in the meantime kept her rooted to the spot. She looked up at the grubby windows of the three-storey building. Litter was strewn over the pavement where she stood. Before long she felt she was attracting attention. She intensely disliked being looked at, as if, looked at hard enough, her secret history would be revealed.

Finally, the mortification of letting Marco down compelled her to abandon her vigil. But there was little conviction in her footsteps. She only got as far as the Duomo when a stronger force, a force there was no escaping pulled her back to the litter-strewn pavement outside the hotel.

Dare, Kiss, Truth or Promise?

'Dare, kiss, truth or promise,' says Myra. Then she performs another handstand. She stays upside down with her dress tumbled over her head for a count of eleven. Myra is always showing her knickers. Jamie though has eyes only for her sister, Rose. Rose is wearing a green ribbon in her hair today. Sunlight afloat in bars lies across her shoulders.

'Why don't we play doctors and nurses again?'

'Boring,' Myra tells Rose. It's always Myra who decides what game they will play. Jamie is often a little frightened of what Myra might say or do next. But this is what makes her presence important. She brings the unexpected closer. She bridges the shyness between him and Rose. Myra is eleven and he and Rose are only nine. Both Myra and Rose always wear a cross on a silver chain around their necks.

'Well Jamie, dare, kiss, truth or promise?'

'Dare.'

'I dare you to kiss Rose's belly button.'

Myra and Rose are in the midst of some private argument today. It is something to do with their father. Some preference Myra perceived he has showed to Rose has annoyed her. Myra wants to cause her sister suffering. Rose, though, has a kind and forgiving nature. He looks to Rose now. He needs to make sure she won't mind him kissing her belly button. He is always considerate of her, always anxious to attend to her wellbeing. To disappoint Myra doesn't bother him. But he is careful to never disappoint Rose. He likes to feel he and Rose can talk to each other without words. She can give value to a moment just by a look in her eyes, make a moment memorable, something glowing he takes to bed with him. He sees on her face she doesn't mind him kissing her belly button. He kneels down at her feet, lifts up her top and presses his lips to her warm skin.

Then it's his turn to ask Myra. She chooses dare but he can't think of anything to dare her.

'You're useless at this game.' As is her habit, Myra looks off into the distance, as if she can see things, important things, invisible to her younger companions.

There are model cowboys and Indians scattered all over the floor of the upstairs playroom. Narnia, the family dog, a scruffy black poodle, scattered them earlier while having one of its fits. It is a dog prone to hysteria. Jamie's mother and father agree that dogs take on the personality of their owner but argue whose dog it is. Rose has picked up a plastic horse with a war-painted Indian chief astride it. He has recently noticed that Rose changes the way he looks at his things. She makes him more uncertain about the things he owns. She likes his collection of marbles which has made them more precious to him. She likes to finger the clothes and bend the limbs of his Action Men. But she shows no interest in his toy cars or toy soldiers.

'Okay. We'll play doctors and nurses.' Myra walks over to the sliding white door of the playroom and seals it shut. 'Where's your mum anyway?'

'She won't come in. She never does.'

'Okay, you're the patient. Rose is the nurse and I'm the doctor. You've been hit by a car.' Myra walks over to the huge train set, laid out by Jamie's father on a three foot high platform against the wall. It has hills, tunnels, roads, a small town and, on the highest hill a white steepled church. Underneath is a kind of cave with a curtain. Myra parts the curtain and peers inside. 'In here will be the operating room.'

They all crawl into the space beneath the train set and Myra partly closes the curtain behind them. They are able to see each other but in a changed light. The atmosphere becomes more consequential inside the shadowed enclosed space. The air feels more alive, more unstable. Jamie thinks they might have entered what he has heard his father call fate – a power you connect with to make new things happen. He knows they have entered a forbidden realm that no adult must be allowed to see. He is both frightened and excited.

'Jamie, you lie down on the floor. Rose, you take off his clothes so I can do the operation. I'm going to scrub my hands.'

He helps Rose perform the act of lifting his t-shirt over his head. There is a new hot sticky tingling throughout his body when she undoes the button of his shorts and pulls down the zip. Rose often takes him to secret places in his mind; now she has taken him to a secret place inside his body. He lifts his hips so she can pull his shorts off. The cold floor against his burning skin is another nice sensation. Fire and ice. He is aware of a tension. They are all listening for any sign of his mother.

'And his pants,' says Myra.

The two girls are kneeling on either side of him. He is not sure he should allow the next thing to happen. They all know it is wrong. Rose hesitates.

'Come on, Nurse. Get a move on. He could die any moment.'

Jamie knows girls have different body parts, but he has never given any thought to it until now. The thing between his legs is a magnetising unsettling presence for the girls. It brings a strange sheen up onto their faces. Jamie is caught somewhere between embarrassment and excitement.

'This looks like a serious injury,' says Myra. She prods his stomach. She has rough reddened hands. 'We will have to operate immediately. Nurse, I need you to hold his thingy while I make the cut.'

Rose frowns at her sister.

'You're such a coward, Rose.'

The moment Rose's fingers close around his private part his entire body is aglow, a network of filaments along which hot light travels back and forth. He becomes the heat of his blood, the urgent throb of his heart. Myra makes a cutting motion across his stomach with her nails. Jamie is staring into deep space with what feels like a look of astonishment on his face. A bigger world of heaving oceans and shooting stars has entered him. A tingling pressure in his groin builds and then bursts and something hot and slimy dribbles out of him. It's the most bewildering and quickening thing. He dares a glance at Rose. She is frowning at her fingers which she then wipes on his discarded shirt.

'That's where babies come from,' says Myra, with authority. Jamie doesn't know what she's talking about, but he feels suddenly ashamed and wants to hide from Rose.

He knows why Myra and Rose don't come to play the next day. He wants to plead his innocence to Rose. It was Myra's fault. Only she knew what would happen. He is ashamed of what happened, but he wants it to happen again.

The next day his mother comes into his room. She makes him sit by her side on his bed. He feels sure she knows about the crime he has committed. He has never known his mother show such concern and discomfort. Usually she seems lost in a world of her own. He expects her to disown him. His first reaction when she tells him Myra has died is relief. He has been given a lifeline. He can return to his old world, all the solitary games he loves so much.

'She was hit by a lorry. It's a terrible thing. Is there anything you want to say?'

He shakes his head.

'How about we go to the sweet shop and get you a treat?'

It's at dinner that evening that he finds out more about how Myra died. His father asks the question. His tone is verging on aggressive, as if his mood has been ruined and he wants to find out who is to blame.

'She was with her mother and Rose. They were waiting to cross Croydon Road. Myra was balancing on the edge of the kerb. She toppled forward just as a lorry was approaching.'

'Going too fast, no doubt,' says his father angrily.

He has to wash his hair and wear his smartest clothes. His mother has even shined his shoes. She rests the palm of her hand on his head as they enter the house next door. They have to squeeze through all the people crowded in the hallway. There are flowers everywhere. An enveloping scent of pollen and sometimes of burning wax. In the living room Myra and Rose's father is standing by the raised coffin. He is howling like an animal. Jamie has never seen a man not in control of himself before. It frightens him that men have this wild beast inside them. He still hasn't caught sight of Rose anywhere. But his heart is beating faster. His mother still has the palm of her hand rested on the top of his head. When she removes it to talk to someone he edges closer to the coffin. He has to stand on tiptoes to see inside. Myra looks like she is asleep but also like she will never wake up. She has an aura of history, an importance that would never now be changed. It's the first time he has ever seen death on anyone's face. He can't stop staring. He is frightened of her face. Frightened it might suddenly twitch into movement. Then he senses Rose's presence. He and Rose exchange glances across the coffin. They alone of all the people in the room know why Myra has been punished. Jamie has to hope he and Rose won't be punished as well.

Raoul

His nervous disposition, making him bounce on his heels, bringing his hands continually to his face, making him sweat under his clothes. This man of the many names. His dyed black hair greased back from his puckered forehead. For weeks he has been a stranger to every place he has found himself in. A man with no known history. A man who answers to no one. Now he has to pass through passport control, the security check, customs. Submit himself to the belittling ordeal of official procedure. Men and women in uniforms demanding to know who he is, where he comes from, where he is going, what he carries with him. It is another indignity, another outrage he has to suffer. If nothing else a man ought to be entitled to keep his secrets. The name on his passport is not the same as the name on his birth certificate. There is a challenging power in the acquisition of a new name. Like walking out into a thunderstorm without a hat. Which is how he would describe his entire life. He has created so many fictions about himself that he gets confused about who he is supposed to be on any given day. He is composed almost entirely of secrets. They are perched in his mind like birds strung along a wire. It has become almost impossible for him to give an honest answer to the simplest questions. When someone asks him anything about his life, his history, his mouth becomes parched and his heartbeat goes up a notch, as if he is about to go out on a spotlit stage, as if he has to earn the trust of a sceptical audience.

He met Raoul in a tavern on the docks in Montreal. He was making a rum and coke last, slowly eking out its fortifying chemistry. He was wary of strangers. He believed they were out to get the better of him in some way. And everyone in the world was a stranger to him. It was at school he learned meanness comes quicker to humankind than kindness. And in prison this conviction was fortified. He met Raoul a few days after he had robbed a brothel at gunpoint. He aspired to be a better person. He believed he was a better person. Allowances had to be made in his favour. Poverty, a missing father, a sick mother. Allowances that weren't made, ever. The world loves some more than others. It's a fact you have to accept. The world has never showed any sign of loving him. It treats him as if he is surplus to requirements. He cannot erase from his mind the expression of hatred on the madam's wet raspberry red lips as she reluctantly passed him the wad of grubby banknotes. It has always pained him to feel he is disliked. It is his weakness. But he needs to buy himself a Canadian passport. He needs to procure a merchant seaman's papers. His plan is to flee to a country where he cannot be extradited. He has been loitering about the docks in the hope of hearing about a passage on a freighter, of coming across a drunken sailor whose papers he might steal. He cannot face the prospect of returning to prison and its prevailing commandment that manhood should be aggressive, that manhood should show no sympathy. He is too sensitive to survive the brutalising roleplaying of bored hardened men. Raoul was wearing oversized black sunglasses. He never removes them, not even in the darkest corners of smoke-filled underground rooms. They make him look like an insect under a microscope.

'You tell me you were in the armed forces. Posted in Germany. But that has nothing to do with who you are. That's just a piece of your litter. Your name isn't Eric. A secret name is how we try to escape the world of bald facts. You like to keep people in the dark. There is power in keeping people in the dark. And it's where you yourself have always been forced to live. But are you even sure the thoughts you think are who you are? Has it never occurred to you that you might be someone else?'

He liked the things Raoul said, he liked the interest Raoul took in him. It came as a relief to find someone to whom he could tell truths about himself. He told Raoul about the grocery store in St Louis he had robbed at gunpoint. He didn't tell him he wouldn't have shot the guy had he refused to give him the money. That he didn't have it in him to physically harm anyone without provocation. The man behind the counter in the grocery store didn't know his life wasn't in danger. The man was frightened. He wondered afterwards if there was something unbalanced about the look of his face that inspired fear. It bothered him. He has no desire he knows of to inspire fear. He told Raoul about his arrest and the twenty-year jail sentence he had received. The excessive injustice of it. Raoul asked how much he had made from the robbery and laughed when he told him about one hundred and twenty bucks. He told Raoul about his escape from Missouri State Penitentiary. But not about the details of his escape. It troubled him that at a subsequent encounter Raoul asked him what he had felt while hiding inside the empty bread basket in the delivery van.

'I didn't tell you about the bread basket,' he said and then licked his dry lips.

'You mumble. And you have a private grin. It's a cross between a smirk and a sneer. Private grins hint at personality disorders. You ought to put away that private grin or smirk or sneer, whatever it is.'

He had the feeling Raoul was winking at him behind his shades. Even at the time he thought the escape was too easy, as if it had been facilitated by unseen powers. He had tried to believe these unseen powers were just good fortune finally paying him a visit.

'I want to know how you know about the bread basket.'

'You allow yourself to get bogged down in details that don't matter. The important thing here is, I think you're a man I can work with. You need to make your activity productive. I can help you with that. What I do is covert. You'll have to trust me. I think you're a man capable of rising above his allotted station in life. Nothing in a man's life should be allotted. My hunch is, you're made for a bigger destiny. A noteworthy life is all about identifying a new connection and acting on it. Think of me as a new connection.'

There was no denying Raoul possessed an air of entitlement, of being a custodian and trader of classified information. It spooked him how much Raoul seemed to know about his history. There were times when he was close to believing Raoul was a figment of his imagination. In a time of crisis even age-old certainties crumble. There was no such thing as ordinary in his life anymore. His mind was a maze of obfuscations, ellipses, shadows and dizzying lusts. He was so confused at times he thought his head might explode. In bed at night he felt as weightless as a snowflake and he was falling and falling.

The first assignment he carried out for Raoul almost ended badly. He was stopped at US customs. He didn't know what it was he was smuggling over the border. When the border guard began searching his car he gave some thought to making a run for it. It was what his body wanted to do. But a senior official walked over and put an end to the search before anything was found. It was the first proof that Raoul wasn't all bluff and posturing. That he had friends in high places.

Raoul continued to give him money. Just enough to tide

him over. Never enough for him to break out on his own. He signed up for dancing lessons. He tried to learn the rhumba and the cha-cha. He had to fight through outer layers of embarrassment, shyness, uncertainty. Words had always failed him. Maybe he could get his truth across better through dance and its magical powers of suggestion. Maybe he could dance himself into a better world. He was tormented by the luxury and elegance depicted in advertisements. This was the world he wanted to live in. His desire to improve himself, make himself more attractive always though lacked some concluding thrust. He took his dirty clothes to the same dry cleaner every Thursday. He counted the number of women with blonde hair he encountered on the street. The number of passing white cars. It gave him a tighter grip on the functioning of his mind to interpret the world through numbers. He often found himself counting down time. He liked to make calculations of how many minutes remained before he could move on to the next thing in his day. He prepared his rudimentary meals at the exact same time every day. Heating up gruel from tin cans. He permitted himself two chocolate bars every day, one at four in the afternoon, the other at nine in the evening. He didn't allow himself alcohol before six in the evening. He read self-help books. He made resolutions. He made promises to himself he never kept. He made no friends. Now and again he treated himself to a prostitute. He had little desire for their bodies which he imagined were diseased. Only the moment of release the rote ministration of a woman's hand provided.

Raoul became his puppet master. He had to follow instructions which often baffled him in their senselessness. Raoul withheld information, as if it was capital. Raoul gave him money to buy a new car. He bought a used white Mustang which Raoul occasionally borrowed. In October he met Raoul in Mexico. Together they crossed the border back into the US with something contraband smuggled inside the spare tyre. Raoul gave him $2,000 and promised he would provide him with travel documents and enough money to set himself up in a new country. Raoul told him the endgame was in sight. Raoul remained a puzzling contradiction to him. He was like a small time criminal with high level security clearance.

He has slept through another empty afternoon. He sits on the bed of his motel room with the feeling this anonymous room is making a statement about the emptiness inside him, about the way he squanders his life one day at a time, his only company the small squalors of the human body. There's an unfolded map on the coverlet by his side. He likes to study maps. As if among all the grids and coordinates, the creases and stains is a still unknown place that is his home. He sits on the bed of his motel room caressing the bristles on his chin. Another empty vodka bottle by his feet. Sometimes when he has a mind to establish where it all went wrong he returns to the fairground when he was sixteen. The air sultry and sticky as if impregnated by the pink candyfloss evident everywhere. Balloons of otherworldly colours hovering over people's heads. Clear metallic sounds ringing in the air. Coloured lights made broken rainbows between him and the girl. She was sitting on a crate. She caught his eye and lifted her dress and began using it as a fan. She was like a world apart. In his limited experience girls had little inkling of how beautiful they could make the world. This girl though knew. She had an air of difference from all the other people around her. She allowed him to see her naked thighs and white panties for a few racing heartbeats. He didn't know what to do. He waited for some wiser voice to give him instructions. It occurred to him she might be making fun of him and his grubby adolescent yearnings. But the moment she stood up and walked off he decided she had given him the gesture as a gift. It's the moment of his life he would most like to replay and revise.

Except he still doesn't know what he might have done differently. Only that he has been searching for the feeling she gave him ever since. One night he dreamed he was following her footprints and they ended at the sea.

He can't sleep. He can't stop thinking about the things that might go wrong in his body. His skin as sensitive as the antennae of an insect. Every day his body produces some ailment for him to study and fret about. A new whispered warning of malfunction, of deterioration. He puts on his scuffed cowboy boots. The act of working them onto one raised foot after another as familiar to him as the touch of his tongue on his teeth. He goes outside. The sharp cleanliness and clarity of the air is like a childhood adventure. He is possessed by a ghost of himself climbing a tree, diving into the river, lighting a Christmas firework. He walks past his white Mustang in the parking lot. The only thing he owns in life that has any market value. He walks over to the wide empty street with its chalk white markings. Traffic lights on green. The blue grey light. The sense of the surrounding vastness tickles his armpits as if he is about to grow wings. He might be the last man on earth. It is a fallen world he sees. A world that understands him. He looks up at a trail of clouds like bubbles blown out of the mouth of a giant. They are so sharply defined he feels he can run fingers over their edges. He hears a train rumbling past nearby. For a moment he imagines himself on board. Travelling with its lights through the night. Towards a new life. The stars in the big sky are paling. The stars often make him think of his mother. The frame house with its porch where they lived. He can recall the knots in the wooden bannisters, the shadow pattern on his wall at night, the kitchen chair with the shorter leg, the view granted by each and every window, the smell of his mother's shampoo when she soothed him every time he woke up from the dream about the pursuing black beast. The last time he saw his mother was when he escorted her on the bus to the hospital. After the doctor gave her details about the operation he was soon to perform on her she took his hand. He could feel how frightened she was. But she so rarely touched him that he was uncomfortable with the warm press of her fingers and quickly extricated his hand. This is another moment he wishes he could relive and revise. He should have made more effort to give his mother some comfort instead of thinking only of himself and his embarrassment. He left her there alone. He returned from the hospital alone on the bus. He still feels he is on that bus, that he can't get off it.

He meets Raoul in Atlanta. Raoul wants him to buy a rifle. 'I need an example to show our client.' In the shop he forgets the make of the gun Raoul named. He knows next to nothing about rifles. He buys the wrong rifle and annoys Raoul with his incompetence. Raoul isn't his friend. He suspects Raoul doesn't even like him much. He has to return to the shop the next day to change the rifle. When he drives back to the motel there's another white Mustang parked outside.

'There's a guy outside who looks like me. And he's sitting in a white Mustang like mine. Except it had Arkansas plates.'

'I'm impressed you know what you look like. To my mind that's the hardest thing of all to work out. What we look like. One of the life's most puzzling mysteries I'd say.'

'Same build. Same haircut. Same hair colour. Similar clothes.'

Raoul adjusts his sunglasses in the motel mirror. 'I'm trying to imagine you buying clothes. But all I'm getting is a black hole. I can see you walking up and down aisles. I can see your eyebrows meet in an effort of concentration. But your criteria. That's a mystery to me. The moment of decision. The instant you single out one article from the hundreds on offer and carry it to the cashier. There is the mystery for me. You like check shirts. You seem to believe a check shirt reveals some secret truth about you. What is it you think check shirts say about you?'

'It's not something I give much thought to.'

'To a casual observer it might seem you dress like you don't want to be remembered. But isn't that what we all want, to be remembered? Sometimes when I look at you I can't help wondering how many lies you tell in an average day. I don't mean the lies you tell other people. I'm talking about the lies you tell yourself.'

He watches Raoul open and close his fists. His powerful forearms straining at the material of his jacket.

'Anyway, we're nearly there. Next port of call is Memphis, Tennessee. This is where I'm meeting the international gun-runners. And this is where you and I will part company. I'll give you all the documents you need for your new life. You need to bring the rifle with you.'

He spends consecutive nights in motels in different locations. His habit of pacing his rooms as if they are cells. Every new mirror alters with sly mockery the way he looks to himself. In the glass he might look like a stranger but within himself the boredom, the frustration he experiences with himself undergoes no alteration. He lets his face go out of focus in the glass, the pouting bottom lip, the anxiously drawn eyebrows. As he paces back and forth, around and around, moments appear again out of the past. The moments he will carry with him into the future. The stained coverlet, the bare light bulb, the threadbare carpet, the dripping tap all want him to admit defeat. He is wide awake when he should be asleep; asleep when he should be wide awake. Sometimes he wants nothing more than to be able to say sorry to his mother.

He turns the radio up loud in the car. So he doesn't have to think. He sings along to country songs, out of tune, so horribly out of tune it occasionally brings a smile to his face which he looks up at in the rear-view mirror. And whenever he finds himself amusing he thinks about the woman somewhere out there in the world he can't find. The woman he might make laugh and lift up in his arms and carry over the threshold into a new life.

The rooming house in Memphis is in a poor rundown part of town. Its scarcity of privilege like something that intimately belongs to him, like his fingerprints. He would like to share with someone his idea that the world seen at close quarters is invariably ugly. Only distance redeems it. Distance in time, distance in space. He turns into the kind of street where the same people do the same thing at the same time every day. A kind of insurance policy against accidents. He leaves the car in a parking lot. Before getting out he rolls up the sleeves of his shirt, an act he feels compelled to perform at least once a day, as if there are moments which demand a further degree of nakedness. He walks into a bar for a beer. Here a man gives him a look he doesn't like. A kind of sticky look. It's like the man is shining a light into his eyes.

Then he returns to his car and drives to the rooming house. He rents a room for a week. Room 5B. The room is like the culmination of every disappointment he has faced in his life. It makes him think of thwarted intimacy, misplaced anger. The cracked linoleum floor, the bare bulb with a dangling length of string, the small disused fireplace, the lumpy mattress with sagging springs. The greasy window looks out over a lot overgrown with bushes and, beyond, a mustard-yellow motel with turquoise doors. When Raoul arrives, he seems more agitated than usual. There is a glaze over his face as if he has been hypnotised. His underarms give off a pungent cut onion smell. He throws the rifle down on the bed. He says he is about to execute the first stage of the gunrunning deal. He has what looks like a walkie-talkie sticking out of his jacket pocket.

'What name have you used for the register?'

'John,' he says sheepishly. His disobedience always has a churlish note. He is holding the blue plastic zippered bag for his toiletries he has owned for two years now.

'That's not what I told you. You're supposed to be Eric. I thought I made that clear. You don't listen.'

He takes to heart Raoul's insult. He takes to heart all insults, sometimes when no insult is meant.

'I'm not comfortable being Eric here.'

'Okay, I need you to buy a pair of infrared binoculars. The client has expressed an interest. I'll probably take him somewhere out of town to try out the rifle. Here's two hundred bucks.'

Outside he buys himself an ice cream. It will be the last time for weeks he experiences life as leisurely. He watches a man fix the tyre of a bike outside a repair shop. He admires anyone who can put things back together. It seems to him the supreme talent. He can't put anything back together. The shop he tries doesn't sell infrared binoculars, so he buys a regular pair. When he returns to the bar beneath the rooming house to buy himself a six-pack of beer the man who gave him the funny stare is there except this time he doesn't look at him. He mentions him to Raoul. Raoul shows impatience. Raoul looks at his watch for a second time.

'Okay, you need to make yourself scarce for a while. Leave the car. I need it. Why not go see a movie?' There's a wobble of anxiety or excitement in Raoul's voice.

Outside, he thinks he ought to get the spare tyre of the car fixed before Raoul uses it. He catches a glimpse of his ghost in the showroom window of a paint and wallpaper firm. He drives a few blocks to a gas station, but the attendant tells him he's too busy to fix his tyre. An ambulance races by, its lights flashing. He drives back towards the rooming house. A highway patrol car is blocking the street. Reminding him as he is reminded every day that he is a fugitive from the law. His instinct now is to flee. He takes a series of turnings in the direction of the Mississippi river and is lost for a while. He is careful to keep within every speeding limit. He turns the volume of the radio down. People who listen to loud music, the social commentator in his head says, are more likely to break the law. His body absorbs the rhythm of every song on the radio without him being aware of it.

He has crossed over the state line into Mississippi when news comes on the radio that the black minister has been killed in Memphis. In an interview after his arrest he will claim he didn't give much thought to the news that Dr Martin Luther King had been shot. A later news update announces the police are looking for a man driving a white Mustang. It takes a moment before he realises they are talking about him. There is a rocket thrust in his chest. The world suddenly goes quiet. He finds it difficult to keep his hands still. He leaves the interstate highway and heads towards Atlanta on back roads. He talks to himself constantly as he drives. He appeals to his wiser self for explanations, for solutions. He abandons the car in a parking lot. The wind blows dust and scraps of paper about. He is wearing a dark suit and a crookedly knotted tie. He is wearing his fake alligator loafers. He boards a bus for Canada. He sinks low into the greasy seat. He is fifteen again, returning from the hospital after failing to give his dying mother any comfort.

'It doesn't quite add up, does it? The evidence points to a conspiracy but it's hard to believe James Earl Ray wasn't involved in Dr King's assassination, at least in some way. How could he have no inkling of what was going on? Wilful ignorance only takes you so far in life.'

'What else do you think?'

'I think you're overly inclined to see a government conspiracy because you're irritated by the idea that an irrelevant individual, a nonentity could bring to an end the noble endeavours of a good man. You need to believe only large complex forces could bring the dream to an end.'

'Maybe he knew all along he was involved in a plot to kill Dr King? Given his background and demographic he was probably a racist. But it had probably never occurred to him they were going to frame him as the assassin. And once he was arrested he couldn't tell the truth because the truth was he wasn't entirely innocent. So he made up this Raoul character who was probably a composite of several individuals he had dealings with. And no doubt he was thinking of what happened to Oswald a few years earlier. To stay alive, he pleads guilty. Otherwise he's a dead man walking.'

'Why have you added fictional details? The images of the girl at the fair and his mother at the hospital create some sympathy for him but they aren't true.'

'You know how I can't help letting my imagination run away with me. It's not that I feel much sympathy for him. He almost certainly would have ended up spending his life in jail anyway.'

'Maybe you're burrowing yourself in this story because you miss me?'

'I do miss you. Why did you have to die?'

'It's death itself you're angry with, isn't it? You think we all have a Raoul in our lives. A covert force ushering us step by step towards our fall. Perhaps you even think you were Raoul in my life. Or I was Raoul in your life? There's always a bigger picture. And we all perform a purpose in this bigger picture that is unknown to us. I was brooding about the argument we had at the breakfast table when I stepped out into the road without looking.'

'I knew that. I've always known that.'

The Girls of his Youth

The alarm hauls him out of his dream. The ice glare of his dream. The alarm moans out its one repeated note. The alarm hauls him back into his body. His body with all its missing weight. His body with all its missing time. The alarm hauls him back into his mind. Back into the snowstorms of his mind. The sandstorms of his memory. He lifts his head. In the armchair. The unfamiliar armchair. The walls close in around him. He looks up at the television. The television on its bracket high on the wall. He looks up at footage of a forest fire. A fire in a forest. Another fire in another forest. The air is not fit for breathing. The television is always there. The television pretends to bring the world closer. But the television moves the world further away. The television is never not demanding attention. But the sound is always turned off. There is no volume. The news of the world is silenced. The news of the world goes unheard. Earthquakes, explosions, wars, famines. Floods, hurricanes, draughts, fires. The news of the world. Unheard.

The woman in the armchair opposite has drool on her chin. The woman in the armchair opposite stares into a void. *I know your heart is broken too.* There are other women seated in armchairs. Slumped in armchairs. They too live with the emptiness. They too live with the horror. Blank-faced women inside limp and brittle sickening bodies. The air is not fit for breathing. He changes position in his chair. The stiffness in his joints. The wear and tear of his organs. The struggles of his respiratory system. There is nothing to look at but emptiness and horror. The monotony of emptiness. The monotony of horror. *Where are my songs? Where is my music?*

He looks back up at the television screen. The television on its bracket high on the wall. There is footage of an ocean on the television screen. A storm-tossed ocean. A heaving ocean. An ocean rising and falling inside a shroud of mist. The sea keeps rising. All the seas keep rising.

Abandon ship! Abandon ship!

The sound of his voice shocks him. The sound of his voice shames him. He has broken protocol. He has stepped out of line. He can sense in the alerted air he has broken protocol, he has stepped out of line. There are eyes studying him. The bleary eyes of ailing women. The bloodshot eyes of sickening women. There is both disapproval and amusement in the eyes studying him. He cannot say the things he thinks. The words disappear before they reach his mouth. But sometimes he says aloud things he has not thought. Things he has not given himself permission to say. Like *Abandon ship!* And then he is made to feel he has broken protocol, he has stepped out of line. And he wants to hide. Hide his face. His bewildering old man face. Hide his body. His bewildering old man body. His body with all its missing weight. His body with all its missing time. He looks up at the television. The television on its bracket high on the wall. He looks up at footage of heaps of coloured plastic garbage on the shore of the ocean. The waste of the world. In his mind all is laid to waste. In his mind the sea keeps rising. In his mind the fires keep burning. In his mind the air is not fit for breathing. His mind like a radio moving from station to station with frequent bursts of static.

Then there they are again. In the midst of all the emptiness. In the midst of all the horror. The girls of his youth. *We will never meet again.* Where are they now? The girls of his youth. *I know your heart is broken too.* The girls of his youth all have something urgent they want to give to him. *The tide is pulling me back to you.* Nothing else is of importance. Only the girls and what they want to give to him. Only the girls and where they want to lead him. The girls of his youth. The girls of his youth break his heart. The girls of his youth make his heart whole again. He catches glimpses of them. They are laughing. They are frowning. They are laughing in their underwear. They are frowning in their winter coats. The girls who played hide and seek with him. The girls who played the adult game with him. The girls of his youth want to give him back his story. The story of his life. But he can't reach them. He can't give them back their names. If he can reach back to the girls of his youth, if he can bring into focus the girls of his youth his story will be returned to him. The story of his life.

The alarm hauls him out of a dream. The ice glare of his dream. The alarm moans out its one repeated note. The alarm hauls him back into his body. His body with all its missing weight. His body with all its missing time. The alarm hauls him back into his mind. The snowstorms of his mind. The sandstorms of his memory. He lifts his head. He is laying in a bed. An unfamiliar bed in an unfamiliar room. The walls close in around him. He is wide awake. He has been time travelling by night. He has been crossing borders. He has been crossing continents. His eyes widen at the fading memory. He is laying in a bed. An unfamiliar bed in an unfamiliar room. He is wide awake. He has been time travelling by night. He has been holding hands with the girls of his youth. The girls of his youth have been singing for him. The girls of his youth have been dancing for him. *We will never meet again.* There are things he wants to say to the girls of his youth. He wants to thank them for their beauty. He wants to thank them for their generosity and for their truth. He wants to tell them there is no beginning and no end.

He swings his legs out of the bed. He is light on his feet

with all the missing time. With all the collapsed time. He touches the wall. He leans on the wall for a moment. He walks over to the window. The unfamiliar window with the unfamiliar view. *This is not my home. This is not where I want to be.* There is a pair of slippers on the floor by the bed. He puts on the slippers. They fit his feet to perfection. He walks over to the door. He is a little dizzy as if the floor is tilted. He does not know what world lies beyond the door. He cannot remember what world lies beyond the door. In his mind he sees a bridge over water at sunrise. In his mind he sees an outgoing tide on a beach at sunset. He opens the door. He opens the door and walks out into a corridor. There are dim lights at regular intervals. There is a faint buzzing noise. Otherwise all is quiet. Otherwise all is still. There is no one to remember him. Only the girls of his youth. The girls he kissed and the girls he didn't kiss. The girls who gave him songs to sing. The girls who said yes and the girls who said no. The girls who granted him a wish. The girls who refused him a wish. *We will never meet again.* He walks along the corridor. The carpet springy beneath his feet. *The tide is pulling me back to you.* He walks down stairs. In this house of sleepwalkers. In this house of deception and lies. He touches the walls. The walls close in around him. He can't remember where these stairs lead. He can't remember what world waits at the bottom of these stairs. But he has the feeling all stairs lead to the girls of his youth.

He walks into a reception area. He walks into a wash of brighter light. He walks towards a clock ticking on the wall.

Abandon ship! Abandon ship!

The woman behind the desk wears a surgical mask. There is disapproval in her eyes, in the line of her eyebrows. She is speaking to him.

Now then, what are you doing up and wandering about at three in the morning, Mr St. Aubyn?

Mr St. Aubyn, he says. The name takes him by surprise. His name. The name by which he is known. He remembers that sometimes he cannot remember his name. The facts of his life elude him. The facts of his life play games with him. He remembers what he has forgotten and forgets what he has remembered. He is constantly remembering and forgetting. Life is consumed with remembering and forgetting. One thing he never forgets is his written signature. This he remembers. The memory is in his fingers. When he wants to remember his name, he picks up a pen and watches his hand inscribe his name. Michael St. Aubyn. The memory of the girls of his youth must be in his fingers too. The texture of the fabric of their clothes. The pulse and warmth of their skin. But his fingers have lost this memory.

The woman behind the desk stands up. The woman in the mask. The woman behind the desk is speaking to him.

Shall we get you back to bed?

I'm medicated. Cloud nine. How are you?

Are we enjoying a moment of lucidity, Mr St. Aubyn? Good for you. But we still need to get you back to bed.

The woman in the mask takes his arm and escorts him up the stairs. The walls close in around him. He says something which makes her impatient with him. What was it he said to make her impatient with him? It troubles him to inspire dislike. It leaves him lost in the snowstorms of his mind. Lost in the sandstorms of his memory. The carpet is spongy underfoot. The woman escorts him back to the room that is not his room. *Where are my songs? Where is my music?*

The alarm hauls him out of a dream. The ice glare of his dream. The alarm moans out its one repeated note. The alarm hauls him back into his body. His body with all its missing weight. His body with all its missing time. The alarm hauls him back into his mind. His mind like a radio moving from station to station with frequent bursts of static. He is laying in a bed. An unfamiliar bed in an unfamiliar room. He is wide awake. He swings his legs out of the bed. He is light on his feet with all the missing time. With all the collapsed time. He touches the wall. He leans on the wall for a moment. He is a little dizzy as if the floor is tilted. He walks over to the window. The unfamiliar window with the unfamiliar view. *This is not my home. This is not where I want to be. Where are my songs? Where is my music?* There is a pair of slippers on the floor by the bed. The stiffness in his joints. The wear and tear of his organs. The struggles of his respiratory system. He puts on the slippers. They fit his feet to perfection. He walks over to the door. He does not know what world lies beyond the door. He cannot remember what world lies beyond the door.

He opens the door and walks out into a corridor. The carpet is spongy underfoot. There are dim lights at regular intervals. There is a faint buzzing noise. From behind the walls. The walls that close in around him. Otherwise all is quiet. Otherwise all is still. There is no one to remember him. Only the girls of his youth. The girls he kissed and the girls he didn't kiss. The girls who gave him songs to sing. The girls who said yes and the girls who said no. The girls who granted him a wish and the girls who refused him a wish. *The tide is pulling me back to you.* He walks along the corridor. The carpet is spongy beneath his slippered feet. He walks down the stairs. In this house of sleepwalkers. In this house of lies and deception. In this house of exile. In this house cleansed of memory. In this house disinfected of dreams. He touches the walls. He can remember now where these stairs lead. All stairs lead to the girls of his youth. The girls of his youth want to give him back his story. The story of his life.

At the foot of the stairs he looks to his right and he looks to his left. He hears the ticking of a clock on the wall. He walks away from the ticking of the clock. The ticking of the clock is the enemy. Time does not restore what we have lost. He walks down a corridor. The carpet is spongy beneath his slippered feet. He grasps the handle of the first door he comes to. The metal is cold on his fingers. He pushes down on the handle. The door opens with barely a sound. He steps into a room. The carpet is spongy beneath his slippered feet. He can make out the outline of a bed by the window. The moon is a sheen of brightness on the window. He can make out the outline of a woman in the bed by the window. He can tell she is looking at him. She is looking at him and she is smiling. *You are the dreamer and I am the dream.* He asks himself if he has ever entered a girl's bedroom uninvited before. A girl of his youth. Their kisses tasted so sweet. The girls of his youth. Their hands carried so much excitement. The girls of his youth. They had so much to give. And so much to take away. The girls of his youth. He walks over to the window. He picks up a vase of flowers on the sill. He puts the vase of flowers down on the floor. He opens the window. The window opens outward on a hinge, but only so far.

Abandon ship, he says. He picks up a chair and moves it to the window. He climbs up onto the chair. He clambers from the chair to the window sill. The stiffness in his joints. The wear and tear of his organs. The struggles of his respiratory system. He squeezes his body through the narrow space between the window and its frame. It is a difficult manoeuvre and demands all his concentration. He can sense the woman in the bed is smiling again.

I'm on medication. Cloud nine. How are you? he says. To the woman in the bed who is smiling in the darkness. He jumps down from the window. He jars his ankle. A pain shoots up his leg and lodges in his lower back. He has to catch his breath. He breathes in the scent of blossoms. He tries to remember the name of this blossom from its scent. The name seems important. Another piece of the map. The treasure map. The map he has lost.

He walks across a silvered lawn. Breathing in the scent of the blossom. Trying to remember the name of the blossom from its scent. He can smell rain too. Recent summer rain. He looks up at the summer stars. All is radiance, all is wonder. By a hedge of leaves shined by rainfall he sees an animal. He tries to give a name to the animal. The animal looks hard at him. The piercing eyes of the animal, the way the animal fixes him with her eyes, confuses the way he sees himself. Then he remembers. You're a fox, he says. His body performs a pleased jig. The fox scurries away. Leaving him as a strange being to himself. A strange being beneath the summer moon and the big night sky. Breathing in the scent of the blossom. Breathing in the scent of the earth softened by rain.

He walks into a bed of flowers. He paces back and forth in the midst of the flowers. Their stalks and stems brushing his legs. Droplets of collected rain dampening his pyjamas. He breathes in the scent of the flowers he crushes underfoot. He looks up at the summer stars. They make him feel closer to the girls of his youth. He wipes his eyes on the sleeve of his pyjama shirt. He walks out onto a road. His legs move with a purpose he doesn't fully understand. He takes note of the muscles in his legs, his unsteady legs. He is aware of his vertebrae and his gravitational force. The activity of his body stimulates activity in his mind. He is grateful for the open air and silence. Grateful that walls no longer close in around him. The pavement is hard beneath his slippered feet. The road has no name for him. The road is strung with pale yellow lights. He tells himself he is vanishing into the night. The night is black and silver. The night is yellow and many shades of grey. He is a shadow in a world of shadows. All the birds are asleep in their nests. All the people are asleep in their beds. The world is strange and quiet. There is no one to remember him. Only the girls of his youth. The girls he kissed and the girls he didn't kiss. The girls who gave him songs to sing. The girls who said yes and the girls who said no. *We will never meet again.* The girls of his youth want to give him back his story. The story of his life. If he can reach back to the girls of his youth, if he can bring into focus the girls of his youth his story will be returned to him. The story of his life.

He turns into another road. The road is empty. All the roads are empty. He looks up at the summer stars. They bring the girls of his youth closer. There is no greater incentive than catching a glimpse of the girls of his youth. Of returning for a moment to a scene in the stories they made together. He and the girls of his youth. The stories that remained unfinished. The stories that had no beginning and no end. He wishes he could give them back their names. He wishes he could give them back their stories. *I know your heart is broken too.* The girls of his youth. But the line goes dead. The connection is broken.

He walks down the middle of the road. He walks in the moonlight. He is grateful for the open air and silence. Grateful that walls no longer close in around him. *Love is at the heart of everything.* What is it that makes him think this? He catches the wisp of a familiar smell. He follows the familiar smell down an alley. The darkness thickens. The darkness consumes him. But there is a light in his mind. A breaking light at the centre of his being. The familiar smell grows stronger. It is the smell that brings the light. He exits the alley. Darkness falls away. He stands at the edge of an immensity. He stands looking out at the wide sweep of sea. His eyes widen at the discovery. He blinks his eyes. He wipes his eyes. The world is vast and alive again. *Love is at the heart of everything.* He stands to attention. He lets the noises of the world come to him. The whoosh and slop of the waves. The sigh of the waves withdrawing over shingle. The waves carry flecks of light. The waves carry flecks of light into his mind. Scattered flecks of lights that appear and vanish. The lights bring in the faces of the girls of his youth. He blinks his eyes. He wipes his eyes. He slides down an incline of shingle. The noise the stones make is happening inside his body. Like the girls of his youth. They too are happening inside his body, inside his mind.

He takes off his slippers. Grains of sand lodge themselves between his toes. He picks up a pebble. He rolls the pebble in his hand. He caresses its universal form. The smooth unbroken fluidity of its shape under his fingers. He has hold of a piece of eternity. The beginning of time and the end of time. His feet sink into the wet sand. A pool of water gathers around every step he takes. The whoosh and slop of the waves gains in volume. The surf turns to smoke on the sand and on the shingle.

He walks into the sea. The girls of his youth lead him into the sea. The waves slop over his bare feet. The cold bolt of shock empties his mind. He rolls the pebble in his hand. He caresses its universal form. The smooth unbroken fluidity of its shape under his fingers. He has hold of a piece of eternity. The beginning of time and the end of time. The waves buffet his knees. The waves reach his waist. The buoyancy of the water, its rhythmic lifting and cradling of his body has returned him to memory of his mother. His mother is holding his hand and leading him into the sea. His mother is telling him not to be frightened. He is alone with his mother beneath the moon, at the edge of the world. He has returned to his mother. His mother is telling him not to be frightened. He is a child again, responding to a dare. He is all the wishes that came true. He is all the wishes that didn't come true. He is all he is. He is all he has ever been. Responding to a dare.

Restoration

'You'd be amazed at what can lurk beneath a painted surface. Of course, often it's just a sketched underpainting which undergoes changes of design as it's worked up, but sometimes we come across a completely different image hidden beneath the top layers of paint.'

Mrs Wells-Llewellyn's smile is indulgent as if he is a child telling her about a game he played earlier.

'Your English is very good,' she says.

'Thank you. I studied at the Courtauld Institute in London for three years.' His girlfriend, sitting opposite at the table on the terrace of this restaurant in campo Santa Margherita in Venice, looks across at him. He can read her eyes as if they send typescript in code. The look in her eyes makes him feel he and she are like secret agents engaged in outwitting an enemy.

'But you restore pictures rather than paint them? I would imagine that is rather finicky work.'

Phoebe's mother makes this seem a slight. Every other thing she says to him has a barb in it. Or perhaps he's being over-sensitive. He has failed to infect her with the love he feels for his work. It's like she is determined to remain unimpressed by anything he might reveal about himself. As if she possesses one piece of knowledge about him that overshadows everything else. And she clearly has no intention of revealing to him anything personal about herself. She has already made him dislike his German accent. And she has quizzed him about his family. Made his father's job as a foreman for a construction firm appear somehow shaming. Now he feels like she is drawing attention to the lack of manly qualities in him. He is also irritated by how little credit she is giving him for rejuvenating Phoebe's spirits. Before coming to Venice, Phoebe had tried to commit suicide. She had thrown herself in the Thames. She was rescued by a man in a passing boat. Though she is still on Prozac and sometimes suffers panic attacks it must be apparent to her mother that she is in a much better frame of mind. He likes to think this is largely down to his own influence.

Across the table Phoebe is laughing with her father. It is the first time he has met her parents. Phoebe warned him her mother might subject him to the equivalent of a job interview. She also told him a story about her father. One night when she and her father slept in the same bed he had taken her hand and placed it between his legs. She had been fourteen. Every time he speaks to her father he feels this knowledge he possesses gives him a moral advantage he is uncomfortable with. He is not someone who enjoys passing judgement. But it's like Phoebe's father is trying to sell him a painting he secretly knows is forged.

Later, when he and Phoebe are in bed, she tells him her father liked him.

'But not your mum. She doesn't think I'm good enough for you.'

'You're not.'

'I kept thinking about what you told me about your dad.'

'I shouldn't have told you that.'

'You don't think it's done you any damage? I mean, the conscious mind gives us only one version of events. Sometimes there's a deeper darker reality from which a poison seeps out without us being aware of it.'

'It was such a fleeting moment. He might even have been half asleep and thought I was my mother.'

'It doesn't appear to prey on his mind. It's obvious he adores you. He kind of flirts with you.'

'Both my sisters are jealous of our relationship. I've always been his favourite.'

For a moment he listens to the gentle slop of the tide of the canal which reaches him through the open window. It's like the sound of his gratitude for the beautiful world he has managed to create for himself. He kisses Phoebe on the mouth which tastes of *limoncello*.

Inexplicably and revealed by an infrared camera, someone has painted over parts of the picture he is working on. Every painting hides secrets. It's an aspect of his work he loves. The uncovering of hidden information, the piecing together of missing parts of a story. With a swab doused in a solvent gel he has taken off a layer of varnish and then, painstakingly, microscopic flakes of 18th century paint from the 17th century paint below. Slowly the subject of the painting is beginning to acquire more identity. He feels he can read deeper into the eyes of the bearded man in the portrait. He feels he and the mysterious man are having a deeper conversation. He has endowed the man with a deep baritone voice. Cleaned of the centuries of grease and engrained dirt layered on the painted surface and the puzzling reworked parts of the picture, the man looks more formidable, perhaps even a little unscrupulous. He is no longer working with solvents. Just a scalpel and water now. His work essentially involves training his eye to pay constant attention to detail. He has learned how much knowledge and vitality are generated by close observation. To pay attention is to remain in a state of eager suspension for the next moment. He is marvelling that while sitting for this portrait this 17th century Venetian nobleman had no inkling of what would happen to the painting, no way of foreseeing any detail of this moment three hundred and fifty years further down the line when his phone rings. It's his sister in Hamburg. He peels off his blue latex glove, takes off his magnifying headband and hangs it on the easel. Then he walks over to the open window where the pungent smell of the canal water is thick in his nostrils.

'Did you ever talk to Grandpa Muller about what he did during the war?' she asks him without any preamble.

'One time I asked him about it. He said there was no point in talking about it because it was a completely different reality back then and no one who hadn't been there could understand it. His mouth went small and tight when he said this. Why are you asking?'

'But we were told he was in the Wehrmacht. A regular soldier. That was the family story. He fought in Poland and Russia. Well, he wasn't a member of the regular German army. Someone has posted a photo of him on my Twitter page. It's definitely him. The lazy left eyelid gives him away. And he's wearing the uniform of the order police. He's standing in front of a huddle of terrified naked women and children. The only thing in his favour is he isn't smiling like the man next to him.'

'Hang on. Who posted this photo?'

'What does it matter? Someone called Fascist Hunter 007. I've done some research. I'm pretty sure Grandad was a member of Battalion 101 of the order police. They were based in Hamburg. The only true thing we've been told about him is that he wasn't a member of the Nazi party. But neither were over seventy per cent of the other men in his battalion. We have this idea that anyone not in the Nazi Party was less guilty, but these men, non-Party members, killed women and children. They were sent to Poland in 1942. Their first major assignment was to round up about 1,800 Jews in a place called Józefów. All the healthy men were sent to a work camp. The women, children and elderly were taken to a forest. As they got down from the truck each policeman was assigned a specific victim who he accompanied further into the forest. The Jews were made to lie on the ground and shot in the back of the head. The executions were carried out by Grandfather's company. It's almost certain he murdered women and children first hand. Actually fired the shot into the back of the heads of children. Mum would have been three years old then. He had his own daughter at the time. He knew what it felt like to be a parent. Yet he was able to shoot a child with his own hand. The hand that touched us. The hand that ruffled my hair. A few months later his company participated in another massacre. This time the Jewish women and children were made to undress and shot in a large pit. This is probably where the photo of him was taken. Basically, Grandfather never once faced the enemy in battle. All that is bullshit. After carrying out the large-scale massacres his job for two years was to hunt down and murder hiding Jews. One by one. And when he wasn't actually killing them he was loading them onto cattle trucks. The killing of Jews was his daily bread. This is why he never spoke about what he did in the war, Jurgen. I haven't told Mum any of this.'

'Thanks heavens for that.'

'Look, I'm sorry to burden you with this. I know how much you idolised him. But it's become too much for me to deal with alone. I was so disgusted and ashamed last night I wasn't sure I wanted to go on living. The loathing I feel for Grandfather has infected me. As if I share some of the blame.'

'You don't share any blame,' he says, but it is nothing but a nervous hollow reflex remark. Otherwise he is lost for words. His predominant emotion at the moment is irritation with his sister for bringing this unwanted information into his life.

He invents an excuse not to see Phoebe that night. The first time he has ever done this. There has been little he has felt any need to hide from her. But the voice in his head he generally obeys tells him not to tell her what he has learned, no matter how much it troubles him. For more than an hour he sits on a landing stage of the Grand Canal searching for peace among the lights on the dark water. He barely notices the wintry sting of the wind while he sits beside the line of creaking moored gondolas.

He cannot deny the information about his grandfather has darkened his understanding of himself. It is a habit of his to make lists when he is grappling with anxiety. He types them into his laptop and regularly updates them. He has a list of his favourite moments with Phoebe. His favourite works of art. His favourite films. His favourite songs. His favourite meals. But there is no list he can compile tonight which will ease his foreboding. He studies himself in the mirror, loathe to find any resemblance on his face to his grandfather's features. While convincing himself he could under no circumstances, in any hypothetical world, murder a child, he finds himself recalling an incident from his past, the one time perhaps he came loose from his moorings. It's the first time he has recalled the moment in years. He was about thirteen. A friend dared him to throw a stone at one of the lighted front room windows they were walking past. Without thinking, he hurled the stone at the rectangle of light across the dark lawn and was running when the sound of shattered glass reached him. He had stepped over a line in his head that evening. Had he been apprehended and charged with his crime his entire life might have been very different. He envisaged embittering years at a remand school, his formative years spent in the company of crude and rowdy juveniles who found coherence in criminal acts. He still struggles to recognise himself in the anarchy of this submissive response to a dare. It's like he had turned himself off for a moment and performed an act which had nothing to do with who he was.

His grandfather has been dead for three years. He had given

little thought to him of late. Now, of a sudden, he has become like one of those words you frequently come across but never quite learn the meaning of. It's true what his sister said. He *had* idolised him. It was his grandfather, not his father, who took him to his first football match. It was an evening kick off. The heart of winter. The closer he and his grandfather got to the ground the more contagious became the air of expectation. He had never been so excited. They walked through the heat and stink of the hot dog stalls outside the ground. Everyone was wearing red and white scarves, even the old men. Age mattered less here. It was probably the first time he had felt part of a community. Not spinning around in an orbit of his own. The moment he first caught sight of the pitch washed in floodlights was like standing on tiptoes and peeping at a world you were forbidden to enter. Never had he seen colours ache with such pristine beauty - the tiny players in their red kits, the green grass and its chalked white lines had looked like some magical kingdom beneath the liquid snow of the floodlights. And it was his grandfather who had escorted him into this magical kingdom where you were allowed to publicly shout and curse and give bodily expression to joy.

Nevertheless, he believes now he always sensed there was something in his grandfather he didn't want to know about. When he pictures him now he sees a grim-faced, constipated-looking man who avoids eye contact. He recalls the things he made him do he didn't want to do. The boxing lessons. The press-ups and sit-ups. He wanted him to build up his muscle. Like the Nazis, he was preoccupied with an ideal of physical fitness. As he himself got older and began to think for himself, a distance intervened between them, like stretches of frozen snow. His grandfather didn't like his long hair. He didn't like the music he played in his room. He didn't like his left-wing politics.

He keeps telling himself that whatever his grandfather did

has no bearing on his own identity. But, two weeks later, he is still reluctant to tell Phoebe about what he has learned, what is troubling him. She begins to notice he is not himself. He blames it on a particularly difficult piece of restoration work. He smiles privately to himself afterwards. *I'm trying to restore the absolutely filthy portrait of my grandfather.* He would like to x-ray his grandfather's painted surface the way paintings are x-rayed. It is a constant source of bewilderment to him how his grandfather managed, throughout his life, to justify what he did, how he found the moral strength to go on living. He feels like his grandfather has become a physical presence in his body, a heaviness in his limbs. It is like standing in the dead of the night to realise this knowledge is now a part of him forever, a burden he will always have to carry. He will live in dread of it being exposed. If he has children, he will have to hide it from them. It's as if all beauty in his life will now be tarnished with a layer of grease and dirt which no amount of restoration work will ever be able to remove.

More and more often he catches himself staring down at his clenched hands. They never do not feel dirty. He loses weight. His clothes feel different on his body as if they belong to someone else. He plays endless games of spider solitaire on his laptop. It's irrationally important that he wins.

At a dinner party with members of Phoebe's class at the jewellery school she attends he barely says a word all evening. He sits hunched forward, like someone in a waiting room. But inside his walled silence he feels compelled to find fault with Phoebe's friends. He is accustomed to perceiving himself as a neutral observer. This compulsion to belittle others is new. He suspects it's because he himself feels shrunken. Phoebe's teacher, a very good-looking Argentinian man who also gives private tango lessons, especially annoys him. How pleased he is with himself. How vain of his physicality. He emits sexual heat. He can sense Phoebe is attracted to him. He eventually picks a verbal fight with him. Smiling with undisguised insincerity across at each other, they argue about something wholly irrelevant, and Phoebe is angry with him afterwards.

He finds himself more and more often finding fault with her. They stop making love. When she tells him she is going to take tango lessons with Angelo he loses his temper. The force of his anger disturbs him. His grandfather has cheated him. He coaxed him into giving love where it was ill-deserved. Now it is as if he cannot any longer give love without agonising over whether or not it is merited. But more than anything he feels he himself is unworthy of love.

The restoration of the painting is finished. He stands staring at the man's face. Willing him to speak. He detects a subtle expression of impatience on the bearded man's face. He can't work out if it's in his eyes or the line of his mouth. But he takes it personally. A current of enlivening reproach reaches him through the centuries from this mysterious man's face. The light he has shone on this small piece of history pierces through the new darkness in his mind. He knows now it has been a mistake not to tell Phoebe about his grandfather's history. This is what the nobleman's expression of impatience tells him. His concern is whether or not he has left it too late.

As he walks towards her jewellery school he recalls something she said the previous evening.

'It's like you no longer want to be loved,' she had said. She was wearing the blue cardigan which always to him brought alive all the beauty of her face. 'I've always known how quickly one can fall in love. I didn't realise how quickly one can fall out of it.'

He had interrupted her. He had not been paying close attention. She made him feel a ghost of who he used to be. Now he tries to puzzle out who she was referring to. Did she mean she had fallen out of love with him? He looks down at the reflections in the water as he crosses a small bridge over a canal as if the answer might be there. He walks past a couple staring down at a map. It's like they are there to impart a message to him - that you can always find your way again in life. Phoebe, he knows, is going to be the jury at his trial. Her decision will determine if he is still entitled to feel blessed in the world. He takes heart from the fact she has overlooked a criminal act of indecency on her father's part. In his heart he doesn't feel she will hold him accountable for what his grandfather did. But it's possible she will think less of him. He rehearses what he will say. He will play down his grandfather's role. Point out there is no evidence he actually participated in the killings. Only now does it occur to him that he has already forgotten the names of the places where his grandfather committed his crimes. It seems a good augury, as if he might yet eventually forget the entire affair. It won't always be uppermost. It doesn't have to be forever.

Philosophy

'Thing is, now she's acting like a complete fucking stranger I've fallen in love with her all over again,' shouted Reg, watching a long-legged blonde girl shimmying on the dancefloor. 'Does that make sense?'

'You need to give me some more forensics before I can answer that, mate,' shouted his drinking companion, a scrubbed and heavy-set merchant banker with a big wristwatch.

'I've got a rival. I'm on the verge of losing exclusive rights. It's fucking humiliating. It's like everything I own has lost its market value overnight. I thought my wife was a Picasso. Turns out she's a bloody forgery.'

'Who is he? The rival. Anyone we know?'

Reg fingered his signet ring. 'No one *you* know. But someone you know of.' Out of tune, horribly out of tune, Reg sang the chorus of a recent hit song into the ear of his companion.

'I'm not following you, mate.'

'My rival is Matt Fleet,' shouted Reg over the thump and shudder of the dancefloor hip-hop.

'As in *the* Matt Fleet, singer of The Recycling, the coolest frontman on the planet?'

'You like this news. I can tell. Your eyes have lit up for the first time tonight. You've finally found something that interests you. I've provided you with some entertainment. That's what we want from our friends. Her sister knows the bass player. Violet met the coolest frontman on the planet at her sister's twenty-first. I was in fucking Dubai. Trouble shooting.'

'I'm trying to get my head round this.'

'Not that hard to understand. He's better looking than I am and he's got more money. He's also got a fucking fan base.'

'You need to play it cool. She'll come around. Accrued interest and all that. She's in your debt, mate. In the meantime, buy her a few presents. Take her somewhere with scenery.'

'At least if I have to slap Matt fucking Fleet it's a scrap I'll win. I doubt if he's ever set foot inside a gym.'

'He paints his fingernails and swans around with a woman's handbag over his shoulder.'

'I had this dream last night. I forgot all my pin numbers and passwords. I was no longer allowed to be me in the world. I was locked out. Like Fred Flintstone.'

'Who the fuck is Fred Flintstone?'

'Cartoon character. Violet's turned me into a fucking cartoon character.'

'Yeah, well you know what I've always thought...'

'What?'

'Violet - bit of a cold fish if you ask me. Always get the impression she doesn't like me much.'

'She doesn't. It mystifies her how you make so much money.'

'I knew it!' The banker snapped his fingers several times in succession close to his chin, as if he had answered a quiz question successfully.

'Look, the honourable Olivia Parkinson is shaking her booty on the dancefloor.'

Both men were wearing pink shirts and pin stripe suits. Their voices were loud and brash - a studied pantomime of upper class arrogance spiced with overtones of raucous football terrace coarseness.

When his drinking companion joined the honourable

Olivia Parkinson on the dancefloor Reg consumed another two vodka red bulls quickly and was then joined at his table by Clemmie Aynsford, a childhood friend of his family. Her sequinned short silver dress in the firework strobe lights was like a rippling flame.

'You look like shit,' she said.

'Rub it in, Clemmie. I've got sensitive skin tonight.'

'Want some coke?'

He put a cigarette in his mouth which he wasn't allowed to light. Then he twirled the box in both hands. 'Why do they put these idiot messages on packs of fags now? Tobacco smoke is toxic. What isn't toxic? When was it decided we ought to live our lives as if the world is a fucking nursing home? Who cares if they die at seventy-five instead of eighty-three? You're doing the world a favour by dying seven years earlier. One less motorised fucking wheelchair gridlocking the pavements. It's a shame more people don't die seven years earlier. The planet might breathe a bit easier. What does anyone achieve between the ages of seventy-five and eighty-three? Why don't they tell us the positive effects of smoking? Smoking reduces your chances of going to prison or ending up in a psychiatric ward by eighty percent. Smoking shows the world you're willing to take risks.'

'So what's the real dilemma?'

'In love with my life, innit.'

'I hate my life.'

'I meant to say, in love with my wife.'

'Lucky man.'

'Actually, life's a lot easier when you're not in love with your wife. You notice less. You have more freedom in your mind. But then you're a woman.'

'I'm very flattered you noticed, Reg.'

'Hard not to notice in that dress, babe.'

'Do you like it?'

'What I like better is your voice, Clemmie. Women have beautiful voices. Nearly all women. The sounds that come out of a woman's mouth. Only takes a handful of words and, in your mind, you're led into their bedroom. Or else back into the arms of your mother. Either way it's the beginning of feeling safe in the world. How sexy would you say Matt Fleet is?'

'That's like asking me how sexy sex is.'

'Sex isn't always sexy. It can be fucking sordid.'

'True. When did you become a philosopher? Anyway, why are you asking me about Matt Fleet?'

'Me and him, poles apart, right?'

'I'm surprised you give him any thought.'

'How come we never shagged, Clemmie?'

She laughed - a deep throated chortle which didn't engage her eyes. 'The closest we got was when I was seven and you were ten. You made me put my hand inside your trousers in the playroom while our parents were out hunting.'

'You remember that?'

'Don't we all remember the first time? For better or worse it's the benchmark.'

'Is it? Why don't you put your hand inside my trousers tonight?'

'Because we'll both feel shit tomorrow morning.'

'My sins have never stopped me functioning efficiently. Thing is, I'm not a good person, Clemmie. Had I been around in Nazi Germany I probably would have joined the SS. Career prospects and the smart scary uniform and all that. That's the truth about me.'

'What the fuck is the matter with you?'

'Violet is the matter with me.'

'I did warn you. She's too complicated for you.'

'What's that supposed to mean?'

'You like simple pleasures, Reg. You like making money and getting drunk and driving fast cars and winning arguments. Violet likes looking at herself in mirrors and pretending she prefers poetry to Pimms.'

'Ha ha!' Reg laid his head on the table, in the ash and sticky stains. 'But what's it all about, Clemmie? What is our purpose? What's the end goal? To procreate? To produce offspring? And then return to the dust. The dirt. The muck and the mire. Most of the things we tell us about ourselves are fictions. An attempt to make our life a page turner, a best-seller. When the body is in crisis and needs some protective comfort the hand goes straight between the legs. I mean, in a platonic sense. My hand wants to go there now. Every other hug in life is an artificial substitute. Is that the same for women?'

Up went Clemmie's expensively manicured eyebrows.

'Do you know what I think? I think the chances are that when we're lying in our deathbed, when we're thinking about our history, when we're trying to write the book of our history, it will be our lovers who tell us the story of our lives. Our lovers who let us know what kind of person we were. We'll nuzzle up in memory again to the brave souls who stripped naked for us. I think this is why Violet is on the verge of offering her naked body to Matt Fleet. It's for her portfolio.'

'Hang on. Violet and Matt Fleet? You can't be serious.'

'It won't last long. Because if there's one thing Violet can't stand it's being at a disadvantage. And how can you hold any kind of advantage over someone who has the world at his feet? She won't be anyone's puppet. Not even Matty fucking Fleet's.'

'Violet and Matt Fleet are an item?'

Reg lifted his head from the table, rubbed his eyes and finished Clemmie's drink. 'Have you noticed that in every film ever made there's a scene with a woman entering an empty room alone? And you get the sense you can read her mind. It's the backstage moment. I like to watch Violet getting dressed. It's one of my favourite things. Because that's the closest I get to seeing her backstage. The trouble is, I'd also like to watch you getting dressed. The entire performance. From beginning to end. I can almost see you naked, your back to me, rummaging through your underwear drawer. How can I demand exclusive rights when there's so little will in me to reciprocate?'

'I need you to get some focus into your eyes, Reg. I need you to tell me this story. The story of Violet and Matt Fleet. From the beginning.'

'It's just the same old story, Clemmie. This follows that. The hot and sticky followed by the damp and cold. The real story is always somewhere else. For as long as I can remember there was always somewhere I needed to be. Somewhere else. Somewhere I caught glimpses of. I thought Violet might get me there. But she's led me on another fucking wild goose chase. We think we've got somewhere in life and then we find ourselves sitting on another fucking train. Sometimes me and Violet catch ourselves looking at each other in unguarded moments and what I see is a stranger. I never have a clue what it is our eyes are sharing or disagreeing about. And yet we all persist with this insane idea that there exist magical combinations of words that can change a person's point of view. It's this weariness with the insufficiencies of language that leads to men becoming violent. Once we've learned the futility of language all our frustration makes for our fists. After three years of marriage I'm still tentative around her, still stilted, as if I've never trusted her not to be cruel. Did you know the first time we slept with each other it was after I crashed the car I was driving? Wrote it off. We couldn't continue the journey. Had to stay the night in a hotel. I was driving her back to England from Italy.'

'You're not answering my questions, Reg. Violet and Mattie Fleet. Tell me the story.'

'The story is this guy can get a hundred thousand people

in a field to sing back to him songs he's written. He can get a hundred thousand people in a field to move their bodies in time to music he's written. Beautiful women throw their underwear at his feet. Won't be long before it's all over the Internet. And yours truly will acquire some fame as the cuckold. That's my designated role. I'll be forced to see myself through eyes other than my own. I'm the archetypal spoilt rich kid. As far as the world's concerned whatever knocks I suffer serve me right. Money and aristocratic blood don't count for much anymore, do they? Fame – that's the only hard currency now. The rest of us, those without fame, me and you, no matter how many titled ancestors we have, are the proletariat, the new riff-raff. I should have learned to play the guitar when I was twelve instead of shooting fucking birds. That's what Violet's taught me. That's what life has fucking taught me.'

Jerusalem

The blood in your body is aglow. You want to skip. You want to make spinning wheels of your arms. Your body's need is for celebration and dance. But your grandfather holds your hand. Your grandfather holds you in check. You are walking with him through the streets of Jerusalem. It is day three of a five day holiday. You are ten years old. And you have a new secret. It gives off such a bright light you feel it must be visible on your face. But your grandfather hasn't noticed any change in you. Your grandfather is talking. He is always talking. He is telling you things he thinks you ought to know. Your new secret creates more distance between you and your grandfather. Your new secret makes it more difficult to listen to what he is saying.

In a market you see a dog with only three legs. It is the first thing you have seen today that distracts you from your secret. You are fascinated by how gamely it hops over the cobbles. You can't take your eyes off it. You swivel your head to keep it in the field of your vision. Your heart goes out to it. Your grandfather is telling you about the three million murdered by the Nazis. About cattle trains and gas chambers. But all your sympathy is for the dog with the missing leg. You don't care about the three million dead. You have no room in your heart for the three million dead. Only for the black dog with three legs. You know this isn't the correct response to what your grandfather is telling you. Your feeling is like the wrong answer in a school test. But you are upset your grandfather didn't even notice the dog with three legs. It makes you critical of him.

Now he is talking about the origins of the city of Jerusalem. The Bible, he tells you, is a mix of historical fact and mythology. The first reference to Jerusalem, he tells you, is in the book of Genesis. The Bible tells us, he tells you, Moses led the Hebrews out of Egypt to the promised land. They brought with them, he tells you, a new religion. It was David, he tells you, who united the twelve warring tribes of Israelites and made Jerusalem the capital. It was David's son, Solomon, he tells you, who built the first Jewish temple. To house the arc of the covenant, he tells you, the chest containing the twelve commandments. Today, he tells you, we are going to see the foundation stone of King Solomon's temple. For us Jews, he tells you, it is the holiest place in the entire world. It is here, he tells you, man can meet God.

But you are impatient to return to the hotel. It's already been two hours since you saw her.

You found out her name today. The maid at the hotel. Aviva. It's a magical word in your mind. It takes you somewhere outside the walk of routine time. You keep saying it to yourself. You keep staring into it. As if it has more meaning than you have yet been able to find. Today, in the corridor on the first floor, Aviva smiled at you and ruffled your hair. Hot blood rushed to your neck and face. You can still feel the presence of her hand in your hair. You can still feel the warmth she radiated. Aviva is too beautiful for you to fully comprehend. She floods mystery into your mind. She makes you feel everything around you is part of your being. She makes you live another life. In some way, mysterious to you, you have chosen her. The thought of her brings you more fully into awareness of yourself. That she might appear from one moment to the next makes the hotel an enchanted kingdom. You never want to go outside. You have to suffocate the thought that in two days she will vanish from your life. That you will never see her again.

Before the appearance of Aviva in your life, before coming to Jerusalem, the most important thing in the world to you was whether or not you had been selected for the school football team. The notice is pinned to the notice board every Thursday lunchtime. Everyone crowds around it. When you're not on the list nothing can console you. It becomes a struggle not to hate the boy who has taken your place. Luckily this has only happened once or twice. You especially enjoy the away games when a bus is hired and you sit with your friends in what is an adventure to new unknown places. You cross another new frontier. The map by which you recognise your world, the intimately known feeling of the streets surrounding your home and school, the places you know in a special way, extends outwards. Sometimes your grandfather comes to watch you play. He stands by the touchline. You are aware of his critical scrutiny. You always want to make him proud of you. You gauge your performance through his eyes. He is the measure of your accomplishment.

You walk past a construction site. You walk past old men sitting outside cafes. You walk past souvenir shops with coloured fabrics and religious artefacts. You think your grandfather could at least offer you an ice cream or a coca cola. Many foreign smells reach your nostrils. You like this. You associate them with Aviva because she too is exotic. They keep her close. You pull down the sleeves of your jersey over your hands. It's a new ritual you have copied from a school friend to make a statement about yourself. You copy things other people do that you like the look of. You are discovering more about yourself every day.

The western wall, your grandfather tells you, is a place of prayer. King Solomon asked, he tells you, that every prayer offered here be answered by God. King Solomon's temple, he tells you, was the first Jewish temple. The western wall, he tells you, does not belong to King Solomon's temple. This is the wall of a later temple, he tells you, built on the site of Solomon's temple which was destroyed by the soldiers of King Nebuchadnezzar of the Babylonians. You look at all the bearded young men in black hats, all the bearded old men in white robes, rocking back and forth on their heels, bobbing their heads. Life is more public in Jerusalem. People here do private things out in the open in ways only mad people do in England. If you were with your school friends, you would all have fun imitating the bearded men. You would all exaggerate their ritual gestures and snigger among yourselves. You would all feel superior.

Your grandfather leads you down into a narrow low-ceilinged underground tunnel. It smells of mould or onions. You don't like being underground. The tunnel seems to want to steal your secret from you. It presages with its chill stifling atmosphere the disappearance of Aviva from your life. You are not listening to what your grandfather is saying. Down here there are no men in black hats or white robes. Only old women in charity shop clothes reading prayer books or leaning their foreheads against the old stones. Your grandfather becomes silent. In the oppressive silence you begin to devise a cunning plan. You will flatter your grandfather. You will tell him how interested you are in everything he tells you about Jerusalem. You will suggest you stay on in Jerusalem for another week. You become aware in a foggy sort of way that, if you look hard enough, there is innocence in guilt and guilt in innocence.

You carry out your plan later that evening. In the dining room of the hotel. Your grandfather is flattered. Your face flushes with the sin of your cunning duplicity. But he tells you it is impossible to stay longer as he is expected back at work.

The last time you see Aviva she is carrying an armful of crisp folded white sheets. Because her hands are occupied she does not touch you. You brave a longer look at her face. You would like her to know how important she is to you. It seems the most important message you have ever wanted to give someone. The moment you have to turn your back on her for the last time is the most difficult step you have had to make in your life. It's like you are leaving yourself behind. At school the heartbreak she caused you will help you to understand and experience more vividly scenes in literature. Out on the forecourt of the hotel it becomes incomprehensible, unbearable that you will never see Aviva again. In Jerusalem you learn what exile and the dream of return means.

Provenance and Posterity.

'So, you're like me. No spouse. No children. No one to listen when you have something urgent to say. Perhaps you don't find women attractive? I didn't find men attractive. I found one or two women attractive. But I was too ashamed to admit it, even to myself. In those days, the days before you were born, perceptions were different.'

I didn't contradict her. Instead I thought about the assumptions, invariably errant, we make about people based on a scattering of breadcrumb facts. We are all jigsaw puzzles with an abundance of missing pieces for other people, even perhaps for ourselves. I was sitting in my aunt's living room. It smelled of dust and decay. I was listening closely to her as if she was offering up her final will and testament. I felt I owed her my full attention. I didn't realise then that I would have to recall and repeat what she was telling me in the dock of a courtroom, albeit an imaginary one. My aunt was in her seventies. She had some kind of skin disease. Her face was impastoed with raw red excrescences. Like the fermentation of some secret sin the body seeps out onto the skin in medieval paintings of the Last Judgement. Her grey hair was matted in anarchic clumps and unwashed. I barely recognised her. I could find no trace of a continuity that connected her back to the woman who had played a role in my adolescence. I hadn't seen her in more than thirty years. We were strangers to each other. She created a mystery when she summoned me out of the blue. Especially when she told me she had something valuable she wanted to give me. It's what we want from people, that they can create mystery.

'You got me my first ever job,' I said. 'I collected the orders from shops in the warehouse at Pye records. Pye was probably the worst record label in the history of record labels. They had the Kinks back in the day but after that nothing but garbage. The Brotherhood of Man. Benny Hill.'

'You're forgetting Sandie Shaw. Sandie Shaw wasn't garbage. I couldn't take my eyes off Sandie Shaw.'

She gave me an impish look from her armchair. I could tell it was the only chair she ever sat in in this room. It allowed her to sit with her back to the window and the world outside. There was a scrawny silver-grey cat asleep on the other armchair. I was perched on the sofa. Rain was tapping on the window, misting the glass.

'I remember my first morning at that warehouse. I was terrified I wouldn't be able to work the clocking-on machine. I think I was fourteen. How small I felt but also how visible. As a child you love to hide. But, in that warehouse, I experienced for the first time what it's like to have nowhere to hide.'

'I worked at Pye Records for more than twenty years. Until it folded. And every day I walked there and every day I walked back home. Six miles, round trip. I could time every milestone of that walk down to an exact science. That's what my ghost will do if we become ghosts. Follow those same coordinates over and over again. But let's get back to the reason I summoned you. When I was twenty-one I went to Italy. I went alone. It was the bravest thing I had ever done. It was like removing all the paint I had applied to my portrait of myself. I became little more than a preparatory drawing. A few stylised marks. Rather like the sketch I'm going to show you. The bravest thing I've done and I'm seventy-seven now. I went to Venice. One night I let a man take me home. I was fighting a kind of civil war with my virginity. As I said,

I didn't find the male species at all attractive. Nothing much has changed on that score.' She gave me a smirk. 'Forgive me, for speaking so bluntly. I have lived a very solitary life. I am accustomed to talking to myself.'

I smiled with what I hoped was encouragement and reassurance. The estrangement I initially felt was beginning to diminish the more she spoke. She had a facility for creating intimacy.

'This man wasn't at all attractive. His name was Luigi. He was a good deal older than me. He looked like he might know the ropes. That was his only attraction. If I was going to lose my virginity I wanted someone who knew the ropes. An experienced actor. Needless to say, I found the experience demeaning. I discovered two people can pass through each other with no more consequence than a momentary gusting of wind. But Luigi did have consequences. Because of what he did afterwards. After smoking a cigarette, he left the room and returned with a framed painted sketch. He got back into bed and handed me the sketch. Then he told me a story. A war story. He had been a young conscript in a fascist secret police force. By this time the Germans had occupied northern Italy. He stole this picture from the home of a Jewish family he was sent to arrest. He told me he couldn't remember the name of the family. But they were a very attractive family. He especially remembered the beauty of a teenage daughter. He thought the sketch might be of her. He also thought the sketch might be valuable. But after the war, when he found out what had happened to the Jews he had arrested, he could no longer bear to look at it. He kept it hidden at the back of his wardrobe. He told me more than once he didn't know the Jews he arrested would be murdered. There was a lot of mental anguish in him. He found it difficult to live with himself. In the middle of the night I got up and left Luigi's apartment. I took the sketch with me. My heart was pounding like a hammer. To this day I don't really know why I did that. My justification at the time was that I would try to track down some surviving member of the Jewish family and restore the picture to them. An acquaintance of mine who worked at Christie's thought the sketch might be by Giacometti. In those days Giacometti's work wasn't anywhere near as highly prized as it is now. How much do you think a Giacometti sketch is worth nowadays?'

'I've no idea. I can Google it.'

I did so.

'Giacometti sketches can fetch anything between 25 and 250,000 quid.'

She seemed satisfied with these figures. 'I didn't get very far with my research into the original owners of the painting because one night, not long after returning from Italy, I took a tab of acid and I never recovered. It was the Sixties and acid was a rite of passage in the Sixties. A way of putting an even greater distance between oneself and one's parents' generation. I suspect you never guessed you had an aunt who had taken LSD.'

I nodded in confirmation. 'I've taken it a few times,' I said. 'In my youth. The first time I remember there was a lot of uncontrollable giggling. The last time I became obsessed by the act of breathing. I became nothing more than my breathing. That was scary.'

'Yes, it makes the mind an alien place. It was an experience, a horrible terrifying experience that changed my relationship with the world forever. Afterwards, I could no longer bear to be looked at. If anyone looked at me too closely I had a panic attack. I had to constantly walk away at work. And I couldn't bear to be trapped in enclosed spaces. I had a panic attack whenever there was no immediate escape route. That's why I began to walk everywhere. I had to come up with excuses to my friends not to get on a tube, bus or a train. It always felt to me like I was locked inside a cattle truck and that felt like a memory from another life. If there's such a thing as reincarnation I think I was Jewish in my previous life. I was born in 1945. The timing is there. The only justification for the primal terror I knew on a train was that this was a journey that ended in death. So, rather than get on a train, I often walked miles, sometimes in the middle of the night to get home. I gained a reputation for being eccentric. I began to lose my friends.'

She got to her feet and walked across the room, her arthritic joints giving to the performance a sense of time slowing down. The cat curled on the armchair raised its head and gave her a disdainful look. She picked up a framed painting and brought it over to me. It was a painted sketch of a woman seated in a chair with her legs crossed at the knee. 80 x 54 cm. Oil on canvas. Even to my untrained eye it radiated importance, distinguished origins. I felt I was staring at an enduring truth. An impression heightened by the reverence with which my aunt handled it.

'Didn't you once draw and paint? I remember the smell of turps in your room.'

'I gave that up a long time ago,' she said. 'Do you like it?'

I nodded. I did like it. I suspected my aunt saw something of herself in the lonely, loosely designed female figure rooted to her chair. It seemed to make plain somehow the thin elusive drift of love that had hovered, like light snow, without settling on her life.

'I want you to have this sketch. I had intended to leave it to you in my will but perhaps it's better if it passes hands in a more clandestine way. It's up to you what you do with it.'

And this is how I acquired a painted work attributed to Giacometti. On the train on my way home I couldn't stop looking at it. It made me feel important. It set me apart from the crowd. Something I had been far from feeling while sitting on the train on my way to my aunt's earlier. Then I had been thinking about my failure to ever learn to drive a car. How I had never been able to trust my mind to behave rationally. I didn't trust myself with the murderous power of a car. I therefore now empathised with my aunt. I too had suffered many mental health issues over the years. Madness has always stalked me in the dark alleys of my mind. I took a photo of the drawing and uploaded it to my Twitter page. The world became annoying again when, half an hour later, it still hadn't received a single like. What I haven't mentioned is that I'm a writer. My most fervent wish is that I was a better writer. It's often Vladimir Nabokov, dead though he might be, who tells me I have no exceptional talent. I knew he would have no interest in the novels I wrote. They were way below his standard. And what point is there in writing novels if you don't have exceptional talent? Of course the glaring absence of exceptional talent doesn't stop about 95% of all published writers from writing. So I had resigned myself to joining their gang and Vladimir Nabokov could think what he wanted. I enjoyed writing. I enjoyed the escape into other lives, into other worlds. I enjoyed the rigours of research. But the best I could hope for, I knew, was to become decently second rate. Now, for the first time in my life, I was in possession of something eminently first rate.

I was disappointed there were no labels on the back of the painting. No clues as to its provenance. For the first time I noticed the canvas appeared pristine for a sketch with more than a half century of traumatic history. But I was excited about investigating it. I didn't know where I would start. I envisaged going to Paris. Visiting some art dealers there. Getting them to check through their accounting log books. I envisaged going to Venice. Sitting in some deeply silent archive there amidst sunlit dust. Sifting through a list of Venetian Jews deported by the Nazis. I had decided to do what my aunt wanted to do: restore the painting to its rightful owners. A girl I had known in my twenties was often my conscience. I wanted her to respect and admire me. I felt a need to keep her informed about my life even though she could neither hear or see me anymore, even though, in all likelihood, she probably now barely gave me any thought. That said, twenty years later, I still often had the feeling, looking at her photograph, that she was about to walk back into my arms. Photographs can create this illusion. I suppose the truth though was that whenever we spent time together I always had the sense I was standing closer to her than she was standing to me. And that's why she married someone else.

When I got home I began googling. I spent the next three days googling. I googled Giacometti. I googled Giacometti's art dealer in Paris. I googled Italian Jews deported from Venice. I ordered the memoir of a Jewish man who lived through the Nazi occupation of Venice. I was living in another world. A world, unlike mine, where every decision was of crucial importance, mined with consequence.

I was excited by the prospect of going to Venice. Before making travel arrangements I decided to seek the expert opinion of an art dealer. I made an appointment with a gallery owner near St James' Square. I was unaccountably nervous as I buzzed on the bell, announced myself through the intercom and then pushed open the heavy door. The gallery owner was a man of my age who clearly spent more time in front of mirrors than I did. After the obligatory hopscotch of small talk, I handed him the sketch. He studied it for no more than ten seconds. The ghost of a smirk appeared at the corner of his mouth.

'It's a forgery. Not even a very good one I'm afraid.'

There are many clichéd expressions for how gullible and small I felt in this man's gaze. I was returned to the ineptitude of a child in an adult world. I wanted out of that gallery as quickly as possible. For the time being, I wanted out of the world. Thankful only that I would never have to meet this man with his scornful expert eye ever again. Standing at a red light near the Ritz, I suddenly knew for a certainty that my aunt had done the painting herself. She had set out to dupe me. It had all been an elaborate hoax on her part. But why? Was it some reproach levelled at me? Or did she, approaching death, want to explain herself to least one person in the world and believe I would only answer her summons if there was something material to be gained? I never found out because she died three weeks after giving me the painting. The coroner's report listed her death as suicide.

No Means No

A bewitched forest of figures frozen in poses of drama and poise. I let these figures speak to me as best I could. I allowed them access to my heart and imagination. I allowed them to take me outside of time. Then I left the room of Renaissance sculpture. The stairway in the courtyard of the Bargello is a thing of beauty in itself. But it was still a shock to meet on those stairs the most beautiful girl I had ever seen in my life. We were both alone. And when we walked towards each other and our eyes met something happened to us both. I was sure of this. My appearance had shocked her no less than hers had shocked me. It was like we were revealed to each other in early morning lustre. There was wonder, heightened self-awareness but also a faint chill. An act of recognition had taken place. Somewhere at the back of your mind is a blueprint of the real life you feel you ought to be living. Now and again a moment from this life breaks through into the everyday. I felt this was one of those moments. As if we had both followed footprints in snow to arrive at this meeting.

The second time I encountered her, about three weeks later, also took place on stairs. At night on the crowded stairs of one of the architecture faculty buildings of Florence's university. The students had occupied all the university buildings in protest at some political outrage, the exact nature of which I can no longer remember. Concerts, exhibitions, performances and debates were held every night. All the students looked very pleased with themselves. As if they believed they could change history. This time we were both in company and my friend Paolo knew one of her friends to nod a greeting to. Once again the meeting of our eyes produced what seemed like a quickening of light. I quizzed Paolo about her. He sought to discourage me. I was soon to learn how possessive people were of her, even people who barely knew her. As if her mystique was bound up in some universally cherished idea of her being unattainable. As if the poetic function granted to her was to lead any male who desired her into a Petrarch sonnet. He told me she studied architecture and had never once been known to have a boyfriend. That she lived with three boys who formed a kind of guard around her. That her name was Giuliana and she originated from southern Italy.

I wrote her a letter in which I invented a dream about her. It was designed as a showcase of my imaginative qualities. In other words, I began my quest with a deception. I asked for a meeting and gave her my phone number. I got Paolo to give the letter to his friend to pass on to her. I was taken aback when she called almost immediately. I don't think excessive vanity is among my flaws. Vanity, like insecurity and stupidity, can make one easily prone to flattery. I wasn't though flattered. I had a sense it wasn't eagerness that had prompted her to call me so quickly. More, it was like a need to get something troubling over and done with as soon as possible, like a dentist appointment.

I met her in piazza della Signoria. I was looking up at Giambologna's statue of the Rape of the Sabine Woman when she arrived. She flinched when I kissed her on either cheek. I took in a fleeting draught of her body warmth. A distinctive herbal smell lifted from her neck or hair. She was dressed all in black. She never seemed to wear anything that wasn't black. As if she saw herself as a woman in the midst of winter. I let her lead me. We walked alongside the river for a while, bats flitting around the lamps, and eventually sat down on a bench in piazza Tasso. A working-class area where women sat in groups watching their children play on the swings and slide. She sat with her shoulder nearest me lifted up defensively. Her hands continually twisted the band she had taken from her long black corkscrewed hair. I found I was listening to her and watching her from a deeper part of myself. She told me she came from a mountain village in the Molise. And that she studied modern dance as well as architecture and had ambitions to form her own dance company. I told her my mother had wanted to be a dancer. That was when, no more than six feet away from where we sat, a scraggy poodle attempted to straddle a spaniel with comical ineptitude. We tried to laugh it off, but we were both embarrassed. I think we both felt it was a spectacle that was making fun of us, of the lengthy dissembling preamble humans go through before sexual union can take place.

We spent about three hours together. Then she allowed me to walk her home. It felt like an achievement in itself that I now knew where she lived. Once again I felt her entire body become rigid when I kissed her on either cheek and took in another draught of her distinctive autumnal smell. Any form of physical contact seemed to alarm her. She became like a wild forest creature whenever I extended my hands.

I allowed a couple of days to pass before calling her. I was taken aback when she made excuses not to see me again. She was icy cold. We had got on well together. There had been a lovely seeded intimacy. I didn't understand the dismissive scorn with which she now treated me. I obsessively sought an explanation, combing through my recollection of the time we had spent together like it was a crime scene.

In the following weeks I saw her once or twice on the streets of Florence's *centro storico*. Every time she appeared it was like a flare had been fired up into the sky overhead and the two of us were singled out in its otherworldly glow. She though ignored me as if I was an insignificant episode in her life. Nevertheless I detected a splash of high tide emotion, an inrush of tension in her body whenever I appeared. My intuition was that she was scared of me. It was a new experience for me to inspire fear. I was very thin and grew up modelling myself on David Bowie. I harboured nothing but scorn for male muscle and brawn. I had never inspired fear in anyone.

I began frequently walking past her building. No doubt my endeavours to feign innocence would have been comical, maybe even sinister, to anyone covertly spying on me. I had once seen her cycle across piazza Santa Croce and made a note of identifying her bike. I saw she always chained it in the same place, opposite the church of Santa Trinita. Therefore I knew when she wasn't at home. One time I sat myself down on her saddle and became a bit creepy to myself.

I was big on psychoanalysis in those days. I used it to explain myself to myself. My mother had always left me feeling unloved. You expect unconditional love from your mother. My mother though had demanded her love be earned. And she was a hard taskmaster. Therefore I expected, perhaps even courted, rejection from women. To be rejected kept me on familiar ground. Ensured I never had to cross a border into unfamiliar intimidating territory. My track record with women wasn't good. My longest relationship had lasted no more than a month. I had a tendency to betray my girlfriends. Twice I had done so with their best friend. Sabotage seemed like the unconscious agenda of my psyche. I liked to believe I had a talent for forging a bond of intimate friendship with women, but I knew I was unreliable as a lover. The best place for the lover in me was probably exile, forced into yearning over an insurmountable distance. Exactly what Giuliana was giving me. That said, before going to study in Italy, I had seen the film of *A Room with a View*. EM Forster tells us no from a woman doesn't always mean no. I believed EM Forster wasn't mistaken. I just needed the right setting - the meadow of golden corn and poppies. And the accompanying operatic aria.

Perhaps with this in mind, I walked up into the hills outside Fiesole one day and stripped a meadow of its wild flowers. I believed I was fashioning the moment to what was in my heart. I felt vulnerable carrying my bouquet into the urban streets. People looked at me with heightened attention, especially the women. They smiled back at me. Giuliana's bike was chained outside the dance school where she studied most afternoons. It took a while for me to pluck up the confidence to enter the building. There was a secretary at a desk when I entered. She too smiled at my flowers. I asked if I could see Giuliana. She smiled and pointed at a door. My entrance silenced and froze the several dancers in the mirrored studio. Everyone waited for me to explain myself. I held out my bunch of flowers to Giuliana. She skipped over to me. I had never seen her so spontaneously light on her feet, so nakedly pleased with the moment. She gave me a kiss on either cheek, the first time she had kissed me.

She let me walk her home and asked if I thought she was cruel. It seemed to bother her that I might think this. I told her I thought of her as a worthy opponent and she smiled. Outside her building I told her I was thirsty and she invited me up to her apartment. The three boys she lived with made little effort to hide their hostility. They looked at the flowers she held with contempt as if they were an agent of disease. There was no one who wanted Giuliana and I to become lovers. Once or twice I had been tempted to confide in the baker below my apartment. When he greeted me he always touched my shoulder and left a handprint of flour there as if it was a message of encouragement. I felt he might be sympathetic, might lift my morale with his kind smile and silver walrus moustache. Giuliana led me into the kitchen. Standing by the sink with her back to me she told me I didn't attract her physically. I could sense her shoulders tighten with fearful anticipation.

She filled a vase with water and arranged the flowers inside. Then she poured me a glass of water. Still with her back to me she said, 'Why can't you understand that you simply don't attract me? You might as well not have a body as far as I'm concerned.'

I had scant defence against such dismissive words of scorn. I felt I could see the collapse of my self-esteem on my own face. She turned to face me, handed me the glass of water and then stood there with her arms folded over her breast.

'You've invented someone who doesn't exist. I'm not the person you imagine me to be.'

The bestowing of the flowers had been forgotten. I was baffled. Why was she so suddenly angry? Her dark eyes challenged mine. I felt she was daring me to push past her prohibitions. To violate her defences. To kiss her against her will. It was *A Room with a View* again. But it was like being challenged to steal something from a shop whose keeper knows your intention and is prepared to counteract it. I was tied in knots. She was demanding of me the kind of unheeding passion I didn't have it in my nature to summon. There was too much imagination in my desire, not enough hot blood. I wanted her to give me the answer without having to ask the question. I was a prisoner of my shortcomings. I felt I had only words. And therefore I merited her scorn. There are few things more potentially humiliating than the expectation of a woman that you act like a man. If indeed this was her covert challenge.

When I called her a few days later the tone of her voice was as cold and sharp as shards of ice. We were back to square one again. It was like being strapped in on a plane that never took off, that never left the runway.

My next inspiration was to spread the rumour I was

about to return to England. If I held no attraction for her she wouldn't care much if I was leaving. She soon called me. I allowed myself to get my hopes up again. We met on ponte Santa Trinita when the afterglow of the sunset was still a reflection on the river water. As usual I let her lead me. We walked together from one piazza to another. Sometimes she was affectionate, other times her anger returned. She was constantly calling me to account. At one point I asked her if she had been abused as a child. That for me was one possible explanation for her disproportionate sexual anxiety. She gave me a fiery stare and again told me she could never be my girlfriend. That I didn't attract her physically. In the moment she said these things they carried all the high voltage of truths because, I believed, she was speaking from her borders, not from her depths. She told me she hated her body. That she couldn't bear to look at herself naked. We were now sitting on the steps outside the Ospedale degli Innocent in piazza Santa Annunziata. At one point she stretched out her body, threw back her head and thrust up her hips. This overtly sexual gesture disconcerted me, but it wasn't sexy; it was more like the clumsy caricatured sexual flirtation of an adolescent girl. Again I had the intimidating impression she wanted me to violate her defences. To kiss her into submission. As if the kiss on the mouth was the thing she most feared and the fear she most needed to overcome. That only then would the ugly toad she felt herself to be become the beautiful princess. I was no longer in a Petrarch sonnet. My instinct now was that I was in a bedtime story. Of course it's not difficult to turn Florence into a fairy story kingdom, especially when the old stones and their fabled histories are ashimmer in moonlight. But I couldn't perform the gesture the fairy story had set me. It drove me crazy that I was unable to rise to the challenge of the moment. The icy fervour of her fear stripped me of all assurances. It threw me from my saddle, it unmanned me. It's when we aspire to something that our shortcomings make themselves felt.

The same game of cat and mouse continued. Except I felt like the mouse pursuing the cat. Then I learned her dance company was giving a performance in the central piazza of Castiglion Fiorentino, a small medieval hilltop town in Tuscany. I was excited at the prospect of finally seeing her dance. I felt it might provide an answer to the maddening riddle of her amorous ambivalence. She trained her body to dance. She underwent sacrifices to hone her body into an instrument of aspiration and grace. She submitted it to daily routines of strict discipline. She heavily censored what entered her body. Sometimes, she told me, she ate nothing but carrots. (Afterwards I left an entire crate of carrots outside her door.) I had begun to believe she had chosen dance as an alternative to sex, the quintessential dance, as if she had been forced to renounce the one activity to pursue the other.

I'm back in that piazza again now, forty years later. I have returned to the small hilltop Tuscan town. I've been told I have about three more months to live. It has cost me much of my remaining strength to make the journey from England to Italy. I never married. I have never owned any house I have lived in. There were other compelling women in my life but they all, like Giuliana, detained me at the border. Family life became an exotic dream beyond my realm of experience. My broken heart was my home. For a long while, until the fatal diagnosis, today might have been yesterday. This week might have been last week. This year might have been last year. Giuliana was a prophecy of what awaited me. A loveless life on the sidelines. I came to realise this was why her appearance always seemed to produce the firing of a brightening flare up into the sky overhead which stopped the world and made me see myself more vividly in it. The umbrella of electrifying light was trying to open my eyes to secret knowledge. I was face to face with a messenger from the future. I was having my fortune told.

I'm sitting outside a café with a glass of prosecco while the sun sets. The night of the dance I was stranded in this piazza. The last bus had left. The last train had left. When the performance ended, Giuliana and the other dancers entered a house in the piazza and stayed there until sunrise. I was sitting on the steps of the church opposite. The dance had bewitched me. Had made Giuliana still more attractive to me. I sat there all night. I imagined her looking out of a window at me and felt myself a pathetic creature. A harmless stalker. If such a thing exists.

I finish my glass of prosecco. I'm thinking how everything I do now might be the last time I ever do it. This might be the last time I ever see an old woman smile. This might be the last time I ever see a firefly. In the encroaching final darkness I often find I can differentiate myself more clearly. But I'm still baffled by Giuliana. I feel she owes me an explanation. I look up to see a party of children dressed in fairy story costumes emerge from a building and troupe out into the piazza. They are all delighted with themselves. As if a wish is on the verge of being answered. The gift of wings. I had been granted my own fairy story and I had failed the task set for me. At least, that's one way of looking at it. The other is that EM Forster was wrong. There has been a hashtag of late used by many women on the internet. #No means no. I suspect I will go to my grave not quite knowing if this is always indisputably true. If no always means no. Or, for that matter, if yes always means yes.

Guilty Party

Freddie: We were walking by the river in London. The ghost shimmer of the lights on the moving black water. We were talking about our childhood memories of hotels. I suggested we spent tonight in a hotel. Instead of returning to our separate homes. We booked into a sleazy hotel near Charing Cross station. Kate and I had been very close friends for three years, but this was the first time we had slept together. I was unofficially the boyfriend of her flatmate. Kate's father died when she was young. She has made him into an idol. Her most pressing need was to feel he would be proud of her. His great unfulfilled passion was to study philosophy at university, specifically at one of the Oxford colleges. Kate took on his ambition. She made it her own most urgent wish. She didn't though get into Oxford. She was in her third year at Hull University. I think she saw something of her father in me. That perhaps was part of the problem.

Kate: I don't want to talk about him.

Lucy: It's midwinter and, at the moment, I just want to devour all my books and make them a part of my mind for the rest of my life. Nothing arrives discreetly in Hull. The harsh blistering winds bite. The shadow of the tree outside my window looks like figures dancing on the lawn. I live days that I feel don't belong to my life. I am ashamed of how much time I kill. Shame comes too easily to me. Perhaps a legacy of my schooldays at the convent in Lincoln. When I look at my face in a mirror I feel it has lost some of its freshness. I share a flat with Kate in Hull. We have become good friends. I feel I have got closer to Kate than I have to any other female friend. I have always known she is in love with Freddie. Though she is reluctant to talk about her feelings for him. He is the choreography of her secret life. Freddie was my boyfriend for a while. Then we broke up but continued to be good friends. I still got into his bed at every opportunity. It was an arrangement that suited him. Never did I refuse him my hands, my mouth, my body. No matter what I might think, hold onto me was always the plea of my body. Last summer I was often naked in his bed. Then the three of us went to Brighton for a few days together. I won't pretend it wasn't awkward. My loyalties were tested. I shared a room with Kate while Freddie slept on the floor in the living room. One night I got up in the middle of night and crept under the covers of Freddie's bed. Then I returned to the bed I shared with Kate. I think she was annoyed with me. But she wouldn't admit it. She got her own back. I didn't know Freddie had slept with her over the Christmas break until she told me she was pregnant. Of course I felt betrayed. But Kate now has a more pressing problem than my hurt feelings.

Freddie: I have moved into a hostel not far from the Tower of London and Traitors' Gate. It's not a scenario I could ever have imagined. The hostel is inhabited mainly by young males who look as though they use industrial detergents on their skin instead of shower gel. They hang around the corridors with cans of beer, making a raucous song and dance of their masculinity. They have mock fights, throwing pretend punches at each other while the fire alarm goes off yet again. I don't go down to the canteen. The stagnant prison atmosphere there makes a mockery of everything I want to believe in. Instead I resort to heating stuff in tins on the toaster. As if I'm living in a tent. As if I'm living at the edge of the world.

Kate: I don't want to talk about him. I will though talk about pregnancy. Being pregnant is to be taken over. You have no control over what is going on in your body. It is horrible. If this had been planned then such an experience could be tolerated – and no doubt rejoiced in. All I think is how unfair it is. I'm burning up energy at a frenetic pace. I feel far away from myself. My fingers are numb. Every morning I wake up nauseous. The complaints of my body stop me thinking my thoughts. Then the ravenous hunger arrives, another unwelcome visitor. But such a fussy hunger. One day it was eggs. I just had to have eggs and lots of them. The next day, pickled onions and spaghetti on toast. Nothing else would suffice. And then Twix bars and Kit-Kats. Yesterday it was tomatoes and lemon juice. Today it is parsnips and leeks and jam. The thought of coffee disgusts me. My tutor says I'm not a good advertisement for pregnancy. She is going to drive me to Doncaster for the termination. I feel as if what is going on in my body is not as it should be. My insides hurt and burn in a peculiar way. I have thought my decision through on every possible ground – emotionally, ethically, rationally and practically. I don't have a person in me. I have a cell. And millions of fertilised eggs are rejected. I cannot, will not see abortion as a criminal act. Am I angry he has not offered to be by my side? Yes, I am angry. I'm waiting to hear if Oxford has accepted me. This pregnancy could not have happened at a worse time.

Lucy: I have still not learned to accept the person I am and live with her. I am all Virginia Woolf's leading ladies, I am the mistress of Seurat. I am Whistler's *Lady in White*. Today I'm wearing red and green. I have arranged to meet Freddie tomorrow in London. I'm remembering the most precious moments he has given me. I will never forget him washing my feet after I wore out my shoes walking around London with him. On the beach at Brighton I dried his hair with my skirt. I loved doing that. I could still throw my dress over his head and love every minute. There was always an atmosphere of moonlight in our being in bed together that I've never known with anyone else. His physical frailty made me more tender. His body is the body of a child. Thin and delicate. His bones obtrusive, traceable. I felt as though I could break him. I remember kissing. His mouth ardent, probing, demanding. It was childish pleasure. The increased heartbeat, like spinning on the spot. One time in bed he said, *Let's play a game. Only you mustn't tell me what the game is.*

Freddie: Was I jealous that Kate had her heart broken by someone else? Probably. I believed her heart was exclusively mine. Except I never had any desire to sleep with her. Until I did. As soon as I did that I had to make a choice, I had to start comparing Lucy and Kate. This was a maddening and futile exercise. Kate is better at getting me to talk from the heart. Lucy is at her best when clothes are discarded. Touch is her element. She can put so much of herself in the caress of her hands. Her problem is she has so little confidence in herself which can make her deceitful and clinging. I couldn't give her everything she wanted. But I saw no reason to break things off with her. The morality applied to our conduct of relationships is often farcical. As if it's a crime to do anything with less than the whole of the heart behind it. But how rarely this is possible in life. I loved spending time with Lucy. We went to the cinema together, we went to concerts, we went to London's art galleries, we laughed together and commiserated with each other in London's parks. Why should I end the relationship just because I knew there was probably someone else out there better suited to me? Kate and Lucy - they are both precious to me.

Kate: There's an electrical storm. The lightning makes my light flash on and off. The rain is lashing down. And then a searing crack that makes me jump. As a child thunder and lightning always made me seek safety under my father's pyjama top with my head buried in his armpit. I wish I had my piano to play. Instead I'm going to eat some ice cream. This is very serious, as serious as the longing of my cat to explore the inside of the wardrobe in my bedroom. Lucy has gone to London for a job interview at the Hayward Gallery. I could tell she wasn't going to tell me she had arranged to meet Freddie. She began to cry when I demanded to know. She uses tears to coax you into sympathy. Tears are like her substitute for affirmative gesture. I won't say I don't feel betrayed. I know she has to sort out her feelings. But at moments I shake because I feel I have no support. Freddie and my father are finally at loggerheads inside me. When my father died I remember I could not bear to be touched by any man for a long time, not even my favourite uncle. No man was my father and it angered me that they tried to impersonate him. I feel like that again now. I don't like men. My father gives a purpose to my life but there are times I feel blinded by his invisibility. I am all that remains of him and this can make everything seem so frail. At moments though I can see him so clearly. I would love to tell my dad about all the things I do. There is such a worthwhile energy to be reaped when some certain person is proud of you and I would glow gold to know he is proud of me. At every landmark in my life, after every achievement, every transition, I want my father.

Lucy: I remember how the older girls at the convent whispered and laughed as if possessed of secret knowledge and how disdainful they were of how much us younger girls still had to learn. Sometimes I still feel like the excluded younger girl I once was. I used to watch the nuns from the choir loft. There was one particular nun who would always appear as though she was in a trance. She seemed transfigured. The others around her were picking fluff off their jumpers or putting their veils straight while being blessed. I only ever believed in that one nun as having a vocation. She seemed to stand in a circle of light. Freddie too is like that. He too seems to stand in a circle of light. At his best, he can fill you with spirit. But all that he gives he later takes away. He has a rare talent for making people feel good about themselves. He helped me enjoy my youth. But he showed me what I cannot be as much as he showed me what I can be. There were times with him when I have never felt more alive. One thing I will say, he has never articulated his fears and phobias to me. In the dark I sometimes got an inkling of his demons. He is not the kind of person who reaches out for your help. He likes to think of himself as self-contained, a law unto himself. He once told me people treat him as if he is a fairground. He's like a famous person who isn't famous, at least not yet. I think we all expect him to become famous. I admire the eloquence with which he shares his thoughts. He has an exciting mind. I've never known anyone who makes it so easy to forgive them as Freddie. You can't hold a grudge for long. But he is quick to become disappointed in people. There were always other girls, anticipating his next move. *Tell me what it's like to be loved.* This is what I wanted to ask him. Almost all the music I listen to has come from him. Kate is the same. We laugh about it. We decide we need to discover music he knows nothing about.

Freddie: Yesterday I went to the British Museum again. A bronze Etruscan dancer spoke to me. And I was mesmerised by the crack running across a tiny delicate Minoan bowl in the alarmed glass case in the Bronze Age room. It was brushed here and there with the faintest, prettiest blue. An otherworldly colour. In Tavistock Square I smoked a cigarette outside Virginia Woolf's house and then I walked to Regent's Park. Now there is a knock at the door and immediately a key turns in the lock. The door swings abruptly open. The Maltese maid fills the space like spilt ink that saturates a blank piece of paper. She rams her withered broom between the door and its frame so that I am exposed to the world. This hostel is like a terminus. You cannot make a home in a terminus. I summon my social self, the purser in me with the ready smile. She chatters away and bustles. Complaining of her bad back and her sweats. I can imagine her cruel and kind in equal measure. She makes a joke about my unruliness. Picking up my copy of *As You Like It* from the floor. I fell in love with Rosalind again. Rosalind in her petticoats. Rosalind in her breeches. I spend so much of my time in books. Outside of books, I feel absent from the place I should be.

Kate: Freddie reminds me of an ant. His mind I mean. It never stops. I can't imagine him ever not thinking. He shuns the world in which you have to appear professional, respectable, accountable. His feet and especially his hands used to mesmerise me, because they seemed different from the rest of his body. Maybe because they best expressed him, apart from the things he sometimes said. I'm leaving aside his face because everyone's face is a kind of miracle in its power to summon feeling. I used to imagine extracting him from my life and I would go numb. I was as if confined to only the front of my head, a reception area where I performed the tasks of daily life. Only when I put him back did the deeper waters begin again to swirl and move. He can be too farsighted for his own good and he's also dogmatic. Considering I hate dogmatic people it's puzzling why I liked him. Perhaps it's because he was funny too. He made me laugh a lot. In many respects he is the most audacious individual I have ever come across. He is so acutely honest with the world that I wonder it hasn't already swallowed him whole. All the doubts he cast over himself used to make me angry sometimes. As if he was willing me to become disillusioned with him. He retreats into himself whenever anything falls short of an ideal. He is too vigilant, too exacting. His reliance on others is as indirect as he can make it. Even the way in which he shares a moment of pleasure is screened. He reminds me of my plant, trailing everywhere but in a pot. I used to wonder if the things I held back from Freddie weren't really me. He could make me feel everything he didn't approve of was face paint. I don't feel that anymore.

Lucy: Kate was angry when I told her I had arranged to meet Freddie. Instead of defending myself I cried. I often feel helplessly suspended between points of view. I can be a hollow shell. I cry too often, as a last resort. It's often my tears that lead me astray. Afterwards I realised it's me who should be angry with her. She had been deceiving me for weeks. There was a belittling cunning in the stories she spun for me to hide the fact she was sleeping with Freddie. In tutorials I'm sometimes criticised for not theorising enough. It's probably true that I let my body do too much of my talking. Last night my father asked me if I was still seeing Freddie. He says Freddie's name with contempt. My mother doesn't like Freddie either. She thinks he is effeminate. A cardinal sin in any man for her. Is that why she married a bully? I still envisage Freddie watching me when I'm in the midst of an awkward situation. I imagined him watching my parents try to belittle and outlaw him. It made me want to put my hands in his hair and undo the buttons of his clothes.

Freddie: I had no experience of Kate's anger until this happened. It's like we've been shifted out into some outlying hinterland of our relationship where it's hard to get my bearings. I angered her when I said the pregnancy felt like a punishment for deceiving Lucy. I angered her when I said I felt that if I didn't have this child I would never have a child. I angered her when I put forward the theory that her getting pregnant was an unconscious bid on her part to get rid of me. I had too much power over her. I was a star pulling her from the orbit her father has established for her. Now she will be able to do her PhD at Oxford without my gravitational force in her sky. They were nothing but half-baked thoughts flitting through my mind I shouldn't have spoken aloud. But she appeared so rational and in control of her decision making that I was taken off guard. I didn't realise how much underlying guilt she's going through. I can no more imagine what's going on in her body at the moment than I can imagine what's happening on the surface of the planet Jupiter. What can a sinner do to be reprieved? I've tried contrition. That didn't work. I've tried the confessional. That didn't work either. I'm in purgatory and she's not letting me out. I was not born to walk the holy road. I'd like to be with her when she has the abortion, but I get a panic attack whenever I find myself behind a door I can't open with my own hands. Trains and buses and planes are out of bounds for me. I should tell Kate this but I'm ashamed of this malfunction of my mind, this weakness. I don't anyway think she would be very sympathetic. My feelings are like a tripwire for her unless they perfectly align with her own.

Kate: When I'm frightened I take comfort in my make-up, my clothes, my books, my music collection. They are always kind to me, they help bring me back to my lifeline. I've discovered more about my tricks. I'm scatty, very scatty, but it is a game I have liked to play. I need to stop playing this game. It's because I was so accustomed to viewing all I do and say as inadequate. Now I feel I have acquired some basic certainty about myself, even if what I know is never quite resolved. For a long time, Freddie filled the black hole inside me. He helped me to stop seeing ugliness everywhere. My anger about my father subsided. I was less blindly frightened and more desirous to live. Now he has brought anger back into my life. Now I feel a need to get away from him. I even bought a denim jacket yesterday. Knowing how much he would hate it.

Lucy: Freddie looked more like himself than ever. I don't know why I expected him to look different. That way he has of lifting one eyebrow, as if he knows more about you than you know about yourself. He was nervous for a while. I always know when he's nervous because he wets his lip with his tongue every few seconds. It was both unnatural and difficult to withhold so much of myself when I was with him. My toes were constantly arching and fidgeting inside my shoes. I spend half my life pretending to be a responsible fully formed adult when I still feel like a child. Before meeting him, I debated for half an hour whether or not to wear my fishnet tights under my skirt. I eventually did. I often do things to spite myself. I didn't want to feel attracted to him, but I did want him to feel attracted to me. I wanted him to experience some heartbreak at losing me. His words didn't reach me as sparks and flame like they usually do. Once upon a time his smile could make me feel blessed. That did not happen today. It's strange how the same face on a different day can lose its repertoire of magic tricks. Perhaps he too was wearing a mask. It was like stage lighting had been deployed to give our meeting an atmosphere of finality. I realised how often I look at his face when he talks instead of listening to his words. His thinness made me feel fat as usual. It was strange to be with him and yet have to deny him access to my hands and mouth. I waited for him to blow that bubble of longing into my mouth that swirls a hungry emptiness around in my pelvic basin, gives a little lift to my hips and heats up my entire body. It didn't happen. Does this mean I am over him? I would like to move forward now. He has a way with words. I'll say that for him. He can argue any idea he chooses into truth. But I think we both knew when we embraced and said goodbye outside the NFT café that it was a never again moment. It will never happen again. That is such a sad sentence, such a lonely thought. I had my first taste today of what middle age will come to mean. A lonely walk towards a greying horizon.

Freddie: Lucy, as always, was generous. I love the way she warms to the stories she tells about herself. As if it's a marvel anyone is willing to give her attention. I wish I had been able to give her more confidence in herself. I felt so much affection for her. Affection that no longer has any purpose because it can't reach her. All the good things she did for me were there before my eyes. In many ways she is the person who has suffered the most. She has been betrayed on two fronts simultaneously. There was a moment she let down her long red hair and the ghost of all the beauty we had made together was in the air. The sight and smell of Lucy is like the smell of the sea for me. I always want to wade in. All prohibitions seem senseless. We will never see each other again. I knew this as I walked away and I felt some resentment towards Kate.

Kate: On the day of the termination I fainted three times. All the other girls were accompanied by boyfriends. I don't think I can ever forgive Freddie for not being by my side. I have been accepted by Oxford. I feel this is a validation of the decision I made. I was terrified Oxford would reject me. Now I need have no misgivings. I did a dance and waved the acceptance letter in the air as if my father was standing in the room with me.

Lucy: The headlights of my car are burrowing into the wet darkness. Now I am sitting in the devilish red glow of the tail lights of the car in front. I didn't get the job at the Hayward gallery. I keep asking myself what it was in me the man didn't like. Did I try too hard to please? My cardinal sin. My father told me it's time to stop all my artistic daydreaming. He's found me a job. Working as a secretary for an insurance firm. He says it's time to show him some gratitude for all he's done for me. I hate him. It pains me to hate him. He doesn't understand anything that burns from inside. Last night I imagined it was me Freddie got pregnant. I would have had the child. I would never tell Lucy this. I think I will be a good mother.

Freddie: I'm sitting on the night train to Venice. I've taken two Valium to keep the panic at bay. I have begun my exile. I have escaped the fate of becoming a husband and a father. I cannot lie and say it isn't a relief. I know I will never see Lucy or Kate ever again. I don't know how often my thoughts will turn to the child that never got born.

The Audition

Blue lights flickered through the foliage. Here came the police again. About twenty of them. Scuttling through the garden's shadows with their set faces. The local residents were outraged we had squatted in the large Georgian house in that leafy road of expensive cars. In the next room Bill was perfecting the Jimi Hendrix solo on 'All Along the Watchtower'. The amp turned up at full volume. I envied him his talent. The articulate knowledge in his fingers as they danced over the frets mesmerised me. It was my most nagging regret that I couldn't play any musical instrument.

The police were soon at the door. Three officers entered the apartment. They might have been aliens for how little I felt we had in common. I kept my eyes fixed between my feet, like a commuter, the epitome of a law-abiding citizen in my mind. There were no drugs in our apartment. I didn't really hit it off with drugs. I'm not a great fan of relaxation, nor do I like feeling over excited. All the drugs were in the apartment below where Rags, the local dealer, lived. But I had acquired a criminal record the previous month. Some nights don't go to plan, some nights surprise you with their outcome. On an exceptionally good night you might end up kissing a girl you didn't know existed the day before. On an exceptionally bad night you might end up the victim of a random act of violence or incarcerated in a police cell. I was caught in possession of an illegal substance. In truth barely enough weed to fill a single joint. I was leaving a concert at Chislehurst Caves. I picked up an empty beer can and kicked it high up into the air. Its descent was caught in the headlights of a police car. I had a red vinyl woman's handbag slung over my shoulder. I was wearing eye-liner. My appearance brightened the mood at the police station. I spent three hours in a cell with a man who had punched his wife and broken her nose. He smelled like a butcher shop. At four in the morning I was charged and released. The empty high street was a joyous place after the prison cell. I hitchhiked and was picked up by a lone man. He stopped the car in a deserted place and asked me if he could look inside my mouth. The energy coming from him fizzed with dark dirty matter. I wrenched open the door and made a run for it. I didn't wear my handbag or eye-liner in court. I wore a suit and tie. The policeman who arrested me said he didn't recognise me. The local paper reported my thirty quid fine for possession of marijuana and mentioned where I worked. A woman made a formal complaint to my boss. She found it morally reprehensible that he was employing a drug addict.

I worked in a record shop in Penge. I worked there alone. The takings every week were paltry. I remember there were these three Rastas who came in to listen to new dub singles. I ordered records especially for these three guys even though they never bought anything. They were civil with me, but never what you might call friendly. Everything they said to me was mumbled, begrudging and distancing. I think they resented me for being the custodian of their music, so to speak. Which I could understand. I wanted them to like me but accepted we were alien beings to each other. They occupied a level of coolness I would never reach. Unless I became a rock star. The wife of my boss arrived every Thursday with a delivery from the other shop. I liked my boss but I was never sure about her. She took me aside one day and told me I should stop encouraging the three Rastas. 'They never buy anything and they put other people off coming into the shop,' she said. My response was feeble. I was at an age when you measure every impression you make. This wasn't one of my best. This didn't score me very high points. Passive silent resistance, all told, differs only negligently from collusion.

Music had been and still was the key factor in my forging of identity. I was on the constant lookout for mirrors and windows. The male musicians I liked the look of gave me an aesthetic template. The songs I liked gave me clues to the nature of my sensibility. As an adolescent, listening to my transistor radio under the bedclothes was like intercepting secret messages – my first experience of making a map of myself. My parents lived in the perfunctory. Daily life was conducted with controlled reserve and conformity. It was important I found a different path to their deadening routines. By the time I met Daisy I felt I had almost crafted a fitting complimentary image of myself. I was the man who fell to earth. I liked the way Bowie had toned down the make-up for that persona. I liked the more classical aesthetic of his clothes.

I was crouched down on my knees with a bloodied nose. There was an ejaculation of orange smoke from a flare behind her when I first met her eyes. As if the colours of reality were already in the process of undertaking an alteration. That's how Daisy first saw me. I immediately liked the shape of her mouth. She said her first impression of me was of a man who had never once made it into any school sports team. I had inadvertently strayed into the midst of a protest march. I had strayed into the wrong side of the barricades. Two factions of society were locked in ideological combat. Giving vent to hate speech. I was jostled by the racists and homophobes waving their union jacks. (I can't help seeing a ghost of the swastika in every display of national flag waving.) My hair was dyed black with a bleached blonde streak that fell over my eyes. I was wearing eye-liner. I was punched in the face.

'Are you all right?' This was the first thing Daisy said to me. Like a bad actress playing a nurse. But I enjoyed people who sent themselves up. It was zealous and earnest people I struggled to connect with.

'I'd feel better if you gave me your phone number,' I said. I was surprised I had come up with a decent line. It made one or two of the bystanders smile. It also made Daisy smile. That I could change her mood seemed to sharpen her consciousness of me. She rummaged in her bag, found a lipstick and, pushing back my fringe, wrote her number in wet fuchsia digits on my forehead. She performed this act to the accompaniment of chanting and the enraged bluster of a male shouting into a megaphone. And then the calamity shriek of an ambulance or yet another police van.

I could still feel her hand in my hair while trying to concentrate on TS Eliot's *The Wasteland* in bed that night.

It was Daisy who suggested we went to see a double Jean Cocteau bill at the Gate cinema in Notting Hill. My excitement all day differed only very little from dread. I found myself pivoted on a new axis. More than once I gave the wrong change to customers. The ash from my cigarettes rarely found its way into an ashtray. Penge East station, the starting point on my journey, was a forlorn forsaken place. A place people left their litter. The clock at Victoria station alarmed me. I was running late thanks to the train unaccountably wheezing to a halt between stations every five minutes or so. I had never taken a black cab before. The experience daunted me, embodying as it did an ideal of sophistication. I was nervous I would display to the driver some comical glitch in my worldly stagecraft. The driver became the latest adjudicator of my social prestige. I was still forging my relationship with central London at this time. Every week I opened a new window, like on an advent calendar. The cab took me past Buckingham Palace, Marble Arch and Hyde Park, all afloat in streaming white light. London was the means by which I recognised himself in relation to history. It made me feel electrically contemporary in a privileged way.

For my date with Daisy I used Marcello Mastroianni in *La Dolce Vita* as my model. I wore black framed spectacles of clear glass, a black suit and a retro white shirt. Daisy demanded to try on my glasses and discovered the deception. But she warmed to it, as if deception played its part in her stagecraft too.

Daisy was at drama school. A prolific talker. As if she talked herself into being. It often seemed she was giving me a performance of herself rather than herself. But I enjoyed this, even though her mimicking of authenticity maintained a distance between us. I was wonderstruck by how comprehensively she filled my eyes. It was hard for me to look anywhere else. I took encouragement from the fact she often seemed out of breath, as if my company induced in her body quicker intakes of air. She also liked to give herself up to laughter. I was heartened by how easily I could make her laugh. At the beginning of a relationship you have to take stock of your life. I still felt I was little more than a reflection on glass. Managing a record shop in Penge was nothing to shout about. I possessed no accomplishments to parade before her. Except perhaps that I had read Virginia Woolf, most of Shakespeare's tragedies and several works by the romantic poets, though without understanding a lot of the time what they were getting at. I decided these constituted pointers about myself and dealt them into the conversation along with a list of my favourite music. I tried not to succumb to discouragement that none of my favourite books or music made it onto Daisy's lists. Every song, every book she mentioned I would acquire and bring back to my bedroom. I set myself the task of playing an active part in all her enthusiasms. I was dismayed to discover she had a thing for musicians.

We went to Camden Market together. I learned a lot about her intimate relationship with colours while watching her caress the second-hand clothes. We went to the Tate Gallery. Every painting she admired quickened into eloquent animated life like an entire world for me. We went to see lots of bands in various London venues. This was when, watching men on stage, I was most insecure, most envious. But we never kissed. It was as if I had no sexual smell for her. I saw the shape of her long legs through her cotton dress by the side of a canal. I knew precisely the measure of her breasts and now snugly they would sit in the cup of my hands. Her perfume lingered in my nostrils at night. I swung my mental torch into every corner of the time we spent together. Searching for signs of encouragement. Nothing generates more intensity than thwarted desire. But every time I saw her the possibility of a sealing kiss diminished. I began to feel we were making the same memory over and over again. I told Daisy our relationship was like a book abandoned on a lawn, the same pages turning back and forth in a breeze.

'Isn't that what all of life is like?' she said.

We were sitting outside a café by the river when she told me she had begun seeing Peter Moss, the lead guitarist of The Exhibition. She seemed to expect me to be both pleased and impressed. It didn't seem to occur to her that this was a breach of contract. Only now did I have to accept there was no contract. I hid the pain this news caused me. This concealing of my true feeling was to become a frequent imperative in Daisy's company, almost a mechanism.

Daisy began cancelling things we had agreed to do together. Often at the last minute. The cinema nights came to an end. We never saw *The Nightporter* or *Death in Venice* together. Never sat through any of Fellini's films with our elbows brushing in the darkness. Daisy was effusive in her apologies. Always telling me how important my friendship was to her. But even her voice on the telephone began to sound long distance.

I first met Peter Moss at a dinner party Daisy gave in her Battersea flat. The table was scattered with rose petals and lit by scented candles. Daisy was wearing more makeup than she ever did to meet me. There was no denying Peter Moss' physical beauty. The standout face in any crowd. I could find no flaw in his face. His thick dishevelled black hair fell over vigilant laughing blue eyes. His cheekbones were vampiric. His wide mobile mouth promised wisdom and wit. He performed every task to a rhythm as if there was a constant music in his body. He talked as though he was being interviewed, as if everything he said would be preserved in print for posterity.

'Our dreams are the only thing that saves us,' he said in the unassailable manner he had.

'No one can tell me some minutes don't pass quicker than others. Science can't explain that,' he said.

'Respect is gleaned in the showing, not in the telling,' he said.

I made a point of screwing up my face every time he delivered one of his trite maxims. But I noticed how tethered and pliant Daisy became in his company. In my company she never seemed unsure of herself. She was like a professional magician in full control of all her tricks. With Peter Moss around she appeared an inexperienced amateur. Her voice was pitched higher and ran faster when his eyes were on her. I could tell she had told him I was in love with her. It was a selling point, another part of her publicity campaign to ensnare him. His aim, as the evening progressed, was to belittle me still further in her eyes. First of all, by pretending he thought my name was Andy and not Archie.

'Were you bullied at school, Andy?'

I knew it would make me appear churlish to give myself

my correct name and I knew this was exactly what he wanted. Everyone was looking at me, as if this was my moment to perform a magic trick.

'It's just that you have that vibe about you,' he insisted in his thespian voice.

I hadn't been bullied at school. But somehow he had made it a facet of my personality the other guests now bore in mind when they spoke to me. The loathing I felt for him made my neck and shoulders ache. He took me to the darkest places of my mind. I became peevish. I spoiled the mood at the table, but I was unable to stop myself. Everyone else was blowing out iridescent bubbles; I was emitting bonfire smoke. It got worse when he brought up the three Rastafarians. I looked across the table at Daisy – I wanted her to squirm at this evidence that she had committed an act of perjury.

'Let's be honest, Andy. You want your three Rastafarians to like you and they never will,' said Peter. 'You want them to make you feel good about yourself. Why should they? Because you grant them the privilege of allowing them to listen to King Tubby tunes.'

I went home crushed. The dinner was like the equivalent of a military defeat; it had pushed back a border in me, left me cut-off from my oilfields and mineral deposits. I watched car headlights flicker on the window by my bed and then fan a fleeting glow over my ceiling. I thought I could make out the outline of a sinister creature in the shadow patterns made by these passing lights.

The Exhibition's first album came out. It was a high energy *soupçon* of punk and pub-rock. I listened to it obsessively, picking apart its flaws as if unravelling a scarf from a single loose thread. My self-esteem hit a new low. I felt I was on my knees. I began to hate the record shop, as if it was an indictment of my mediocrity. I went to see The Exhibition at the Marquee with Daisy. She revelled in having access to backstage, as if that was where she wanted to live her life. There were other beautiful girls making eyes at Peter and I felt sure he was taking full advantage of the erotic opportunities available to him. Daisy was more insecure and jealous but this only strengthened her attachment to Peter Moss. I had been relegated to a bystander in her life, a character witness.

One Thursday while sitting behind the counter reading the *Melody Maker* a notice in the ads section caught my eye. The band Neon Edges were auditioning for a singer. I liked Neon Edges. They were much cooler than Peter Moss' hackneyed band. For the rest of the afternoon I listened to their only album over and over again, singing along when no one was in the shop. I was encouraged the former singer didn't have a wide vocal range. I was soon drafting in my mind the scene in which I told Daisy I was now the singer in Neon Edges. I revelled in the new light she would see me in. I made the call the next day.

The rehearsal studio where the auditions were taking place was at the Elephant and Castle. A large eviscerated building, dimly lit and makeshift inside. Sitting on a black sofa with torn cushions spilling foam stuffing I recognised the band's lead guitarist.

'You're here to audition, right?' he said. I felt the boy appraising my appearance and I could tell I had passed the first test. The boy liked the look of me.

'I've brought a notebook of lyrics and poems and stuff,' I said, my tongue gummed to the roof of my mouth with nerves.

I sat down next to the boy on the sofa and handed him my notebook. I was quite proud of my wordsmithery. It was perhaps my only talent, apart from looking like someone who might be famous. I liked to compose lyrics to non-existent songs. I myself was like a song with words but no melody lines. I could tell the boy liked some of what he read. It occurred to me that if only I could sing I would probably get the gig. That was the moment I admitted to myself I couldn't sing. I couldn't dance either. But I tried to believe a miracle might happen and my voice, carried aloft by amplifiers, would take on a newfound resonance and lustre. But when the boy got to his feet I felt sick. I considered for a moment faking illness and bolting for the exit. I knew I was about to damage myself.

The drummer was sitting behind his kit and the bass player strapped on his guitar when I entered the rehearsal room. They both looked closely at me without seeming to. The guitarist asked me which of their songs I wanted to sing. I had spent all the previous evening memorising the lyrics to track one, side one of their debut album. Ritual Moment, the song was called. The guitarist thrashed out the opening chords, the drums and bass pounding. I wanted to fly away. I was so light on my feet flying didn't seem wholly farfetched. My singing voice came back to me through the monitor speaker as the most belittling infliction of mockery I had ever suffered. The embarrassment in the studio was palpable. My voice became more flat and jarring with every new line I sang. Never had I experienced myself as such an ugly ridiculous anomaly in the world. They all thought me delusional of course. I found I had to agree with Peter Moss that some minutes last much longer than others. I was horrified that I still had another verse and chorus to get through. But I was also dreading the crash of the final chord when I would have to meet their eyes.

A couple of days later Daisy called me. 'Did you audition as a singer for Neon Edges? Peter was talking to them and they mentioned a comically bad guy called Archie who auditioned. Peter described you and you fitted the bill perfectly.'

'I can't sing in tune. Why would I deliberately humiliate myself by auditioning as a singer?'

The Dance Teacher

The eight young Italian girls stand in a half circle. All bare-footed. They look to him aglow with the precious secrets of their young bodies. The circle is completed in the wall of polished mirror glass. They gaze at him expectantly. He can't help wondering what they see when they look at him in this primed way. They frequently make him wonder. Do they see anything more attractive than what he sees when he looks at himself - a lonely, once handsome fifty-five year old man who has missed his opportunity? They sometimes surprise him. Ivana, Melissa, Claudia, Francesca, Paola, Cristina, India and Safara. They can make him feel better about himself. He is grateful to them for this. It touches him the solemn earnest-ness with which they answer his questions, as if they stand with their hands pressed to their hearts. He would like to think he has some attraction for them as well as authority. He knows a compliment from him is cherished. A criticism taken to heart. He is careful with this power he possesses. He has two hours with his girls three times a week between five and seven in the evening. I am among angels, he once joked to an acquaintance.

'I have some beautiful words for you today. Comanche. Arapaho. Shoshone. Cheyenne. Sioux. Cherokee. Anyone know what I'm talking about?' He is English, a Londoner but he can speak Italian like a native. That he is articulate in another language is perhaps the most unexpected accom-plishment of his life.

'They are all Indian tribes,' says Claudia. Her eyes flit to his face. This shy intensity with which they communicate with him.

'Exactly.' He tells them to sit down. He watches them arrange themselves on the maple floorboards. A sheen of the sunset enters the window. He opens his laptop and shows them footage of two Native American pow-wow dances. Women of all ages in feathered costumes dancing to the pounding heartbeat of big elemental drums and a choral chant of unearthly voices. He plays each video twice. He is glad to see the girls are fascinated. Then he demonstrates the passages he wants them to learn. He spent hours in his lonely apartment practicing these steps in front of the mirror last night. He was magnetised by himself in the mirror while he danced in his bare feet. His bare feet, the stark nudity of them, had shocked the girls initially. It was as if, when he took off his shoes and socks, they became the only thing in the room. But now all the girls revel in dancing barefoot, the beautiful arabesques of their spines, their hair knotted up in unravelling buns.

'They dance in a moving circle,' he says. 'You notice how their feet never quite leave the ground. It's like they're pawing the earth and at any moment might take flight. This dance apparently represents the butterfly emerging from its chrysalis. The aim is to appear as if you're fluttering.' He wants to incorporate passages of these dances into the end of term performance when he will present a choreography at the Roman amphitheatre in Perugia. He is excited by the prospect of watching his young girls channel this animal grace through their bodies. He cherishes a hope his choreography will be noticed. He has imagined it trending on social media.

He turns up the volume of the soundtrack. The pounding drums and strange forlorn high-pitched chanting. He wants the girls to share the excitement the earthy music arouses in him. The girls begin copying the movements of the dancers on the screen. He walks among them, offering criticism, offering encouragement – the two cardinal pivots of all friendship. He nods in approval to Francesca. He presses his palm to the base of Melissa's spine. Were he twenty Melissa is the girl he would be attracted to. Sometimes, when he works the girls hard, there is a scent of sweat and musk in the mirrored room and it is hard not to see the girls as sexual beings. He has always disciplined himself to quickly shut down these carnal imaginings. But these girls, and Melissa in particular, evoke the illusion of being able to give him back what he has lost. Aesthetically, Melissa is the personification of everything he longed for when he was nineteen. He is aware he touches her more than he does the other girls. His justification is that she is the laziest of his students. Nevertheless, he knows the other girls notice his preferential treatment of her. He is aware of the hierarchy that exists among the girls. The circumspect power struggles. The fragile bonds. The covert exchanges of overcharged glances. The careful custodianship of every new discovery which makes them special to themselves. He has seen how easily two girls can destroy a third girl's confidence if they choose which they sometimes do. For these young girls everything is a rehearsal for the real thing. He can tell they find it hard to distinguish what is theatre and what is real life. They make him realise life is different now than when he was their age. It is more narcissistic. Social media has seen to that. Everyone sees themselves more in their own light. Everyone has become their own publicist, their own agent and PR office. They follow trends. They succumb to fads. The first thing they do when the class ends is to look at their phones. They are reluctant to shut off their phones even for the two hours of the lesson, as if the world is going on without them. He likes to believe he can speak their language, enter into their world, but at times they make him feel like an alien being, a relic from some redundant bygone age.

The last of the leaves are falling from the chestnut and plane trees, the elderly women are wearing their furs and the morning frosts have begun. Every day he walks through the Etruscan gate in the city wall and strides out into the Umbrian countryside. He walks until his legs ache. It is how he keeps himself in shape. It is how he gives clarity to what's in his mind. It is a relief to leave the confines of the tiered, walled medieval city. He has never been able to forge an affectionate bond with Perugia. Though many of its vistas are pleasing to the eye, photogenic, he finds it a mean and darkly spirited city. The people, on the whole, are unfriendly. Even the staff in the bar where he goes every morning for his cappuccino treat him as if they have never seen him before. He has been unable to make a home in Perugia. He has been unable to strike up a kinship with anyone in the city. He cannot find a quiet place within himself here. At night the *centro storico* becomes a sinister deserted place. It's like going back in time to when hooded cloaked figures with a concealed blade stalked the labyrinth of stairways and heavily shadowed corners. Despite its medieval grandeur it is difficult for him to ever escape a feeling of oppression. He thinks of it as a city where everything seems to have already happened. A closed book. As if the story, in which he has no role, has ended.

All his life he wanted to be a dancer. His mother encouraged him; his father was aggressively derisive and noticeably relieved when he brought home his first girlfriend. He never cared much for his father's good opinion. His father was like a man undone by some former act of cowardice. He possessed little authority. It was always his mother he wanted to impress.

His mother though was diagnosed with breast cancer two weeks after he was accepted by Pina Bausch's *Tanztheater* dance company in Germany. Because of his commitments there, or so he managed to convince himself, he only saw her once before she died. Not a day now passes that something doesn't happen to remind him of her. Her shadow is always close. She has left him with a residue of guilt. A longing to make amends, to correct things he did badly at the time. It is still hard for him to believe he will never get the opportunity.

Pina was preparing a choreography entitled *Palermo Palermo* at the time of his mother's fatal illness. It was to be staged in the city of its title. He exalted in the rehearsals. It was to be his first performance for the company. Because he was one of the few males who wasn't gay he was popular with the female dancers and was sleeping with two simultaneously at the time. He had never been so contented with his life at the time his mother was dying. His insensitivity to her ordeal appals him now. If only he was given one more chance to do things right. It's the refrain that most often echoes in his head. It is his mother who most frequently makes him consult his heart. He sometimes thinks the devastating stage fright that ended his career as a dancer was a punishment. Do we in some way choose our misfortunes? In the wings of the stage of the theatre in Palermo the unrelenting surge of panic made him unrecognisable to himself. The only way to appease it was to flee. So he fled. He didn't want to know how his absence had affected the performance. He hid out in the unknown city of Palermo. It was exciting in its way to experience himself as a renegade. To stalk the streets with an accelerated heartbeat. The salt on his skin, the smell of fish in his nostrils. He tried not to dwell on the chagrin he had caused Pina. He tried not to dwell on his shame. By the docks, watching men with more useful professions, he wrestled with this new idea of himself as mentally deficient and a coward. Arduously he had trained his body to obey his commands but had failed to master a control over his mind. Ironies accumulate. This is one thing life has taught him. He couldn't work out if he had become the frightened child inside the man or the child inside the frightened man.

It was probably stage-fright that ended his marriage too. His wife's presence was like a spotlight, his role as husband like a performance scripted for him by someone else. His marriage only lasted two years. He has not heard from his ex-wife since. There were no children. He married at the lowest point in his life. He discovered many things about himself he didn't like. Especially how prone he was to petty irritations. And how cemented was his intolerance to obeying the grating urgency of other people's rules. He was forced to admit there was a lack of generosity in his nature. He decided he was not suited to life in any spotlight. His life in Perugia is solitary. The only person he speaks frequently to is himself.

Something happened at the end of class today that continues to bother him. After he had put on his shoes and socks and gathered his belongings, Melissa collided with him. For a moment she pressed the full length of her body against him. Did she rub her small breasts against his chest as a dare? All the other girls were watching as if the act had been choreographed. One night recently, alone with his computer, he noticed social media was awash with the outrage of women who made public incidents of sexual abuse they underwent as young girls. The subject inspired a dialogue in him, self arguing with self about the challenges male biology presents to the mind and, subsequently, the importance of mastering with the mind the body's urges. He has never been able to work out if his stage-fright originated in his mind or in his body. Either way it was with his mind that he had to master it and he had failed.

But then he remembered an incident from his past. It

had taken place at a house party in the Italian countryside. The girl he liked had gone to bed early. She was ten years younger than him. A beautiful shy girl with an air of poetic loneliness with whom he had struck up a fledgling friendship while walking through the woods. He entered her bedroom uninvited, told her he wasn't in the mood to participate in the drunken rowdiness and asked if he could take refuge in her bed. He assured her he sought nothing but sleep. She was too shy to say no. He was careful to behave impeccably, ensuring there was always space between their bodies in the large bed. Until the following morning when a fellow male guest entered the room. Then he had scooped her up into his arms, manhandled her, as if they were lovers. He gave no thought to her feelings. It was a gesture enacted to impress the male who had entered the room. She was mortified. He could afterwards sense the deep humiliation he had caused her with this stupid act. And it was not an act he could blame on male biology. He never told her he was sorry. He wishes now he could tell her he is sorry.

The light is draining from the sky. Outside the premises of the dance school a man and woman are standing by a parked car. There is an air of consequence about them. Somehow they possess the enormity with which objects loom in dreams. They change the colour of the waning day. He senses this even before he notices the look of disgust on the woman's face when she looks at him. She nods to the man. The man strides forward and delivers a right hook to the bridge of his nose. The blow, the shock of it, knocks him off his feet. He is on his back in the gutter. His assailant bellows out abuse as if he is on a battlefield. He struggles to make sense of the gist of the man's rage. He tries to convince the man it is a case of mistaken identity.

'*Sei un pezzo di merda,*' the man retorts, spraying spittle.

The director of the art institute appears in the street. In

her tweed suit, lacquered hair and gold jewellery. She sets about appeasing the raging man. Assures him she will sort things out. He notices Claudia and the Senegalese girl Safara who have arrived for the class. They are staring at him aghast. As if he is naked. There is blood on his hand when he wipes his nose. The director leads him into her office.

'A complaint has been levelled at you by one of your students. Melissa Conte says you pressed yourself against her and fondled her breasts.'

His bewilderment keeps him silent for a while. He is still dazed by the shock of being hit. It is the first time since schooldays he has been struck in the face. The shocking intimacy of it, the violation of a sacred boundary, the brutal awakening of the helpless infant within. He feels like a child now. A child charged with a misdemeanour in the office of a principal. He wonders if there's even any such thing as growing up. *I'm too young to be this old.* It's a constant refrain in his head, a recurring regret in his heart. He is still waiting for the discovery of another self. When he is about to refute the charge he is taken off guard by the memory of the shy girl whose body he had used as a stage prop. She becomes for a moment his mirror. The director, maintaining a stern countenance, wants to hear his side of the story. She taps her fingers with impatience on the desk. He looks up at a framed diploma on the wall behind her. He is overcome by a sapping weariness. He believed the girls all loved their dancing classes with him. Often their small triumphs, the shine of wonder at themselves in their eyes, were all he had to show for his day. Had they always held him in scorn? Waited for the first opportunity to bring him down, get rid of him? He sits back in the chair. Once again the shy girl whose body he used as a stage prop becomes his mirror. He doesn't hold up his hands but it's as if he did. Guilty, not as charged, but guilty all the same, he thinks.

Acknowledgements

For inspiration, sustenance and feedback, thanks to: Charles Cecil, Freddie de Rougemont, Georgiana Calthorpe, Emily Pennock, VJ Keegan, Rupert Alexander, Justin Sparrow, Anna von Kanitz, Jessica St. James, Talitha Stevenson, Paola Rosà, Gina Monaco, Alex Preston, Judith Kinghorn, Annabel Merullo, Charlie Campbell, Hamid Khanbhai, Christabel Brudnell-Bruce, Charlotte Raymond, David Flusfeder, Tim Atkins, Eloise Anson, Vanessa Garwood, Hugo Wilson, Antonia Barclay, Sarah Haybittle, Lucy Corbett, Chiara De Cabarrus, Kim Macconnell, Stuart Bridgeman, Paolo Cristellotti, Katie St. George, Tiarnan McCarthy, Ebba Heuman, Cristina Zamagni.

Milton Keynes UK
Ingram Content Group UK Ltd.
UKHW010708201023
430994UK00004B/114